Contingently YOURS

DIANNA ROMAN

WILD ONE PRESS

For information address diannaromanbooks@hotmail.com

Published by Wild One Press
Cover design by Wild One Press

Editing by Jennifer Green

ISBN: 978-1-959553-38-0 (Trade Paperback)
ISBN: 978-1-959553-39-7 (Hardcover)
ISBN: 978-1-959553-37-3 (eBook)

Content Advisory

This work of fiction is not intended for readers under the age of 18 and contains the following content. Please read at your own discretion.

- explicit adult language
- explicit consensual sexual content
- accidental intimate touching
- teasing and name calling body hair by one MC, which is later revealed as a kink of that MC

Dedication

to my readers –
thank you for giving me
this wonderful job

Why do I hear noise? It cannot possibly be anywhere near ten a.m.

Cracking an eye open, the light coming from my bathroom strains my cornea. A curvy, toweled figure with a pleased smile emerges. She saunters past the end of the bed, flaunting her state of consciousness. Devil woman. It's like she knows she woke me up and is proud of it.

"Ugh. Why are you mobile? Sleep time," I mumble with my lips squished against my pillow and close my eyes again. "*Still*…sleep time."

An ethereal laugh and the soft steps of feet against the carpeting tell me she's gathering her clothing and ignoring the important fact I've just voiced. Sleepovers are not supposed to be interrupted by early risers.

"Not everyone has the luxury of working for their family," comes Veronica's teasing reply. "Some people's work days start before noon."

Grunting, I ignore her bitterness disguised as mockery and roll onto my back. Flexing my toes, I yawn and run my hand down my stomach under the covers, trying to coax my body back to sleep.

"Come back to bed," I murmur, unsticking my cock from my thigh and giving it a good morning stroke. "You make more money than I do. You can miss a day."

"I don't think you need me," she chuckles. "Looks like you've got yourself covered."

Opening both eyes now, I locate her on her way back to the bathroom. Snickering, she stops by my dressers and flashes an accusatory look at the outline of my fist where it's underneath the comforter. Yeah, my hand is on my dick, but that doesn't mean anything. I just wanted to snuggle. Snuggle and sleep.

"I had an itch."

More laughter. Dropping her towel, she brandishes a clean pair of underwear from her purse like it's a Giving Tree and shimmies into them. "Drew, I've never seen anyone touch their cock as much as you do. I'm not even sure why you call me."

"What?" My hand freezes on the cock in question, but I realize doing so probably makes me look guilty when I have nothing to feel guilty about. "That's not what... I just don't like it sticking to my thigh first thing in the morning. You'd know this if you wouldn't get out of bed at an unreasonable hour," I grouse. Closing my eyes again, I give myself a comforting stroke. "Someone's clearly salty because they didn't get enough sleep and are trying to take it out on me now."

Her chuckle is subdued this time. I hear the shift of more clothing and then the clip of heels on my bathroom flooring.

Jeez. She really is leaving. She's a sadist.

Playing possum, I still my hand on my cock as I hear her approach. Soft lips grace my forehead, and her lilac scent wafts over me. Just as she starts to move back, I snake my free arm around her waist and tug her closer.

"You know, I'm kind of awake now after all that noise someone made."

Laughing, she presses a hand to my chest. "Sorry, Sleeping Beauty, but I have to go. I'm leaving for Brussels tomorrow and have to pack."

All pretenses and realities of being sleep deprived evaporate on that info bomb. My eyes flare open, taking in her long auburn locks spilling over her shoulders and the unflappable look on her face. Is she serious?

"Brussels? For how long?"

"Two months, I think."

"Two months? What am I supposed to do for two months?"

It's not until the words are out and Veronica's head rears back with a curious look on her face that I realize how monogamous that sounded. Monogamous and desperate. I am neither, by any means.

"Uh…the same thing we've always done?"

I know she's referring to our no-strings-attached arrangement, but she's never been out of the country for that long. And, truth be told, I honestly can't remember the last time I slept with another woman. Made out, sure. A few oral exchanges, yeah. But sex… Well, I think it's been a little over a year since I've dipped my nib in another pool. What can I say—I'm happy with our dynamic. It's easy and requires no effort. I tell her when I'm in town, we meet up, and vice versa. Convenience at its finest. Her leaving for two months is going to be highly inconvenient.

Glancing at my recent birthday gift from my parents, I see that it's only just after nine. Veronica is so being a dick getting up this early and dumping this news on me, but it's not the time that annoys me as much as it is the sight of my gift. I'm officially thirty-five as of last week. I'm starting to feel…old. Not like arthritis and I-need-a-back-pill old, but the kind of old that makes a guy reconsider his routines.

Most of the women I meet anymore are much younger than me, and while I enjoy a night of rolling under the covers, it kind of kills the mood when they tell you you're hot for an older man.

'Older man.'

I still remember that comment from a woman I went home with from a club last year. She understood none of my jokes or references. I was never the type of person who needed an emotional connection, but damn, it would be nice to not feel like I was just thawed out after two decades of cryosleep.

Sitting up, I slide my hand down to Veronica's and give it a squeeze. Flashing her a smile, I lean on my reliable charm. Thirty-five or not, I know I've at least still got that.

"What if we keep doing the same thing we've always done, but just… with each other?"

Why is she doing that head-rearing thing again? Arching a brow, the corner of her mouth ticks up. "Are you…asking me to be exclusive with you?"

My phone starts buzzing on the nightstand, but I ignore it. This conversation needs to happen, so I'm not at the mercy of hitting the bar scene and hook-up apps anymore. It's too fucking tiresome.

Shrugging like it's no big deal, because it isn't, I stretch my arms behind my head, lacing my fingers together. "I mean, why not? We both get each other and know what the other likes. We both work and travel all the time. It works. It'd save us the disappointment of shitty hook-ups. Right?" Snapping my fingers, I chuckle, recalling the perfect example. "Remember that guy you said you met at that convention in Denver last year? The one who grunted every three or four sentences and kept telling you he liked your eyebrows? Think of all the weirdos you could avoid if we just met up more often."

"Wow, Andrew, that is…a tempting offer," she chuckles, straightening up. "But listen to what you're saying. If you want to settle down, then make the effort and go find someone to settle down with. We've never been *that* to each other. We have…fun. That's all it is. That's all it's always been."

"Who said anything about settling down?"

Rolling her eyes, she moves back to my dresser and fetches her purse. Slinging it over her shoulder, she calls back, "Being exclusive, sleeping with only each other; that's almost the same thing as settling down. It might be fine and dandy until the other person meets someone they want to settle down with, but then what happens? Someone's left disappointed. So, in the end, it's not any better than what you're used to. The outcome will still be the same, just prolonged."

God, I hate when she wakes up before I do. It gives her time to be more mentally cognizant than me. And how did this become a deep conversation when it should have only been a really good offer that would solve both of our problems?

"Well, you won't have to worry about *me* meeting someone to settle down with. Are you trying to tell me you're waiting for Mr. Right?"

Turning around, she pinches her eyes shut and groans. "Andrew," she huffs with a laugh, "most people want to settle down eventually. Just because I work and travel all the time doesn't mean I don't keep my eyes open."

Ew. Who is she? How come I never knew this?

"That's disgusting. Please don't ever talk like that again."

Snickering, she rolls her eyes and grabs her jacket off the hook on the wall. "Don't worry. I haven't met him yet. I'll call you when I get back."

Folding my arms, I grimace as my phone buzzes again. I was dead to the world and wouldn't have heard it if she hadn't woken me up to the worst fuck-buddy goodbye in history.

"I'll answer if I'm available," I call out, hoping I sound as spiteful as I feel.

"Sure," she says, sounding way too amused. Shaking her head, she blows me a kiss. "For now, why don't you answer the call you do have? It could be Lou."

This isn't funny. The first offer of being something close to a boy-friend I've ever made to anyone is being received with mockery.

Swiping up my phone, I see that it is, in fact, my Uncle Lou's real estate office. Son of a bitch.

Turning the phone so she can see the screen, I waggle it in the air. "See? You *do* know me. Think of how convenient it would be not to have any surprises. You could be waking up next week to some guy's phone going off in Brussels, thinking he's Mr. Right, only to find out it's his mother calling him to come do her weekly chin whisker trimming for her." Clicking on the *accept* button, I sneak a peek at Veronica to see if my words of wisdom are sinking in. "Hey, gorgeous, what's up?"

It's not Lou. It's our sixty-year-old receptionist, Vera. She also hap-pens to be my aunt, but you get more flies with honey than vinegar.

"I know you don't mean that, but it's always nice to hear. That's why I call you."

"Well, I am your favorite nephew."

"No. That would be Chad."

"What? How in the hell is Chad your favorite?"

That is just not possible. My older brother Chad is the most boring human being on the planet.

"He buys me those candles I like for my birthday every year."

Veronica is busy touching up her lipstick in the mirror on the wall by the door. I take it as a good sign that she hasn't left yet. The woman puts up with my shit and has manners. How does she not see that we're perfect for each other? We both love sex and don't get hurt feelings or have to gut our souls with sappy overtures.

"So, listen, nephew-mine," Vera segues. "We've got new clients coming in at ten o'clock. Can you get that tush of yours out of bed and in here by then? I'm worried Lou's in over his head with this one, and it's too good of a deal to miss out on."

A burst of gloating explodes in my chest over the request for my talents. Dad and Chad have curled their lips up at me ever since I started working for Uncle Lou four years ago. It's not my fault Dad canned me from his company. It's also not my fault that I may have a chip on my shoulder about it and am determined to show him I can make a name for myself without working for Broadhouse Publishing. He's the one who put the chip there. Maybe it's petty of me, but each sale I've made working for Uncle Lou repairs a fragment of my wounded pride. It also helps that Dad hates Uncle Lou, so I guess choosing to come work for him *was* a tad bit petty.

"Bed?" I snort. "I'm on my, like, second property viewing of the day already. Ye of little faith."

"Andrew…just because you close more deals than any other agent we have, doesn't mean I don't know you get up at the crack of noon, but that's beside the point. This one is huge. They want to buy three properties. We need all hands on deck today so we look like we're a fully staffed, well-run business."

Three properties? We sell islands and beach front real estate. Holy shit. That *is* huge. Thinking of the zeros that would add to my bank account and how I could rub it in Dad and Chad's faces makes my eyes glaze over. Just because I know how to have a good time doesn't mean I'm irresponsible and can't make it in the workforce outside of our family's business. Landing this deal would be irrefutable proof.

"Oh, good," Vera sighs. "Lucas just texted me back. He said he can make it in."

Lucas Everette? Over my dead body.

"I'll be there in fifteen minutes!" I hang up and jump out of bed. "Fuck!"

"Everything okay?" Veronica asks.

Shit. I totally forgot she was still here.

Scrambling to my closet, I pull out a short-sleeve button-up and a pair of nice khakis. "Yeah. Huge deal coming in. I've got to get to the office before *Dickhead* shows up and tries to steal it from me."

Hopping into my slacks, I realize I didn't even put underwear on, but I don't care. This is urgent. Shaking my dick into my pants, I zip up and fling my shirt around my shoulders, heading toward the door as I do the buttons.

"I don't understand what your problem with Lucas is. He seems like a sweetheart."

Now I'm the one rearing my head back. Clearly, she needs coffee or a psyche eval.

Guiding her by the small of the back, I nudge her out of the bedroom. "Obviously, we're not talking about the same person. Did you forget he assaulted me?"

Finger-combing her hair, she saunters down the hallway with me to the living room, flashing me a dubious look. "No offense, but I kind of got the feeling you provoked him. I've only met him a few times, but the man doesn't look like he'd willingly hurt a fly."

"He's a veteran from the backwoods of North Carolina—the man was basically bred to be in bar fights and then trained to kill people with only his thumb. You're lucky that I have good reflexes."

Rolling her eyes, she clicks her tongue and stops by my front door. Ugh. For someone who disrupted sleepover time, she sure doesn't look like she's in a hurry now. Does she not know how pressing this is? I need to be on the road.

"Drew, you swooped in unannounced with new clients and sold the property on-site that he was showing to some of his own. Of course, anyone would be upset about that."

"Oh, and being more business savvy means I should be subjected to physical violence from hillbilly brutes? He was Lou's freaking helicopter pilot. Just because a gorilla who can handle a joystick gets a real estate license, doesn't mean he can sell real estate."

Her smile looks placating. I don't like it.

"You threw a hissy fit that time I ate the last of your rocky road. All I'm saying is that I know you; you're good at getting under people's skin."

Opening the door, I give her a peck on the lips. "Okay. Good talk. Have fun in Brussels."

Chuckling, she pats my shoulder and steps outside. "I'll see you."

I'm about to close the door, but remember we never finished our conversation, or rather, she kind of brushed me off. Fucking Lucas better not beat me to this client. Uncle Lou likes him for some awful reason that I don't understand. He experimented with too many drugs in the seventies, and it affected his judgment is my guess.

"Hey!" I call out. "Think about what I said. I can't wait forever."

Stopping by her red Corvette, she holds her arms out to her sides and laughs. "My point exactly."

Oh, brother. I never figured her to be one to play hard to get. I have faith, though. She'll come around when she considers all the merits of my proposal. She's a businesswoman, after all. People in business can't say no to logic. For now, I need to deal with my own logic—ruining Lucas Everette's year.

Chapter 2

LUCAS EVERETTE

licensed agent

"You are a confident, capable man. You know this job. You're genuine. People appreciate honesty and compassion," I tell my reflection in the rear-view mirror of my Chevy Silverado. Studying the bags under my eyes, I sigh and add, "You could also pay off your loans and the girls' wedding. You went to war—you can do *this*."

I'm not proud of how desperate I sound, but like Mom always says, you can't hide from the truth. I *am* desperate. I thought piloting for Lou Hanson's island real estate agency here in Wilmington was a damn good gig to get when I got out of the Army. It was a reasonable drive from the house I had just bought in the North Carolina countryside for the life plans I was making, but as the bills piled in and I saw what the real estate agents earned off their commissions, piloting didn't seem like the answer anymore.

I've only been a certified agent for about two years now. While I've made a nice dent in my debt and also managed to put some away for my sisters' upcoming wedding, I'm still far from where I'd like to be financially at my age. I should just be grateful that Jolissa and Julia decided to have a double wedding. If they'd had two separate ceremonies and parties, I'd be feeling the squeeze even more. When I told Mom she wasn't going to foot the bill, I meant it, even if I didn't know how I was going to accomplish taking care of it.

Blowing out a breath, I kill the engine of my truck and search my rear view again. I want to see the confident soldier who was a reliable warrant officer to his men staring back. I need *that* guy today, especially if Lou trusted me enough to call me in for this potential deal.

Tires screech nearby. A black BMW whips into the parking lot. Whatever confidence I hoped to muster morphs into something else entirely as I squint at the rearview and spot the jackass who just double parked behind me. I know exactly who that jackass is.

"What the hell is *he* doing here?" I mutter, watching Andrew Broadhouse bail out of his fancy car with an urgency he never practices. This can't be good. "Shit!"

Wrenching my door open, I bound out of my truck, hating the way these khaki slacks are stuck to my sweaty ass from my leather seats. Yeah, that'll look professional and impress a client. Glancing over at Andrew, a lump forms in my throat. He's made more of an effort with his wardrobe than he normally does, wearing dress slacks and dress shoes today. That means he must have gotten wind of the deal. Granted, his sandy mess of hair looks like he couldn't be bothered to comb it, but he never wears dress clothes to the office or viewings. Why would Lou's lazy, spoiled nephew bother dressing professionally when he can be handed the best deals while wearing shorts and flip-flops like a frat boy?

His gaze meets mine, looking just as suspicious as I imagine I do right now. I'm not proud that I resorted to punching him in his stupid face a few months ago, but I can't say I didn't enjoy the feel of my knuckles connecting with his cheek when he showed up on the property I was just about to clinch with my clients. In my defense, he started it when he threw the property listing sign at me, and it hit me in the balls.

He freezes mid-stride behind his vehicle, and his eyes narrow at me like a gunfighter in a duel. Shit. He will not. Not again.

Something primitive ignites in my blood—a silent war cry in biological form. I narrow my gaze right back, taking a slow breath through my nostrils.

I am a professional. He isn't. I've got this. I don't care what kind of crap or fake charm he tries to pull today. Relative or not, Lou will see that I'm the most appropriate agent to broker this deal.

I keep telling myself that, even as I mirror each hurried step Andrew takes toward the doors of VeraLou Island Properties. By the time we're ten feet away, however, professionalism is a distant memory. We're both full-out sprinting. I despise the immaturity this guy brings out in me.

My hand reaches the door handle first. I cheer a silent victory until I realize that yanking it open gives Andrew the opportunity to step under the threshold first.

He's about two inches taller than me, but I'm stronger. Pushing my feet against the pavement, I lunge forward in an attempt to cut him off. He mustn't know how to walk in his stupid dress shoes, though, because he staggers to the side when my shoulder bumps his. The idiot won't give up and continues to try to press forward at the same time as me. The result leaves us smooshed in the doorway, shoulder to shoulder, our legs snared in each other's as we both try to advance.

"I was here first," he grunts. "Wait your fucking turn."

"Like hell you were." I kick his shin in return after the cheap shot he just delivered with his elbow to my ribs.

"Ouch!" he yelps, completely overdramatized. "Are you going to assault me again because I got to the door faster than you?"

"What in Sam Hill is going on?" Lou's voice interrupts us, booming across the reception area.

I'm too mortified to move or speak. That gives Andrew the advantage. He jerks out of our doorway sandwich and tries to make himself look dignified after staggering into the office. Smoothing out his dress shirt with one hand, he flicks a thumb over his shoulder at me.

"G.I. Joe here just tried to trample me. I warned you he's violent."

Vera's head of wiry black hair peeks out of the conference room door behind Lou. I glimpse a man's back sitting at the conference table and hear laughter.

The clients are already here? Crap. I don't even have time to plead my case of why I'd be a good agent to show them properties.

"What was that noise?" Vera whispers.

Lou waves her off, signaling for her to go back into the conference room. "Nothing. Keep them busy. I'll be back in a minute." Snapping his fingers, he points to his office at the opposite end of the reception area. "You two, with me."

Great. Now I'm going to be reprimanded because of his jerk nephew. Lou was gracious and understanding over *the incident* a few months ago, but judging by how red he is in the face right now, something tells me there's a limit to his graciousness. He's not someone who sugarcoats things. It's why I like working for him. You always know what you're going to get. He's brash and sometimes vulgar, not what I imagined the owner of an island real estate company would be like, but I don't mind it. His blunt delivery reminds me of my counterparts from my military days. I know how to work with people like him—do your job and they're happy. I especially admire how his nephew seems to get on his nerves, but I wonder if he'll choose family over me now that I've been caught in not one but two scuffles with Andrew.

I pause near Lou's office when Andrew looks like he's about to engage in a repeat of the doorway sandwich we just disentangled ourselves from. Glowering at him, I fold my arms and wait for him to pass. He rolls his eyes and strides in, plopping lazily into one of the chairs in front of Lou's cluttered desk.

I walk over to the other chair like a mature adult and take a seat, straightening my tie. Inhaling slowly, I put on my soldier's face, awaiting my ass-chewing like a responsible human being.

"I'm not even going to ask what the fuck that was about," Lou fumes. "Today is too important. The clients showed up early, and I've got to make a decision about who's going to handle their viewings."

"Well, Uncle Lou, I can help you out with that right now," Andrew says cheerfully. "I'll gladly do it. Happy to help, as always. You know I'm your guy."

"Shut the fuck up, Andrew. You don't even know what they want yet."

I lock up a snort over his uncle's quick dismissal and bite the inside of my cheek. Hearing Lou put his nephew in his place will never get old. Maybe my job isn't in jeopardy over the doorway scuffle after all.

Andrew lets out a fake scoff and sits up straight, holding up his index finger. "I will ignore how hurtful that was and blame your outburst on your obvious stress level. But let me just say that whatever they want, I can handle it. I've shown and closed on more properties than almost every agent you have."

Rubbing his eyes with the heels of his palms, Lou mutters under his breath and lets out a sigh. I feel like that's a telling sign dear Andrew has been a pain in the ass since birth.

"If you can't stop talking, then just think about how much you'd enjoy going back to work for your father. That's how close I am to losing my patience right now," Lou warns.

I don't know why, but that has Andrew's yap snapping shut. I know he started about a year before I did, and I've always wondered who in their right mind would have previously employed the pretentious man who always ignored my pre-flight safety briefings like I was a bug on his shoe. I am so glad I had to fly his ass around only a handful of times.

His eyes have gone wide, like his uncle's threat was a bucket of cold water to his face. What is that all about?

He holds up his finger again, since he just can't help himself, despite Lou's warning. "Hurtful *again*, but…I'm listening."

With that, he folds his arms over his chest and finally shuts up. Lou's nostrils flare with an exasperated breath before shoving his hands in his pockets.

"They want to purchase three properties, each on a different continent. One, a private family home that can be beachfront if it affords enough privacy. An island with a club resort, and a third undeveloped property with coastal access to use as a recreational adventure retreat for outdoorsy survivalist types."

"Who's the client?" I ask, unable to hold back my curiosity any longer.

"Mason, Dario, and Keenan Hepperly. Money isn't an object, so needless to say, these sales have a lot of potential."

Andrew lets out a low whistle. "Nice."

"Are they brothers?" I venture, already silently thinking about how I can try to relate to them as someone who has two younger siblings.

"No. They're a throuple who got married a few months ago. They want to make the viewings their honeymoon over the course of a month and stay at some of the properties to get a good feel for them, so we'll have to shoot for furnished or staged properties."

"They're a what?" My request for clarification draws a snort from Andrew. Why does he look so smug? "What?" I repeat defensively.

"A *throuple* is what you call a couple plus one, sweetheart," he informs me, lacing his fingers behind his head before he returns his gaze to his uncle. "See? Told you. I'm your guy."

A *throuple*…as in three men who are all married to each other? That's a new one for me. I've only shown properties to couples, singles, and business partners. And how the hell does Andrew know what a throuple is?

Shit. Now I look like I don't know what I'm doing.

"I'd be happy to show them, Lou. I can relate to all those property types," I offer.

"Yeah. Everything about you screams luxury resort, *Conan*," Andrew snarks.

Just as I glare at him, Lou interrupts. "Knock it off. I don't have time for this shit. If you two could get along, that would make my life a hell of a lot easier right now. It's going to be a lot of work. A lot of travel. I don't want to send anyone out solo on this, but everyone's either got scheduling conflicts or isn't appropriate. Hank's got two showings the week the Hepperlys want to take off. Judy's never shown Oceana properties, Clarence can barely get in and out of a car anymore, let alone a sea plane, and Jeremiah…well, I'm not taking any chances on his lack of filter making us look like Destination Living after what they did to the Hepperlys."

I sit forward at the same time as Andrew. Destination Living is our biggest competitor. If the clients had a bad experience with them, I want to know about it and use it to my advantage, as well as not make any repeat mistakes that may have been committed by our competition.

"They went to Destination first?" Andrew asks.

Lou snorts. It's a smug-sounding snort, which gives me hope. "Yeah, and word is that whoever they got at Destination wasn't a fan of same-sex marriage and made some subtle comments expressing as much. The Hepperlys told them what they thought of that and walked right out, so their misfortune could be to our benefit."

"Are you kidding me?" Andrew sounds off. "They're like the most famous throuple in the world and those idiots decided their shitty opinion needed to be heard? I hope they slap a lawsuit on them." He lets out a bewildered laugh and shakes his head.

"They're…famous?" I interject.

I'm still absorbing the term *'throuple.'* There are famous throuples? My sisters say I live under a rock. I'm starting to feel like they might be right in at least this regard.

Andrew sighs and rolls his eyes. "Uh, ever hear of the band, Renegade?"

Only vaguely, but I'm not telling him that, so I shrug and nod. Are these guys all in a famous band?

"Mason Hepperly is the lead singer," Andrew continues. "No?" he challenges with a smirk, like he knows I'm just posturing. "How about a little show called *Down Under with Dario,* or did the foil fall off the rabbit ears on your television?"

Is he kidding me? *That's* the Dario who's sitting in the conference room right now? I love that show. Every survivalist show on TV usually has over-enthusiastic wannabees, but Dario Kealy is the real deal. He's a wild man who eats grasshoppers like they're M&M's. I had no idea he was gay or…*throupled*.

Is that a word?

"Of course, but he doesn't go by Hepperly on the show," I mutter in my defense.

"I'm supposed to go in for my hernia surgery at the end of next week," Lou informs us. "I've been waiting months to get this done and can't miss it. Vera will have my head if I do, but I can probably help with the tail end of the viewings in a few weeks. I still need two agents to start them out on the front end, though. Andrew, maybe I can call someone from Bridges Real Estate to help you out until I recover, and then Lucas and I can handle the viewings on the second half of the trip."

The commissions from these three sales will be extravagant, but Lou just dispensed some depressing math. Andrew and a Bridges Real Estate agent, and Lou and me? That's a four-way cut. I know even a quarter of the commissions would likely solve all my financial problems, but with my luck, Andrew will try to finalize all three properties during the first week or two.

"No!" Andrew and I blurt in unison. My face blooms over my outburst. While being blunt might be common for my nemesis, it's not for me, so I amend, "I can handle it," but Andrew again says the same words that come out of my mouth.

I fume as we glare at each other. He doesn't need this deal, at least not financially. He just wants to show off to his uncle, or maybe his family, from what Lou said earlier. Can he not be a selfish jerk just this once?

"These people were just shit on by our competitors. I know you're both capable, but understand this—VeraLou is going to be part of their honeymoon. We need to pamper them and show them the love they didn't get from Destination. I want us dining with them, swimming with them, asking them if they need their fucking pillows fluffed. It's more than just showings. We're going to get invited to their damn anniversary parties and kids' birthdays by the time this is over. We're not going to neglect them for a second, and guess what? You have to sleep sometime, so no matter how many sales either of you have made, you're not going to be able to juggle all the travel, off-loading their luggage, getting them settled in the properties for the night, and kissing their asses at the same time. It's just not possible for one person."

Shit. He's serious. I'll hand it to him—it's a good strategy for such a unique situation. We need to be like tour guides. Commission aside, the idea of hanging out with Dario Kealy for three to four weeks is also not an opportunity I want to pass up. How many people can say they got to do that? I never take vacations or do anything for recreation. I know this is technically work, but it's the closest thing to having a good time I'll have had for as long as I can remember.

For some reason, I glance at the sandy-haired jackass next to me. Probably because he's surprisingly quiet. When I find him giving me the same wary expression, I get a sick feeling in the pit of my stomach because I know what he's thinking. Inhaling, his lips press into a firm line, but then he looks back at his uncle with a brighter expression.

"Lucas and I will do it."

We *what?* Did I just hear him correctly?

A trickle of hope filters through me, knowing that *two* people equals fifty percent commission versus only a quarter, but…this is Andrew Broadhouse. I'd probably murder him before we even board the plane.

Lou is a sensible man because he scoffs at Andrew's suggestion. He plops down in his chair, yanking open a drawer. Retrieving a bottle of antacid tablets, he levels a stern look at us. "Do you think I'm fucking stupid? You two haven't even been able to be in the same room as each other since the Panama showing last year. You couldn't even make it through the office door today without playing grab-ass. You'll get our licensing privileges revoked in three countries by the end of the first week, not to mention embarrassing the shit out of me with the Hepperlys," he rants, trying to pry the lid to his tablets open. "Not happening. We either come up with a plan to split it and take turns or ask them to prolong their trip until Hank is free and can go with one of you, which I'd rather not do. The Hepperlys only have so much free time between all three of their schedules, so we need to make this happen now."

Crap. He's right. If we ask them to hold off, they could go through agencies local to each of their destination choices, *and* we'll look bad for not being able to accommodate them. However, a twenty-five percent commission is still not a fifty percent commission. Maybe I can restrain myself from choking Andrew for enough money. My soldiering finally kicks in, reminding me to suck it up in the face of adversity.

"We can do it, Lou," I agree, hoping I sound confident. "Andrew and I have…put our differences behind us."

His weathered skin crinkles at the corners of his eyes as Andrew nods. I really hate deceiving the old man. He trusts me. I can tell he's only considering it because I'm the one who assured him that no blood will be shed.

Popping an antacid tablet into his mouth, he crunches it silently as his gaze pings suspiciously between us. Andrew should really wipe that creepy smile off his mug right now. I'd trust that face about as much as I'd trust someone to wax my chest.

"Yeah? What about the doorway incident this morning?"

Andrew claps his hand on my shoulder and gives it a brotherly looking shake. I can feel his fingertips digging painfully into my muscles. "Just a game we like to play. All in good fun." Turning his face toward me, he flashes that obnoxious smile. "Right, Lucas?"

Fifty percent. Fifty percent, I chant silently as his fingertips dig deeper into my shoulder.

"Right," I concur, nodding to Lou.

Lou's phone on his desk rings. Picking up the receiver, he's silent for a moment as I hear the muffled sound of Vera's voice on the other end, probably asking what she should do since she's been left to entertain the Hepperlys in the other room.

"I'm working on it. Hang tight. I know. I know," he grumbles. Slamming the phone down, he glances at the clock on his wall and grimaces. His gaze returns to us, pinging between the two of us. Except now I'm sporting the same fake smile Andrew is. I'll feel guilty about that later. Sighing, his lips flatten as they press together. "Fine, but hear this—if you two fuck this up, I will personally tweeze out your nuts hair."

Ouch. That's…specific.

I nod, though, because apparently, I'm willing to lose my nut hair for my baby sisters' happiness. Andrew slaps his palms together and pops out of his chair. "You're my favorite uncle, you know that?"

"I'm your only uncle," Lou mutters, leaning back in his chair and rubbing his eyelids.

Andrew doesn't wait, heading for the door with hurried steps like a vulture with its eye on a fresh carcass. I scramble out of my seat and utter my gratitude to Lou for trusting me. He nods, but looks wary as he glances at his nephew's retreating back. I take pride in knowing that means he might have more faith in my professionalism than Andrew's, but how sad is it that I have to be the more responsible of the two of us when I'm not the one who's his own kin?

I catch up to Andrew halfway across the lobby, but he doesn't slow down. Holding my arm out in front of him, I side-step into his path to the conference room door.

"Hold up. We can't just waltz in there. We need a game plan."

"I don't need a game plan. I've got this."

Selfish. He's so damn selfish. I knew this would happen. He's going to try to steamroll me the entire time and make me look incapable.

"Did you hear what your uncle said about nut hair?" I whisper. "We need to look like we get along and act like a team."

"I manscape. I'm good. You can sit this one on the bench and grab the luggage and cappuccinos while I do the important work. Don't worry your pretty little beard off." Smiling, he slaps me on the shoulder and steps around me.

God, I hate him. Racing, I step in front of him again. "You can't be awake 24/7, and it doesn't matter who makes the sales. It's a fifty-fifty commission split, so we need to make sure they trust both of us."

Throwing his head back, he lets out a long breath. "Would you just calm yourself and let me work my magic? You'll get your fifty percent." Shifting around me, his hand is on the door before I can stop him again. "Then you can ride off into the sunset in a new monster truck and we won't ever have to deal with each other again."

I don't own, nor have I ever had the desire to own, a monster truck. He's such a pampered ass with a skewed version of the world. Why can't he be more like Lou? Lou served his country and then worked for everything he has, from the ground up. Andrew was clearly handed a job; first by his father, and then by his uncle.

The door is open before I can retort or even imagine kicking him in the small of his back. I really hate the ideas this man gives me. Just because I was a soldier doesn't mean I have violent tendencies. Every time I see Andrew, though, all I can think of is inflicting physical harm. Squashing the thoughts, I suck in a breath and hurry on his heels into the room.

Vera's brows hike momentarily, but then she paints on one of her charming smiles. "Oh! Good. Here are two of our boys right now."

Andrew bends down and plants a peck on her cheek. "Auntie," he says sweetly. I've only heard him call her 'auntie' when he wants something. "Have no fear. They're in capable hands."

Vera lets out a nervous laugh, but I can't react. Literally, I can't. I find myself slack-jawed, staring at Dario Kealey in the flesh. Oh my God, he just made eye contact with me.

Nodding, he smiles and greets, "G'day," in his signature Australian accent that I've heard countless times only on television.

"I love you," I blurt like some starstruck teenager.

"Glad to hear it, mate, but I'm a bit taken." He grins and gestures to his husbands.

Holy shit. What is wrong with me?

"I…I mean, I'm a huge fan," I flounder, but realize that only makes me sound more rabid, like I'm about to ask for an autograph on my forehead. "You talk about methods that would have come in handy when I was deployed in the Army. My guys would have loved your show if it had been airing at the time I was in."

"Ooh, a soldier," another man coos, making me realize I've neither introduced myself nor acknowledged anyone else in the room. The shaggy-haired blond with the diamond stud in his ear and leather cuffs on his wrists, I'm guessing, is the musician of the throuple. I find myself blushing at the praise in his blue eyes.

The door closes behind Vera on her way out, and I find Andrew looking appalled that I've just somehow gotten points in with the clients. He quickly masks his features, however, and does that thing where he slaps his palms together like a used car salesman.

"So, guys, it sounds like you want to take a different kind of adventure," he enthuses. "I'm Andrew, and this is my partner, Lucas. We are so excited to help you find what you need."

All three men's faces light up for some reason. Keenan, a clean-cut looking man in a button-up that contrasts with the more casual attire of his husbands, arches a brow behind the dark frames of his glasses. "You two are a couple?"

A couple? As in…boyfriends? Me and Andrew?

Oh, fuck. How did he get that assumption? As I scan Dario and Mason's faces, I can see they're curious and excited for confirmation as well.

I'm jostled by a slap from Andrew's hand. His arm stays slung across the back of my shoulders, and he gives my biceps a squeeze. I want to shake it off, but remember that we're supposed to look like two people who can stand each other.

"Yep! Met this cutie when he stumbled into our office four years ago looking for a piloting job." The confounding words spill from Andrew's lips like a practiced speech that is the equivalent of a horror story to my ears. Why did he just say that?

I gape at him, waiting for some punch line or to see how he's going to get his dress shoe out of his mouth as Mason coos, "Aww, you met at work. Brilliant. I love that."

At the same time, Dario asks me with intrigue, "You can pilot?"

Before I can utter a syllable, Andrew's hand moves to the back of my neck, where he gives me a little shake. "He sure can. But don't let this big hunk of man meat fool you. He's both brains and brawn. He got his real estate license last year."

"Two years ago," I correct because I don't need him speaking for me when he doesn't know a damn thing about me, but that was the wrong thing to say.

"Sorry, sweetheart." Flashing the Hepperlys a smile, he adds, "Time flies when you're in love."

Keenan sighs and closes his eyes. "Don't even get me started on dates with these two. Neither one of them can remember what we did last week, but they expect me to remember the anniversaries of our first dates and when we got engaged."

"You're a financier, *Keen*," Dario laughs. "You work with numbers all day. How hard is it to remember a couple of dates?"

They erupt into an affectionate squabble over the significant dates in their relationship. When it looks like we've been momentarily forgotten, I claw my way out of my shock. Did what I think just happen actually happen?

Angling my head toward Andrew, I scathe under my breath, "What in the hell are you doing?"

"Making this happen," he murmurs back out of the corner of his mouth. "Just roll with it."

Roll with it? Is he out of his fucking mind?

The Hepperlys return their attention to us and begin to elaborate on their plans more than what Lou briefly relayed to us. I'm forced to table my protests to Andrew and take a seat. There is no way I'm causing a scene, and I honestly can't think of a way to dig ourselves out of the lie he just told without looking like we're completely unprofessional.

For the next hour, I take notes, writing down every detail that each of the men says. If a client wants a cactus garden and purple curtains like their grandmother had, I make sure to note it, just in case I can make it happen. Andrew...well, Andrew lounges back in his chair with his arm slung over the back of mine like that's enough to pass off that we've laid claim to each other as he mucks it up and agrees with everything they say, throwing out grandiose assurances that we're going to hook them up. How he's sold a single property is beyond me. Lou was right. This is going to be so much work. The travel coordination is going to be stressful enough, let alone now adding in the elephant in the room that Andrew created.

Biting my cheek the entire time, I mostly murmur and nod because I'm too preoccupied trying to decide if we should just come clean now and tell them we're not a couple. That we, in fact, hate each other. How can they not see that? I'm pretty sure I look like I want to vomit—Andrew and his stupid arm and pet names. *Cutie. Man Meat. Sweetheart.* All I hear each time is mockery and disdain. I wish they could hear it too. They seem like nice people who don't deserve to be duped. Clearly, my counterpart has no soul. Surprise, surprise.

When it starts to sound like everyone agrees to leave at the end of next week, I feel a panic bubble in my chest expand. I'm supposed to get my fitting done for the girls' wedding that day. Maybe I can ask them to move it up or back. We've planned to be gone for four weeks because the Hepperlys apparently want to relax at a few of the viewing locations, and they have a three-day stopover in the middle of the trip in Boston at Keenan's mother's house. Lou wasn't kidding about them doubling this as their honeymoon. I'm going to have to try to coordinate the band's playlist and handle all the other wedding tasks for Jolissa and Julia that I promised to deal with from abroad. I'm already feeling the squeeze, and this giant lie on top of everything has my stomach in knots.

The slap of palms snaps my attention back to the present. Chairs start to screech against the floor, and the Hepperlys rise along with Andrew.

"All right then! This is happening," he declares, reaching out to shake their hands. "Honeymoon for five!"

Oh, for fuck's sake. They're laughing…actually laughing. They love him already. How is that possible? Worse yet, I think this means I officially have to pretend to like him.

After the Hepperlys make their way out of the building with well wishes from us and Vera. I wait for Andrew to exchange his quirky pleasantries with his aunt. I like Vera too much to drop the bomb on her that he just crafted in the conference room. We need to have words in private for this disaster waiting to happen. I see no way out of it without completely pissing off this poor throuple and Lou.

Damn it. This is a nightmare. Fifty percent, but still a nightmare.

Giving his aunt's cheek a kiss, he breezes out the door without further notice. The amount of dust on his office computer tells me how much planning he puts into his showings, but I suspect his retreat isn't due to laziness this time. No doubt he's scampering away before he has to talk to Lou. When or if Lou finds out about what he just pulled, I can only imagine the old man will have a coronary.

Giving a quick farewell to Vera, I hurry outside. He's halfway across the parking lot already, the idiot. Already acting like I don't exist. How in the hell are we supposed to pretend to be a couple if he just left me high and dry? The Hepperlys could be driving around the corner for all we know.

"Andrew!" I call out, but he doesn't stop. "Andrew!"

Stopping, his head falls back like the sound of my voice is exasperating. Wonderful. So much for his promise to Lou that our differences were behind us. He's probably going to accidentally, on purpose, forget me at one of the properties, a remote island, no less. I can see it now.

"What?" he asks, sounding bored.

"What the hell were you thinking?" Glancing over my shoulder to make sure Lou hasn't come outside, I add, "How are we going to fix this? They think we're an actual couple."

A puff of laughter. A grin. Stepping forward, he pats my stubble. "There's no fixing anything Sweetcheeks. Did you see how they lit up when they thought we were an item? I saw an opening, and I took it. We're in like Flynn. You're welcome."

Batting his hand away, I glower at him. "First off, that's dishonest." He snorts and rolls his eyes. "Second, we don't even like each other and your first instinct was to tell them we're a couple? It was already going to be difficult enough to pretend not to hate each other for weeks on end, but now we're going to have to act like…like…"

"Like what?"

"Like we're…into each other."

Frowning, he folds his arms. "Wait. You're not homophobic, are you?"

What? Why would he think that? Just because I don't like having *any* conversation with him doesn't mean I'm homophobic. I actually get along with men far better than I've ever related to women, aside from my mom and sisters. I am not the problem here.

"No, but I've seen the way you flirt with female clients, and what about that Veronica lady that comes in sometimes to go out for drinks with you?"

His hand bats the air dismissively. "These aren't female clients, so no issue there, and Veronica's just a friend." Stretching out his arms, he grins, "Don't worry. I'm all yours, lover."

Ugh. He's impossible. This shit is not going to fly for weeks on end.

"You heard what your uncle said. We're going to have to play a part and be with them the entire time. And now, no thanks to you, that means we're going to have to act like a couple of happily paired gay guys 24/7 when nothing about you says *gay*."

"Oh my God. Would you listen to yourself? Do you think gay people are any different from everyone else? I literally just convinced three people that we're in love."

I've honestly never known any gay men, but he's completely misconstruing the point. He's a playboy who can't keep his tongue in his mouth when a pretty woman walks by. "For an hour, not three to four weeks," I digress.

"Just calm your tits. Don't argue with me in front of them and try not to look like you want to cut out my liver until this thing goes contingent, and we'll both walk away happy, richer men," he says like he has complete faith in his own bullshit.

I purse my lips, thinking of all the things I want to say, but I know there is no talking sense to him. I have a temporary boyfriend whom I can't stand, but if I don't murder him, I'll be able to pay off my loans and the girls' wedding.

He holds out his hand, and I scoff in disbelief at the fragile peace offering. I nod and grip it, but can't hold back the words that leave my mouth. "I hate you."

"Not as much as I hate you."

Chapter 3

ANDREW BROADHOUSE
licensed agent

"Teach me how to be gay," I blurt desperately when I finally locate my cousin in his living room.

"Drew?" he squawks, his head jolting up from where it was resting on the back of the couch.

Between his knees, his husband, Terry, pops off his dick and dives to the floor on his stomach, screeching, "Oh, my God! What the fuck?"

Fucking Lucas. What did he mean, nothing about me says *'gay?'* I've known my cousin Shaw my entire life. I guarantee I know more about being gay than the Army Ranger extraordinaire, but fuck it all if I'm going to be the one to screw this deal up.

Moving further into the living room, I head between the coffee table and the sectional as Shaw swipes up a throw pillow and covers his lap with it. What is the big deal? It's a dick. I've seen it before. Mine's better. Case closed.

"I didn't hear the doorbell. Did you even knock?" Shaw asks, straightening up as I take a seat on the other end of the sectional.

"I have a key, remember?" I huff, scooching back to get comfortable.

"He's sitting down. *Why* is he sitting down?" Terry calls from under the coffee table.

Sighing, Shaw covers his face with one hand. "The key is for emergencies. You can't just walk in here unannounced."

"This *is* an emergency. I need your help."

"He's *still* speaking! Why is he speaking?" Terry barks from his hiding place as his hand sneaks out to retrieve his shirt from the floor.

Is he going to stay down there all day? They've been married for ten years, and he's been uptight for the entirety of them. I'm surprised

Shaw was even getting a *beejer* from him in the middle of the day with a personality like that.

"Really?" I look at Shaw as I gesture to the table.

"Terry, just come on out. You know he's not going to leave," Shaw mutters.

Huffing, Terry's reddened face emerges when he pops up like a prairie dog and glares at me. "We could have been fucking. What is wrong with you?"

"I told you—*emergency*."

"Wait." Shaw squints at me. "Did you ask me to teach you how to be gay? Are you…coming out? Is this you coming out?"

Terry's eyes go wide, and he smacks Shaw on the knee. "Holy shit! I freaking called it. Did I not call it?"

Called it? He thought I was in the closet? He might as well dive back under the coffee table if he's that unperceptive. I came here for *good* advice.

"What? No! I'm not joining the club. I just need a day pass to sink a deal at work. The Hepperly throuple wants to make a three-property purchase, and yours truly has been assigned to spend the next month with them doing the viewings."

"*The* Hepperlys," Terry parrots, pausing his shirt halfway over his shoulders. "As in the pop star, financier, and survivalist TV show host Hepperlys?"

"Are there other Hepperlys?" I throw a hand up.

Terry reacts to my sarcasm with a disapproving noise and stomps around the couch toward the kitchen area. Running his fingers through his curly brown hair, he mutters, "That is so not fair that you get to hang out with them." He pauses halfway to the island counter, though, and spins back around. "Wait a minute. Why did you say you need a gay day pass?"

"Lou assigned another agent to show them the properties with me, and they, for some reason, assumed that we're a couple, so…I just went with it."

"You what?" Shaw gapes.

Terry scoffs, but then throws a hand out and looks at my cousin. "See? I'm not the only one."

Why does everyone think I'm gay all of a sudden? It's not my fault Lucas' opening line to Dario was a profession of his love for him. When I said the word *'partner,'* I didn't think they'd take that as a *romantic* partner. Once the assumption was made, I honestly saw no other viable option considering how Destination had just shit on them.

Sighing, I scrub my face, frustrated by this interrogation. "Look. It was out of my hands. Okay? Lucas fangirled over Dario because apparently, he has a giant man-crush on him, and then I introduced him as my 'partner,' but I meant *work* partner. Your dad said they came to us because the last agency was bigoted toward them, so I figured what better way to make them feel welcome and accepted?"

"By lying to them?" Terry chirps. "Ugh. I can't with you." Throwing his hands up, he stomps deeper into the kitchen. Hopefully, he'll stay there.

"So…not only do you now need to present as a gay man, but you need to present as a gay couple with…" Shaw trails off. "Wait a minute. Isn't Lucas that guy who kicked your ass last year?"

"He did *not* kick my ass."

Why is he laughing? It wasn't funny then, and it's not funny now.

"Oh, man. I can just imagine what my dad thinks about this."

"Whatever," I mumble, shifting on the cushion at the thought of steam coming out of Uncle Lou's ears. "Can you help me or not?"

Shaw studies me for a moment and then guffaws. "Oh, brother. He doesn't know, does he?"

Pious people practice vows of silence. Right? You'd think that would mean some kind of higher power would be in their favor, but it does zilch for me at the moment, producing another round of laughter from Shaw.

Sighing, I get up and head to the fridge. If they're going to torture me, they could at least offer me a beverage. "I'll tell him," I throw over my shoulder. "Just…after I get on the plane."

Terry frowns at me when I pull a beer out of the fridge and pop the cap off. As soon as I set it on the counter, he slaps his palm over it and whips it into the garbage can like it was a dirty diaper. Can you say dramatic?

"Cranky much?" I challenge. "*Sorry* I interrupted your fucking."

"Uh, hello. *Not* fucking because of *you*. This was the first time we were both home together in two weeks."

"Well, then make this quick, so you can get back to it. How do I pull off looking like a boyfriend?"

"Oh, my God," he laughs, covering his mouth like he's containing excitement over a secret. "You don't need to know how to be gay, you need to know how to not look like an insensitive asshole."

"What?"

"You don't date. You've never dated in all the years I've known you." Glancing over at my cousin, he calls out, "Shaw? Help me out here. Am I right?"

No shit, I don't date. Terry's not getting a rocket scientist award from me for that remark. I watch Shaw tromp into the kitchen and impatiently wait for one of them to offer something helpful.

"Drew, gay, bi, pan people—anyone who's attracted to men—you can't just lump their behavior, looks, or idiosyncrasies into a collective. That's insulting, even for you."

"Ugh. You know what I meant," I say, speaking to the ceiling because it might listen better than these two. "Only the Hepperlys and Terry think I'm into guys. I just want to keep it that way until they buy some islands, which, I might add, will bulk up your inheritance."

"You are so disgusting," Terry mutters and stalks off to do the dishes, angry style.

"Gee," Shaw deadpans, grabbing a jug of orange juice from the fridge. "That is so thoughtful of you, but I think I've done all right without waiting for Dad to kick the bucket."

I drum my fingers as he drinks straight from the container. Silently, I note that Terry flashes him the stink eye. I know Shaw is right. No two gay men are the same. Some freak out over beer bottle caps being left on the counter, while others drink directly from orange juice jugs. Got it. That's just human nature, sexual preferences aside. But Terry's right, too. I don't date.

While I have an inkling of what it might be like to date a woman, I have no freaking clue what it looks like to date a guy. The part after dating, I fully comprehend. Look at these two ill-matched people, bickering over stupid shit all the time. Look at my parents—copacetic enough as long as they each avoid the other's lengthy list of triggers.

Marriage is chaining yourself to the idea of tolerating a bunch of crap no sane person needs in their life. *That* is why I don't date. And yet, every single one of my friends has fallen down that pit of despair, even my favorite cousin. At least he and Terry don't have kids, so I can still hang out with them without having to hear how they can try to squeeze me in around playdates and little league schedules like my other friends. And that's only if and when they can find babysitters. I stand firm. Marriage is a chain. Children are the anchor attached to it. I am perfectly fine being a parasail zipping by unfettered, even if it does occasionally get boring and lonely.

"I don't know what you want me to tell you," Shaw digresses. "Just be attentive. Look like you give a shit about everything Lucas says or does. Everything he doesn't say or do. Include him in the conversations. I'd tell you to throw out stories about things you've done together as a couple, but—" he holds out a hand, "—here we are."

"I can be attentive."

"Newsflash," Terry pipes in, violently scrubbing a dish. "Attentive means thoughtful. Pulling out chairs, getting his favorite coffee, and rubbing his shoulders when he looks tense. Doing things without being asked."

Shaw sidles up behind Terry just then and starts kneading the muscle at the side of his neck as he places a kiss on his cheek. Terry visibly relaxes, his mouth ticking up at the corner. That is so needy—*gross*.

"So, I'm supposed to be an emotional support dog for the most aggravating man on the planet?"

"You made the bed, bro," Shaw laughs. "It's your choice if you want to sleep in it."

Terry chuckles silently along with him. One minute, he's shrieking, the next he's in stitches over my misery. Why did I come here?

"I'm glad this is so amusing to both of you. Is this any way to treat the best man at your wedding?"

"That was not by my choice," Terry voices, not even trying to mumble under his breath.

Finishing my beer, I grab another from the fridge and slap the cap down on the counter as loudly as possible. Terry's on it like a fly on shit, which brings me a small bit of joy after his hurtful remark.

"All right, fine. Be attentive. I'll kiss Satan's ass like no one has ever kissed ass before, but worst-case scenario here—he's a full-on brute who didn't receive his emotions chip at the hillbilly processing plant when he was created. He's not going to be able to sell this like I am. What do I do if I think they're on to us? I can't come clean. I just can't. I know it's wrong in the grand scheme of things, but I don't want them to have another shitty experience and the seed has already been sewn, so I need a back-up plan in case they suspect we're a sham."

They both turn to face me and go still. Is the answer obvious, or are they stumped?

"I could say Lucas had a head injury at a monster truck rally," I suggest. "Something that makes him emotionally unavailable, moody, and grumpy as fuck. Will that work?"

They continue to stare like I've lost my marbles. Okay, I know that was a little far-fetched, but this is Lucas we're talking about. Talk to him for ten minutes, and it sounds completely plausible.

"No, dude," Shaw chuffs. "There's only one way, but you're not going to like it."

"What?"

Why the fuck does Terry look so damn smug? Kicking his hip out, he rests his hand on it and smirks. "You're going to have to love up your man in front of them."

What…

The fuck I am.

The thought of doing anything physically intimate with that sour-puss, stack of bricks has my dick vowing to play dead for the rest of the year. "Well, that ain't gonna happen." I frown.

Shaw snorts. "Well, then you're fucked. Kiss your commission goodbye." Throwing an arm around Terry's shoulder, he murmurs. "See? I told you he's not into guys. I've known him my entire life. He's not even capable of faking it."

"I can do it," I snap, hating how easily I'm being dismissed. I fake it all day, selling properties. How is this any different? Shaw's amused expression pisses me off even more. "I could!" I reaffirm. "Just…with anyone but him. *Literally* anyone."

Smiling, Terry steps forward and pats me on the chest. "This is one instance that I actually have faith in you, Drew. I have no doubt you could make some unlucky man completely miserable and less-than-satisfied someday."

As I watch his shapely lips dispense that insult, I see an opportunity to redeem myself. I also see a test, a means of practice, in the bleak event that Lucas fucks this all up and I have to rely on their horrendous backup plan.

Fuck it. I can do it. I can.

Grabbing the back of Terry's neck, I hold him in place and slam my mouth against his. He lets out a garbled noise as his nose bashes into the side of mine. His mouth is clamped shut tight like a puckered asshole, which is fine by me. No one said anything about tongue being necessary.

"Drew!" Shaw gasps, letting me know I've pushed the cousin card far enough for one day.

Mission accomplished. Lips are lips. Big deal.

"There! See? I did it," I boast, holding my hands up to indicate I'm no longer a threat to his precious husband, who shrieks and spins around.

Terry wrenches the bottle of OJ out of Shaw's hand and chugs it until his cheeks are full. Then he bends over the sink and spews a stream of the orange liquid at the drain, sputtering like I just smeared battery acid on his lips. Dramatic. Totally dramatic. I still don't understand what Shaw sees in him.

"Oh, my God," Terry croaks into the sink. "Unclean…I'm unclean!"

Shaw grimaces at his husband's wretched pose and sighs, then tosses me a disapproving look. I level my gaze right back at him.

"I *am* coming home with a commission," I inform him with conviction. "Thanks for the advice."

Turning on my heel, I head toward the door, deciding I've gotten as much out of this prom dress as I'm going to get. The rest, unfortunately, will be up to my wits and Lucas.

"Drew!" Shaw calls, stopping me when I hear his footsteps shuffling after me.

I turn around to find him holding out his palm, eyes narrowed. "I'd like my key back."

"Fine, but if you throw your back out trying to pry Terry out from underneath the furniture, don't call me. I won't be able to get in."

"I'll take my chances," he mutters. "Enjoy your trip."

Despite that last disingenuous jab, I spring down their front steps feeling fairly confident about myself. I am going to pull this off, and Lucas is going to get with the program, even if I have to impale him with another listing sign. Or…if I have to lip lock him, I guess. Whatever. I just kissed Terry. As long as Lucas doesn't react the way *he* did, we'll be fine.

Oh, fuck…

I *kissed Terry*—Terry, who just had his mouth wrapped around my cousin's dick. My *cousin's* dick!

I let out something between a wild goose's mating call and a moan that startles some woman across the street who's watering her lawn. If she knew I potentially had remnants of my cousin's dick juices on my mouth, she'd be making this noise too. Ally or not, I draw the line at the transferring of a relative's dick juices.

Staggering, my body turns into rubber, convulsing. If Terry didn't like me putting my beer cap on his counter, I'm guessing he's not going to like me painting their shrubs with stomach bile, either. Serves them right for giving terrible advice.

Chapter 4

"What do you think?" Jolissa asks, angling her phone's camera until a gaudy vase comes into view. It's wide and clear, adorned with tiny white seashells around the lip and sapphire-blue stones adhered to the body. It's hideous.

Shifting in place as I wait for the baggage claim conveyor belt to start, I hold back a cringe. I've done what I can to be optimistic about all the wedding plans, but it's getting more difficult to act invested in the remaining fine details. I don't know if it's because I'm footing the bill or if it's because I'm their big brother and the closest thing to a father figure they have, but the girls have insisted on including me in the decision-making since day one.

"How much are they?" I ask, glancing up when I hear the loud slap of flip-flops approaching.

Andrew saunters toward the baggage claim with a Christmas ornament inside a clear gift shop bag, seemingly oblivious to the fact that it's June. He empties a packet of mixed nuts into his pie hole with his other hand like he hasn't a care in the world. I didn't have to see much of him on the flight since his precious self booked a first-class seat and he showed up at the very last minute when it was time to board the plane. Nice to see he's back to his frat-boy, beach-party image in shorts and a tank top. I guess he only had it in him for one day to impress the Hepperlys.

"Sixty-five dollars…" Jolissa's wary reply comes over the phone.

My eyes nearly bug out of my head. Once she sees my expression, her sheepish look grows even more sheepish.

"And you have *how many* tables again?"

"Fifty-two," Julia pipes in, appearing at her shoulder.

I run the math and assume my eyes bug out even further, given their twin expressions. Holy shit.

"That's like over three thousand dollars just for ugly centerpieces that you're only going to use once!"

"You think they're ugly?" Jolissa's voice rises. "Why didn't you say so when I asked?"

Ugh. Now I've crushed her bridal dreams and look like a tight ass.

Julia hums, inspecting one of them. "They're not my favorite either, JoJo."

"Well, we've been in here for like thirty minutes already. We have to find something. Go find Mom. See what she thinks."

Oh God. Not Kelly. I love my mother, but that woman adores anything that sparkles. These hideous vases are…extra sparkly. Also, while she's as frugal as I am, she's had a much more difficult time saying no to the girls for anything regarding their big day. It also doesn't help that she thinks I'm a big-time real estate agent now.

"No! Wait, just…can't you find something similar back home?" I bargain, knowing they're on some day trip to North Charleston, where everything costs a pretty penny more than back in our rural town of Bolton.

"What, like Buck's Emporium?" Julia snickers. "He'll probably sell us Mason jars with cow bells on them."

Damn. That's brilliant, actually. I hadn't even considered Buck's place. Granted, he sells livestock feed too and the only apparel he stocks is western-themed that no one in our town buys or wears, but I'm sure we could find some country decor there that won't make my bank account sweat.

"What's wrong with Mason jars? You are getting married in a barn, after all."

"Wow. This is disappointing," comes an unexpected voice. "I'm gone for two minutes to grab my bag, and he's already cheating on me with two women."

I flinch as Andrew leans over my shoulder from behind me, grinning at my baby sisters. *Grinning* is being kind—it's more like leering. Turning, I don't care if my elbow just bashed into his stomach. "They're my sisters."

"What?" comes his shocked reply. He angles around me and cups his hand over mine so I can't jerk my phone away from him. "Ladies… how *on Earth* do you two share the same DNA as this silverback?"

What the fuck? Is that a gorilla reference? And why are the girls giggling?

"Half-sisters," they say in unison.

"Ah…that explains it."

I shouldn't be salty about it. The girls have blonde hair and blue eyes like Clark did, God rest his soul. However, this is coming from Andrew; if there's an opportunity to belittle me, he'll find it.

"I'll message you when I get a signal where we're going. Think about the Mason jar idea."

I end the call so Andrew can't further fawn over my siblings or out my compliance with his despicable plan to my family. They don't need to know I'm impersonating as his boyfriend after a lifetime of trying to instill good morals, like honesty and integrity, in them.

"How old are they?" he asks.

"Way too young for you, and they're both getting married next month, so don't waste your time tormenting me with questions about them."

Scoffing, he readjusts the bag on his shoulder. "Easy killer. That's not where I was going. I prefer people born in the same decade as me. They just look like babies compared to you."

"They're twenty-five. They *are* still babies."

"And they're trusting their grumpy old half-brother to be their wedding planner?"

"Thirty-seven isn't old," I grumble, even though my stiff back doesn't believe it. "And I'm paying for the wedding since their father died when they were little, if you must know. So, it'd be nice if you could drop the harassment long enough for us to make sure we handle these sales professionally. Their happiness depends on it."

Frowning, he slaps me on the shoulder, but keeps his hand there. "Listen, *Sticks*. I know math might not be big where you come from, but we will land this sale, and that means you can afford way better than Mason jars for the babies. Okay? Women want Tiffany's and shit like that."

Shaking his hand off, I notice the conveyor is running and that he already has his bag. "Having money doesn't mean you need to waste it on overpriced crap."

Groaning, he rolls his eyes. "Whatever, just go grab your tighty-whities and emotional-support beard oil so we can hit it. We've got to go prep the puddle jumper in about two hours, and I need a snack first." Shaking the last few crumbs from his snack packet, he adds, "These free nuts aren't doing it for me."

Jackass. I don't doubt that was another dig at me. My nuts aren't free. They have to be earned.

Ugh. Listen to me. Never in my life did I imagine I'd have a boyfriend, pretend or not. It's just my luck that the one I get is high-maintenance and bossy as shit.

Two hours later, after Andrew has bought enough snacks to fill his back-pack, I can feel my lip curl as I watch him eat his weight in local British

Virgin Islands cuisine at a café near the dock. At least I have enough phone reception that I was able to call the girls and go over the seating chart to help pass the time after prepping the seaplane. I take another bite of my granola bar and sigh, gazing out at the crystal blue water. It's one thing I love about this job—the scenery is always breathtaking.

"You're seriously going to eat a protein bar at a restaurant? Are you one of those people who think they'll get dysentery if you eat local food or drink the water?" Andrew interrupts my moment of serenity around a mouthful of food, a lack of etiquette I wouldn't expect from a man who comes from wealth.

"They're heart-healthy and filling," I inform him without looking at him.

"When we get to the cay and your stomach starts growling halfway through the showing, tell me how filling they are then."

A taxi pulls up and stops in front of us, bringing me relief over the end of our forced bonding time. That relief is replaced with anxiety, though. It's showtime. I jump up when the Hepperlys pile out of the cab. Andrew takes a sip from his beer and waves. Classy. I still don't understand how he manages to sell so many properties. He's as charming as a Hawaiian shirt with plaid pants.

Rushing over to the trunk, I help the driver remove their luggage. They all flew in yesterday and spent the night at a hotel on the island. I wish I'd done the same, but I can't afford that luxury when I'm pinching every penny I can until this sale goes through.

"What a gentleman," comes Mason's British accent to my left as I heft one of the suitcases to the pavement. "Are you taking notes, Dario?" He smirks, glancing over his shoulder.

"Pack lighter and I'll show you a gent," his husband quips. "Wait'll we get to my neck of the woods. Those hair products are getting tossed in the reef."

Running his fingers through his well-styled blond locks, Mason answers cheekily, "You love my hair. You wouldn't."

Sighing, Keenan rounds Dario's side and extends the handle on the suitcase, rolling it out of the way to make room for the others. "Don't start you two, or this is going to be a long trip."

Mason throws an arm around his neck, pulling him closer and planting a kiss on his close-shaved hair. "It was your idea, love. And it's not my fault that my fans would riot if I buzzed my head like you do."

Hoisting another suitcase from the back, I let out an awkward laugh, unsure how to act. I feel sheltered having never seen two men in a relationship interact, let alone three. Their ribbing and playful touches aren't any different from the way my sisters are with their fiancés. Yet, the dynamic leaves me feeling even more out of my element than usual. I haven't been in a relationship, a real relationship, in almost four years. I haven't been on a date in a decade. Frankly, the sight of anyone in love still makes me uneasy after my disaster of an engagement. Sometimes, even seeing my sisters so over the moon is like a kick in the gut. I'll never have that. I think I even knew I never would've had that with Shannon. It felt…good having a partner, but that was just it—good. Safe. Reliable. The comfort of not being alone. I've never had that drunk-in-love look that my sisters do. Maybe I'm defective.

I sling one of their backpacks over my shoulder and then grab a suitcase in each of my hands. Nodding toward the dock, when their laughing faces turn to me, I inform them, "The, um, seaplane's ready to go, if you'd like to follow me."

"Lucas, you don't have to carry all of that," Keenan admonishes.

"It's fine. I've got it."

A hand slaps me on the shoulder and squeezes. "He does it all the time," Andrew assures them, kneading the muscle at the base of my neck. "Built like a pack mule, this one. Come on." He motions with his head toward the plane and brushes past me. "I'll get you boys settled."

Gritting my teeth, I watch him saunter off empty-handed as the Hepperlys follow him. I thought maybe he was just trying to get my goat when he said I would be handling the luggage while he did all the *important* work, but now I can see how this is going to go. Not that I mind being a gentleman. It's called having manners, something Andrew Broadhouse clearly knows nothing about. I doubt he's lifted a finger for manual labor a day in his life.

Hurrying after them, I have every intention of immersing myself in the conversation, so he knows he can't set a precedent that he's the one they'll come to for property questions. However, as I stow their bags, he's already mucking it up with them, rattling off details about the resort we'll be showing them today with rapid-fire exuberance.

"Fire her up, sweetheart," he calls out, sparing me nothing more than a glance. "Let's hit it."

Swallowing silent curses, I have no argument, since I *am* the one who has to fly the plane. That leaves him every opportunity to continue to run his mouth while I have to pay attention to the controls and our flight path. To my credit, I set us down gently at Moonbeam Cay and get a few claps from the Hepperlys for my flight skills.

Before I even have everything shut down, Andrew has already bailed out and is leading our clients down the dock to the resort. But not before he assured them I'd handle all their baggage. I'm going to murder him before the day is over.

After three long-ass treks to the resort's empty reception area, my back is soaked in sweat, and my heart rate is primed for a cardio workout. I nod to one of the caretakers, who's in charge of maintaining the place while it's officially closed, that this is the last of our cargo. He lets me know the rest of my party is already out back viewing the pool area. Fucking Andrew. He'll have made a sale before I even get peep in.

"Oh, this is great. Look at all the room for patio seating," Mason declares as I come huffing through the doors.

"There he is," Dario greets me, hands stuffed in his cargo shorts. His rugged physique, wavy black hair, and well-worn olive drab T-shirt make him look out of place even if the resort is currently devoid of its intended high-dollar guests.

"What took you so long?" Andrew asks, stretching out his arm like I'm supposed to come to him. Is he kidding me?

I'm not a demanding man, but if I did have an actual boyfriend, this would be grounds for dumping him. I can feel sweat trickling down my spine, and I'm sure I now smell like perspiration. Just the professional image I want to portray for a showing.

I stop between Dario and Andrew on purpose, ignoring whatever the hell his open arm is supposed to mean. I know I don't know the first thing about having a boyfriend, but I'm pretty sure they don't need to touch every second of the day or during a work setting.

"Your bags are all at reception," I inform the guys, offering a smile and trying not to sound winded.

"That was so nice of you, Lucas," Keenan says. "Thank you."

I feel his presence before I see him—Andrew's arm reaches around my back, squeezing my side. "Babe, you didn't have to do all that. I would have helped."

Turning my head, I hope he can see the concealed fury in my eyes. "Really? You could have fooled me."

Gaze shifting, he tracks the Hepperlys as they meander around the pool, surveying it. "Ew, you're all sweaty," he grumbles, releasing his hold on me and shoving me away. Before I can remind him how long the walk from the dock to the reception area is, he scurries off after our clients, spewing more of his zeal about all the other amenities the resort has to offer. I look like an idiot already. A useless, sweaty, pack-mule idiot—the exact image Andrew has of me. How did this happen?

Hurrying after them, I interject helpful facts whenever I can, but it proves difficult when Andrew barely shuts up and is constantly on the move, like this is a sprint. I've at least surmised that Dario couldn't care less about the resort. Keenan interjects a few things about potential revenue, which makes sense since he works in finance, but it's clear that Mason will be the deciding vote. They want to build a small stage for him and his band to host performances several times a year—an exclusive resort named after his band. The property will be an investment for the Hepperlys. While they clearly don't seem to need the revenue at the moment, I have to say I appreciate their collective interest in securing a financial future for them as a throuple. It's…sweet. The kind of thing people who intend to grow old together plan for.

Taking a seat at the bar in the lounge two hours later, I study them in silence. No thanks to Andrew's yammering, I can get away with doing so. They act like three best friends, three sometimes physically affectionate best friends. I'll admit I feel strangely warm each time I catch one of them giving the other a loving stroke to the arm or a side hug, but I'm in awe. I've never found one person to be so copacetic with. How lucky are they that each of them has found two?

My stool jostles, and a knee slams into the outside of my thigh. I know without even looking that it's my very non-copacetic fake boyfriend.

Andrew's barstool is scooted so close beside mine, he's practically enveloped me with his open thighs from the way he's sitting on his. I stepped away from him and shrugged off each of his touches as soon as the Hepperlys weren't looking while we walked around the resort today. I thought he'd have gotten the hint, but apparently not. His arm slinks over my shoulder from behind, effectively putting me on display now that I'm between him and the Hepperlys. I know he's doing it just to annoy me. We don't need to touch each other to sell properties. Steadying my breath, I try to ignore the sensation of his heavy arm over my shoulder and the way he's fingering the pocket on my shirt. I haven't been touched in forever, but it's not the touching that bothers me. It's the toucher who's making it feel…weird. I think sitting still while your archnemesis pets you might actually be more difficult than any of my army training.

"So, you two met at work?" Mason asks, sitting back in a chair at one of the round tables next to the bar that he and his husbands claimed. The caretaker brings over a tray of drinks and deposits them on their table, giving me a moment to prepare myself for our lie.

"Yeah," I concur, trying to smile. I feel dirty already, dirtier than when Andrew's filthy hands are on me.

"Sooo…tell us all the details," Mason croons. "Was it an office flirtation? A secret rendezvous? How did it happen?"

Andrew laughs. Too loudly. Right in my fucking ear. There is no way my smile looks genuine right now.

"He followed me around with those big puppy dog eyes of his for weeks before he finally got the nerve to ask me out."

My stomach roils and my face burns as the Hepperlys coo and chuckle. "I did not," I grit.

"Oh! I always love this part," Keenan laughs. "Two sides to every story. I can relate, Lucas. Go on. Tell us what really happened."

Fuck. How did I go from not wanting to lie to them to being neck deep in it with all eyes on me? My mind churns over every past interaction I've had with the jackass who's now got my shoulder in a death grip, like he's silently threatening me to make him look good. A man can only be so dishonest. Andrew is not good.

Picking up the beer the caretaker set on the bar for me, I mutter as I bring it to my lips. "He stalked me like a menace until I gave in."

Dario cracks up and shoots a look at Mason. "Sounds like someone else I know."

As the Hepperlys laugh, I feel heat at the back of my ear. The death grip on my shoulder tightens. "What the fuck?" Andrew hisses.

As soon as I'm sure our clients aren't looking, I smack his hand off my shoulder. He lets out a gasp like it hurt. The baby. I sit up straighter, pretending to adjust my shirt, but it's just an excuse to put more space between us. I don't want the first time I've been touched in four years to be by someone I can't stand. It's a deception my body doesn't need.

I try to listen to Mason defend his reasons for repeatedly booking Dario's survivalist package and coincidentally ending up at the same off-the-beaten-path pub Dario was at, but I can feel the hostility behind me like an invisible barrage of daggers. Good. I hope Andrew enjoyed getting a taste of his own medicine.

"Lucas," Dario calls, raising his glass with a smile, "you have my sympathies, mate."

"Thank you." I nod, raising my glass in return, enjoying the ounce of vindication it brings me.

I can feel Andrew bound off his stool. His hand clamps down on my shoulder again, making me tense. "Fellas, can you give us a minute to go over some of the arrangements for tomorrow? We'll be right back. The staff's getting some lunch prepped for you now, though, so hang tight."

"Sure. Bit a grub sounds good by me," Dario assures us.

"Take your time," Keenan adds, looking over the property plans with Mason like their digs to each other are already forgotten.

I give Andrew a side eye and am met with a sour expression. His stupid, wavy, sandy hair is starting to curl more in the humidity, making him look deranged. If he thinks he's supposed to be intimidating, he needs to work on it. Gripping the back of my neck, he practically steers me to the patio door. He's got another thing coming if he expects me to ask how high each time he says jump. I hope my sisters have at least an inkling of how much I love them and cherish their happiness. I cannot wait to break up with this asshole.

Is he *trying* to blow this? God, what was I thinking? There is no reasoning with a six-foot-one slab of backwoods meat with the social skills of a porcupine. I am giving this my all, and he's trying to ruin it at every turn.

I pat him on the shoulder, and he shrugs it off. I lean in, and he shifts in the other direction. Does he think that was easy for me? The man is a walking, talking repellent. Still, I even tried to hold his hand earlier when we were showing the Hepperlys the convention room, but he jerked his away. I swear Keenan noticed and gave us a peculiar look. Even now, when all I want to do is throttle him, I've got my hand on the back of his neck like we're life mates.

Speaking of which, why is he so fucking sweaty? Yuck!

Shoving him away from me as soon as we're outside and out of view of the Hepperlys, I wipe my palm on my shorts. Mental note to burn them later.

Folding my arms, I face off with the brute. Glaring at me, his lower lip pouts, causing his cheeks to puff out. It makes him look like a depressed chipmunk. Dario's sympathy should be for *me*. If I were really gay, I could do so much better.

"Are you trying to blow this for us?"

"What?" he huffs, adjusting his shirt collar like I roughed him up. If only.

"You might as well just deck me with how prickly you come across."

Smoothing down the front of his thin short-sleeve button-up, he mutters, "Tempting."

The freaking coward. He can't even look at me when he mouths off. Some badass ranger he is. "Hey, whether you like it or not, we're in this thing together."

"No thanks to you." Folding his beefy arms, he glares out over the tennis courts like a giant bearded baby.

"Oh, for fuck's sake. Are you going to stand there and pretend you don't want the money? Don't think I haven't heard you on the phone nickel and diming your sisters over every wedding decision."

That must have hit a nerve. His eyes flick to mine, and his arms drop to his sides like tree branches. "That's none of your concern. And I'm not nickel and diming. I'm…being sensible. I didn't think they were going to have 300 guests. I only had a hundred at mine and that was only because—"

"Whoa…hold up. *You're* married?"

"No," he blusters, shoving his hands in his shorts' pockets and averting his gaze.

"You just said *your* wedding. Ah, let me guess; you're divorced."

"You have to be married to get divorced." That thick lower lip of his disappears as he purses his lips. Is he…blushing?

"Oh, shit." I find myself snorting even though I know it's not appropriate. "What then? Did she leave you at the altar?"

"No," he sulks. His nostrils flare on an expansion of his chest, and he's quiet for a moment. I honestly don't give a damn to know anything about Lucas Everette, but this is too intriguing, so I wait. "She…left me at the *Piggly Wiggly*," he mutters, kicking the heel of his sneaker against the concrete.

Excuse me? He got jilted?

I mean, it doesn't exactly surprise me. I think I'm more shocked that someone actually wanted to marry him. Well, okay. I guess, *technically*, she didn't.

"Two weeks before the wedding," he grumbles, rubbing the back of his neck like it still bothers him. "In the middle of the frozen food section."

Fuck…

No wonder he's playing wedding planner for his sisters. Someone fucked him up.

I should say something. Even though I can't stand him, logic and decency tell me I should say something. I need his head in the game, after all.

"Damn. That's…cold."

I don't understand why he's glaring at me until I remember where he said she broke the news to him. Ah, shit. I'm a smartass even when I don't mean to be.

I try not to crack up over the thought of him getting dumped, surrounded by frozen peas. A wave of frost settling on him as sad music plays from an overhead speaker in the middle of a grocery store. I'm sure my face gives me away, but then his mouth ticks up at the corner, cracking a smile, and I lose it.

Thank God. Even Mr. Personality appreciated my unintended joke.

"I had to put half the shit back," he scoffs with a hint of mirth, but then sighs. "I wish it had been that easy with all the wedding bills and the house."

"Wait. You got stuck paying for a wedding you didn't even have?"

Grimacing, he shrugs. "Shannon's parents didn't have much, and I'd have never asked them to help." When I don't say anything, he adds, "They're good people. It's fine. I'm about done paying off the loan, then I'll just have the house and my truck to worry about."

Not that I'll ever have to worry about footing a wedding bill or not being able to afford one, but that's messed up. Did he freaking buy a house for two that's now a bachelor pad? And if she's the one who called off the wedding, she should be helping him out with the wedding expenses, at least. What is he, a sap? Or just…

No.

I refuse to even silently think that Lucas is a good person. I don't care if there is evidence. We're getting off track here anyway.

"Well, I'm not Shannon. I'm going to see this thing through to the end, so can you start trying to act like you give a damn about me?"

I don't know how I'm supposed to take the look he gives me. On the one hand, it's shocking. How can such a big, angry dude look so vulnerable, almost like he has trust issues? I will not feel sorry for him just because someone broke his stupid heart. On the other hand, I'm offended. His face says that trying to fake liking me is the most repulsive thing someone has ever asked him to do. I am not repulsive. Yeah, clearly he's not down with dick either, but I'm still a catch.

"No more insults about how we met. No more flinching when I touch you or pulling away," I elaborate, so he knows I'm not asking for his heart and soul.

"They laughed when I said the stalker thing. All couples bicker and tease," he says lamely.

"Yeah, but they also get along, laugh, and smile each other. Did you not see the way they all dote on each other? If you keep up the way you were today, they'll be onto us in no time, and you can kiss our commission goodbye."

His gaze rakes over me covertly before looking away. Huffing, he stares out at the tennis courts again. "Why is it so important to *you?* You've got plenty of money."

If that's his shit way of saying I'm good at this job, he's getting an F in the compliment department. One more thing we'll have to work on in front of the Hepperlys.

"Because…"

Ugh. Isn't there some unspoken rule that you never divulge your weaknesses to the enemy? He just flayed himself about his failed hillbilly wedding that never happened, though, so I guess I can throw him a bone if it helps get him with the program.

"Because my dad and brother think I'm not responsible enough to have a successful career. Never mind that to them, successful means *only* if the career is at Broadhouse Publishing. So, I've been working my ass off for my Uncle Lou to show them I can do just fine on my own, whether they like it or not."

I wait for derision or insults, but they don't come. There's something in his eyes that looks like respect. Fuck him and the surprise that's there too, but the respect part has my face heating. I honestly can't remember the last time anyone looked at me with respect. Maybe it's just weird seeing him not hate me for five seconds.

"Fine," he finally says.

Really? He's giving in that easily? No headlocks or insults?

"*Fine?*" I parrot.

"Yeah. Whatever."

Huh. Strange. Sass him around with logic and he complies. Noted. Maybe he has something ingrained in him from the military to take orders.

Shrugging, I nod. "Okay then."

An awkward beat passes between us as we both glance toward the resort. If he wants to shake hands or thinks we're friends now, this is going to get even more awkward. It's just business.

"So...what do you suggest we do?"

It shouldn't fluff my feathers so much that he's actually looking to me to take the lead. I tried to tell him to do that from the beginning, but I guess some people are slow learners. He's a few years older than I am. You'd think that would give him more life experience, but ruck marching in the military clearly doesn't prepare people for the dirty real world. Alpha boyfriend, it is.

Sucking in a breath, I hold out my hand, hoping he gets the message. "Be as absolutely disgusting as we can."

Glancing down at my hand, his face blanches and his lip curls down at the corner. Such a jerk. I don't have time for his freak outs. Grabbing his big meat hook, I start for the door.

"I said disgusting as in candy-sweet disgusting, not *disgusted*. Lose the grimace."

His arm hair feels like a sherpa blanket underneath my forearm. Why did he go into island real estate? The man's body was not built for warm weather.

"Why are you so hairy? Can't you wax that shit or something?"

"No one waxes their arms," he huffs, reaching for the door at the same time as I do, but then gives up. He jerks his hand away when he passes through, though not as violently as earlier, I'll give him that much, but I can tell we've still got a long way to go.

"And if insulting me is what you meant by disgusting, I doubt that's going to convince them," he grumbles, but waits for me.

Snagging his hand again out of spite, I ignore how meaty it feels in my grip. His palm is surprisingly soft, not covered in calluses like I imagined it to be. Maybe he wears gloves when he chops wood back in the swamp or wherever he comes from.

"Sorry, lover," I snark, squeezing his hand tighter when I notice how limp his grip is, like he can't wait for the second I let go.

The color of his face says he has murder on his mind. Ha! Maybe this won't be as miserable as I imagined. I can play the doting boyfriend *and* piss him off at the same time. I am now committed to not letting go of his sweaty-ass dirt digger until we're done with the showing for the day. If he wants sweet, I'll be as sweet as a freaking toothache.

Shaw did say to be attentive. I have a feeling I'm going to thoroughly enjoy being attentive if it gets under Lucas' skin this easily.

"Smile, baby. We've got islands to sell," I mutter under my breath as we approach the lounge.

His breath is audible. His mouth widens, lips pressed together in a thin line.

"If you call that smiling, they're never going to think we're a couple."

"I'm trying," he grits, but it only gets worse.

"Everything all right?" Dario asks, quirking a brow.

Fuck. I'm not the only one getting angry mutant vibes from my dickhead boyfriend.

"Yeah. Lucas was just bummed that he'll miss a monster truck rally next week when we'll be in Massachusetts."

"Ah shit, mate. I'm sorry."

I can practically feel the hostility rolling off him. Slipping my arm around his shoulder, I hug him to me. "It's all right," I assure Dario and his husbands, who look up from their meal. "I told him I'd make it up to him. Isn't that right, sweetheart?"

Holy fuck. Could he look any more pissed off? It was just a joke. Couples joke.

Crap. Dario looks like he's got our number, his brows now scrunched suspiciously.

Turning Lucas by the shoulder, I cup his beard in my hands to direct his grumpy face away from theirs. The man would suck at poker, wearing his emotions like this.

"What are you doing?" he whispers angrily, scanning my hands like he's terrified by my proximity.

"Paying for a wedding. Don't fucking move," I murmur and hold my breath as I slam my mouth against his.

He lets out a startled noise and clutches my wrist. Only Lucas would make a guy need to resort to his backup plan on day one. If he freaks out and decks me, I'm going to drown him in the ocean.

Clutching onto the back of his fat head, I make a show of moving my lips over his when really I'm just grinding our tightly closed mouths against each other. I'm going to have beard burn after this. That's a new one for me. The shit I do to prove things to my family.

"Yeah! Get it, Lucas!" Mason cheers, letting me know I've sold enough of my soul for one day.

I release him, and he lets out a strange sound. You'd think I just slapped him the way he's gaping at me. His tongue darts out and wets his lips. It didn't feel like a kiss until he did that. Gross. Now I can kind of taste him.

Granola bar. Yeah. Definitely granola.

Someone whistles, probably Mason. He seems like the liveliest of the group. It's enough to clear the strange fog in Lucas' eyes, and he blinks, releasing my wrist. Clearing my throat, I glance over at our amused clients. Flashing them a satisfied smile, I run my hands down Lucas' beefy shoulders to further seal the façade. It's meant to look like a caress, but it feels strange. He's like a damn brick building. A far cry from the slender and curvy female bodies I've had my hands on.

"There's more later where that came from," I tease, patting his furry cheek, enjoying the way it makes his jowls jiggle on his stupefied face.

Fortunately, feeding him turns out to be a good cover to hide his emotions. For a guy who bitched about me controlling the entire showing, he stayed mostly silent throughout lunch and the rest of the afternoon. By the time dinner rolls around, holding his hand isn't even weird anymore. It just feels like I'm guiding around a silent lumberjack out of charity since he's given up sassing me in front of the Hepperlys. He offers one-liners of slightly helpful insights about the property and manages these breathy little laughs that have to be completely forced, but all in all, it's passable. I haven't detected a single skeptical look from our merry clients.

The tour of some of the rooms, the grounds, and a potential area to build a stage all went fairly well. Yet, the trio seems satisfied to wait to give their full opinions until we look at the next property the day after tomorrow. With the investment they're making, I can't say I blame them, even if I hoped we could cut this trip shorter than planned.

Hauling our luggage upstairs, I leave my suitcase by the room we were given and grab one of Mason's from him. "You guys are right here in one of the luxury suites. We'll be right next door if you need anything."

"Andrew, how about a tour around the cay tomorrow?" Dario asks, holding the door to their room open for Keenan. "Can we take one of those boats out?"

"Yeah, of course. That can be arranged. How about after breakfast? I think the caretaker said they'd serve it at eight."

"Sure thing. See you at brekky."

I blink, wondering what he means until Lucas mutters, "That means breakfast."

Oh. How could I forget that Dario's number-one fan is my new roommate? Walking back toward our room, I mumble, "I knew that."

The asshat rolls his eyes and gives me a smug look. I'll give zero fucks about that when I'm sound asleep in an hour.

Opening our door, I roll my suitcase inside, grateful to be done for the day. The balcony doors are open, letting in the cool evening breeze from the cay already making my sun-kissed flesh feel at ease after the long day of travel.

"Why is there only one bed?"

And so it begins…

Tossing my backpack on the dresser, I eye the bed in question. Decent-looking mattress and fluffy comforter. I am going to pass the fuck out as soon as I get crab-ass squared away.

"Because…while *someone* was fucking around with the luggage this morning, I got put on the spot arranging our rooms with the caretaker in front of the Hepperlys."

"And…what does that have to do with one bed? I know they have doubles here."

"Uh, maybe because we failed to plan a backstory where we came from a Mormon community and are saving ourselves for marriage? What was I supposed to do? Ask for separate rooms right in front of them?"

Scoffing, he stands there like a lump with a frown, eyes fixed on the bed like it's a rat trap. "Well…where am I supposed to sleep?"

"The floor? The couch? Out on the balcony?" I gesture carelessly, kicking off my shoes. "What the fuck do I care as long as we walk out of the same room in the morning?"

His gaze goes from the sofa, which upon second glance is actually a love seat, then to the bed, and then to me. "We'll take turns," he lets out finally.

"Like hell we will." Ignoring his appalled expression, I grab my toiletries bag out of my bookbag and head for the bathroom. "And I get the first shower!" I call just before slamming the door shut behind me.

I no sooner get all the Lucas sweat washed off my body and stroll back out into the room in my towel than I hear a knock on the door. My gaze snaps to Lucas. Gross. He actually does wear tighty-whities.

Okay. They're black, but it's the same fucking thing. Did *not* need to see that. Eyes round, he freezes with a pair of clean underwear and a towel clutched against his stomach, glancing at the door.

"Gents? You decent in there?" Mason calls from the other side.

I no sooner yell out, *'yeah,'* than I spot Lucas' makeshift bed on the floor. A pillow and…did he fucking gank the comforter off the bed? What the actual fuck?

"Quick! Get on the bed!" I whisper, swiping up the comforter and tossing it onto the mattress. I nearly forgot the pillow until I trip over it when Lucas' shoulder bashes into mine.

"Watch it!"

"You got in *my* way," he grumps, barreling onto the mattress.

The door creaks open just as I whip the pillow at dickhead's face and spin around with the smile my DNA gifted me. Brushing my damp hair back, I adjust my towel and nod at a freshly showered Mason.

"What can we do you for? Room okay?"

His bare chest displays an array of tattoos and two pierced nipples. A pair of sleep pants are slung low on his hips. I should be at ease that he feels comfortable enough around us to waltz right into our room in such a state, but the grin he flashes after looking past my shoulder makes me cringe.

"Hope I'm not interrupting anything," he says. I can only imagine the bed looks like I just wrestled a bear, but points to shit timing if it planted the wrong image in his brain. Flicking his thumb over his shoulder, he continues, "So, Dario and I decided we'd like to go for a run on the beach in the morning. You know, get all the views that the guests would have. Keenan said he'll save us some breakfast, so I wanted to let you know you don't have to wait for us."

"Oh, all right. Great idea. There are paths all the way around the property, so you should have smooth sailing."

"Can we do the boat tour about ten o'clock?"

"Absolutely. We'll have her ready for you."

"Right-oh. Carry on." He salutes with a wink.

Heaving out a breath, I pinch my eyes closed. That was a close call. Fucking Lucas. Turning around, I find him looking as clueless as usual.

Why is his mouth always parted? Does he have sinus problems or something?

Legs splayed open, he's practically spread-eagled on the mussed-up bed, ruining the illusion of sound sleep for me. He looks like he just got fucked and is still in shock over discovering that orgasms are better than deep-fried pickles. At least, his broken facial muscles are good for something. Either that, or Mason is just shit at reading a room.

"I get the left side," I inform him, chucking his pillow to the other side. *Blink. Blink.*

Yeah, dickhead. You just graduated from the floor, I don't say.

I've not gone through everything I have all day just for one of the Hepperlys to barge in again and find Lucas in a makeshift fort on the floor like we had a lover's quarrel. Eyeing the alternative, my good humor fades. I can just picture his mat of chest hair shedding as I stand here. Yuck.

"And keep your short and curlies to your side." I wave at the dark smattering of hair that covers his pecs all the way down to the slight paunch of his stomach. "I don't want to wake up with a mouth full of your fuzz."

Grunting, he gets up, swipes his Superman-style underwear, and stomps to the bathroom. This commission is starting to sound like not enough.

Chapter 6

It feels like I just fell asleep, and yet I can tell the morning light is coming in through the balcony windows, illuminating the darkness behind my closed lids. I don't want to move yet; the jet lag and exhaustion are weighing me down. Maybe we can miss breakfast right along with Dario and Mason. Reaching out, I hit the cancel button on my phone to silence the alarm, performing the action blind from muscle memory.

It felt like I lay awake for hours last night, listening to the sounds coming from next door. Sounds of pleasure. Pleasure times…three.

I've never heard men make love before. I mean, I've heard myself, but…that's different. And yet, I guess it's completely the same? Pleasure is pleasure. I just…how am I supposed to look three people in the eye today after hearing what they did last night, like I was practically in the room with them? I can't even pretend I'm a boyfriend. How am I going to pretend I didn't hear Keenan yelling, "Aw, fuck yeah!"

Here, I thought he was the quiet one.

Burying my face deeper into the pillow, I grunt at a tingling sensation in my cock. Andrew is right; I have been exceptionally sweaty on this trip. My dick feels like it's in an oven right now, stuck between my thighs or…

Wait a minute.

It can't be stuck between my thighs. I've got underwear on.

The haze of sleep clears like the sun evaporating fog, and my senses come online. There's something warm and solid pressed against my back and something heavy draped over my waist. Something fleshy pressed against my stomach. And something…*gripping* my cock.

"Uhn…" A groan floats over my shoulder, a jaw brushing the back of my shoulder blade. "You snore."

Andrew! Oh, God.

Every muscle in my body locks up as my eyes blink open to the harsh light. I can see the plush comforter cocooned around me. The heat behind me either suddenly burns warmer, or it's my awareness. I'm not just cocooned in the comforter. I'm cocooned in Andrew, telling me I know exactly what that sensation on my dick is.

Shifting my gaze, my breath stalls in my lungs. That is definitely Andrew's arm slung over my waist, disappearing under the covers mid-forearm.

Oh, fuck…

His hand… It just moved. Is he…stroking me?

"*What*…are you doing?" I croak, too stunned to move. What the hell do you do in a situation like this?

"Trying to sleep," he grumbles against my shoulder. His knee bashes into the back of my thigh, and his grip gets tighter, sending a bizarre tingle to my balls. "Why are you so close?"

Is he kidding me? First, he kissed me yesterday, and now he's… stroking my dick while I sleep. Is he into guys? Into…*me*?

It feels like there's a thick lump in my throat, making it difficult to speak. I can't even remember the last time someone hit on me, let alone touched me. I certainly didn't expect that if it ever happened again, it'd be from a guy…a guy that is Andrew Broadhouse, of all people. I thought he hated me.

"Why are you…holding my dick?"

A dismissive snort gusts across my skin even as his thumb grazes the tip of my cock. I never thought I'd get hard because of a guy, but if he keeps this up, I'm about to set a record I didn't know was possible to set. His touch is surprisingly sensual and completely at odds with his personality. I can't take it anymore and latch my hand down over his wrist.

"I'm not," he whines sleepily. "I'm…I'm…"

Trying not to hyperventilate, I hold as still as possible. I'd jump up, but what if he doesn't let go and breaks my dick? Granted, I've not used it in a while, but I'd like to again someday. Some day, when I'm not playing fake boyfriend to the world's most infuriating man.

The silence feels deafening compared to the moans and cries we pretended to ignore last night. Finally, his grip goes slack. He slides his arm back to his side of the bed, taking his wandering hand with him. My cock, unfortunately, is now officially awake, along with the rest of me. Clearly, it doesn't know that it was the Devil who was just holding it.

It's quiet. Way too quiet for what just went down. Andrew never shuts up, and I can tell from the tension I feel behind me that he's not fallen back asleep. He needs to explain. How are we supposed to work together today after…whatever the hell that was?

"What the hell was that?" I call over my shoulder.

"I am not responsible for what I do in my sleep," he drawls. "And why are you so sweaty? *I should have known.* Ugh."

The mattress jostles, telling me he's wiping his hand on the sheets. He's the one who crossed the red line and is acting like I just infected him with cooties.

"Because you were holding my dick," I counter, sitting up and throwing my legs over the edge of the bed. I adjust my junk, but it does little to remove the feel of his hand around it.

"What?" he squawks. "Like my hand was a dick sweater? It was probably all your tuft."

"My what?"

Glancing back, I can't even see him. He's got the comforter pulled all the way over his head, which would explain why he sounds so muffled.

"*Tuft*," repeats the lump in the bed belligerently. "Do you have a freaking sheep down there?"

The cover flies off, revealing his mussed hair and his narrowed green eyes. He bolts out of bed, hustling toward the bathroom. "Gross. Now I need to wash your dick sweat off my hands."

The door slams before I can act as childish as him in return. I'm left sitting here with the ghost sensation of his hand on my cock, feral moans from last night in my brain, the peculiar feeling of his mouth smashed against mine, and the sight of our messy bed. I feel…strange.

I'm hurt when I shouldn't be. Warm over not waking up alone for the first time in years. And there's a foreign sense of longing in my chest at the memory of cries of bliss I know damn well and good I've never made before in my life. This is way too much to process. I…need a granola bar. Maybe my blood sugar is low or something.

Instinct has me wanting to make the bed, but then I remember how Mason dropped in unexpectedly last night, so I leave it and move to my suitcase. I can barely focus on what I'm doing. Am I dizzy? All I know is that we're supposed to take the boat out today, meaning we'll be on the water. I rummage around for my swimsuit and shorts because cooling off sounds like a good way to cleanse my body of Andrew and the peculiar hot flashes assaulting me. Is this what happens when you've been alone for too long—you react to the touch of anyone, even a guy you can't stomach?

The door to the bathroom flies open, and he scowls at me. I've never thought I was near his level of immaturity, but I don't know what else to do, so I scowl back. He's looking at me like *I* put his hand on my dick. He's such a child.

Maybe I am, too, because I'm not about to change into my suit in front of him. I've changed and showered plenty of times in front of the guys in my unit, but none of them ever made crude comments about my body hair or…kissed me. Also, for some reason, my cock is tingling again now that the hand that grabbed it is back in the room. My cock clearly needs a serious dick slap, which I'll gladly give it in the privacy of the bathroom.

Tromping around the end of the bed, I refuse to make eye contact with the perverted menace. Can't he just man up and admit that he accidentally cuddled me in his sleep? He didn't have to be rude about it and insult me. Civilian men have no feelings, not the other way around, like people assume.

Whipping a shirt out of his backpack, he flaps it in the air with a *crack* like he's getting the wrinkles out. Can you say passive-aggressive? Ten bucks says he's going to keep acting like '*the incident*' was my fault.

Reaching the bathroom doorway, I can't bite my tongue any longer. Apparently, spending this much time with Andrew makes me as petty as he is because I get one last dig in before I slam the door. "My dick is *not* sweaty."

Chapter 7

I'd kiss Lucas for docking the boat just now after being on the water for the last five hours, but one—it's Lucas. And two—well, I fucking kissed him already and once was enough. He'd better not cross over to my side of the bed again tonight. It's not my fault that he got in the way of my morning ritual. I guess Veronica was right—I am a morning cock handler.

"How did I end up with two husbands who love the sun?" Mason groans, wiping the sweat from his brow with his bandana.

Fortunately, I've already gotten enough of a tan this year that I won't burn, but he's right. It's hot as shit out here.

"We're buying tropical properties, *Mace*," Keenan points out, gathering up his discarded shirt from the bench where he and Dario had lounged for our tour of the area. "If you don't like the heat, now is not the time to bring it up. How do you plan to perform a show in it?"

"I like the heat, just not five hours of direct sun and soaking in my own sweat. I do enough of that on stage. I don't want to do it on my honeymoon, and at least I have misting machines and fans at my concerts."

At the mention of sweat, I swear Lucas' gaze flicks to mine. I can't be sure due to those dorky sunglasses of his, but my money is on someone knowing they're guilty of being a *Sweaty McSweaterson*. One more reason to get off this boat and wash away the day. He'd better go hose down before he starts smelling offensive.

"Did you happen to see that little shaded cove just off the west side of the resort on your run this morning?" Lucas ventures. "It'd be a nice spot for a dip, if you want to cool off. I was going to go take a swim there before dinner myself."

"Hell yes," Mason groans, climbing out from under the canopy, panting like a dog in the Sahara. "Let me go use the loo and I'll meet you down there."

"Oh my God," Keenan sighs, shaking his head. "There's got to be a diva in every crowd. Sorry, but Mason is ours," he apologizes.

"Nah, it's fine," I assure him. "I'm cooked, too, but I doubt you guys will be spending this much time on the water at whichever resort you settle on. At least you got the full lay of the land, though."

I am not going to admit I'm grateful that Lucas salvaged a moment of unpleasantness for our guests with his swimming idea. Stepping off the boat, I reaffirm some of the features of the resort we're heading out to tomorrow, several miles to the south. We were actually able to get a glimpse of it today from the boat. I nearly missed it, too distracted by the sight of Lucas' bare back when he stripped out of his tank top.

Did he do it to show off to Mason, who stuck by his side the entire trip under the comfort of the shade of the canopy? How inappropriate. The guy is married and his husbands were sitting right there on the boat. Doesn't he know how that makes me look?

When the world's worst and sweaty boyfriend finally meets us on the dock, he keeps up with the Boy Scout attitude he's had all day, waving us on toward this swimming hole to top all swimming holes. There's a fine sheen of sweat across his furry chest, but he's the only one not panting from the heat. I didn't think I could hate him anymore. Is he superhuman?

By the time we're clearing the west side of the resort, Lucas is forty feet ahead of me. It's too far and I'm too hot to yell that we lost Dario and Keenan, who decided to pop into the resort for more bottles of water while they wait for Mason.

Tripping over a rock, I wince when my flip-flop bends underneath my toes momentarily. "This is why I don't fucking date," I mutter under my breath, shaking the sand from my sandal. "They're either inconsiderate or high-maintenance as shit. Who fucking needs it?"

If I'd at least had the chance to fuck with him today, maybe I'd feel better. He was too busy acting like the best skipper to have ever skippered, steering the boat and pointing out every natural formation and species of freaking birds. Did he watch a *National Geographic* marathon before we left? No one cares about that shit. Sure, people put it on brochures to boast whatever they can about their properties, but how many tourists come to the Bahamas to fucking bird-watch?

All right…Dario looked interested, if I'm being honest. But he's a wildlife guy, so he's the exception. He even hopped out of his seat and stood next to Lucas, watching him point out a group of sandpipers or coots or whatever the fuck it was they were looking at. I don't know. I wasn't listening. All I do know is that it was really odd how Lucas seemed to have no problem being shirtless and shoulder to shoulder with his male idol, and yet, holding my hand is somehow repulsive.

Maybe he's not as opposed to male attraction as he lets on and reserves his distaste only for me.

Huh…

I promised myself I was done thinking about it, but now I'm curious to know just how long he let me sleep stroke him this morning before he decided to say something. He did act kind of strange after that not-a-kiss yesterday. I fully expected him to throat punch me, but he just stood there, gaping, almost like he was drugged.

"What the ever-loving hell…"

As I round a grove of small palms where the cay descends to the shoreline, my feet stop so abruptly that the rest of my body lurches forward. I've found Lucas's swimming hole. The problem is that I've found much more than that.

Damn…my eyes. *That* is one big bubble butt.

Once Lucas kicks his cargo shorts and flip-flops off, he straightens to his full height. I now have a clear and unwanted image of the shape of his entire body from head to toe.

Turning around like he senses my presence, his brows quirk together over his sunglasses. "What?" he huffs indignantly.

"What the fuck are you wearing?"

His lower lip bulges as he glances down at himself. Holding his hands out to his sides, his actual response is, "What's wrong with what I'm wearing?"

Am I suffering from sunstroke? How is he oblivious to the many levels of wrong he represents right now?

My brain says, *'Mommy, make the bad man go away,'* but my eyes don't listen, taking in the sight before me one more time. He's wearing a twin to his tighty-blackies, but in bright blue. A much smaller, much tighter, much more *spandex-y* version of his tighty-blackies. How is he still looking at me like his question merits an explanation?

"You can *see* your tuft."

Frowning, he glances down again, as though he doesn't see what the rest of the world would see. Leveling his gaze back at me, his nostrils flare, and his fingers form fists at his sides. "I don't have…*tuft.*"

I'm fucking staring right at it. Literally, staring right at the floofy groin hair that's framing his bright-blue-clad junk and blends into thinner hairs that cover his thighs all the way down his legs. And…he's still staring at me, looking completely clueless. Unbelievable. Does he just enjoy arguing?

Fuck this. I'm hot. It's not my fault he doesn't know how to manscape or dress himself when there's clients around.

Kicking off my flip-flops, I toss my shirt on a rock next to the path to the water and then gesture to the source of his delusion. "Are you kidding me? It's like you've got a full-grown Chia Pet suffocating in there and it's popping out to breathe."

He appears to process that as I start down the path. His face goes red, and his hands move to cover the Chia Pet. "Quit looking at my dick."

I can't with him anymore. Spinning on my heel when I'm in line with him, I march over until we're practically nose to nose.

"How can I look at your dick when I don't have a machete to hack through the tuft jungle in front of it?"

Voices float over the slope that rises to the resort. Lucas's gaze flicks in that direction, and he takes a step away from me, mumbling, "Knock it off. They're coming."

Someone please tell me why he's dropping his hands *now*? What a slut!

It's okay for the guys to see his Chia Pet, but not me, his own fake boyfriend? That's some bullshit.

Taking a step closer, I rest my arm across the back of his shoulders. I haven't touched him all day. I'd better not have to have a repeat conversation with him about who he fake-belongs to. "What's the matter, snookums? Afraid the guys will notice you're having an intimate moment with your man?"

He's tense under my touch, but I don't miss the way his cheeks go crimson. Does the guy do it with the lights off? For Pete's sake, he acts like he's never heard of an R-rated movie.

"It's not intimate," he mutters, pretending there's something incredibly interesting on the ground at his feet. "You're just being an asshole because you're embarrassed you grabbed my dick."

Oh-ho-ho.

So, *that's* how it is?

Slipping behind him, I sidle up close until my chest is flush with his back. I have a brother, a gay cousin, played soccer in college, and am very secure with my body and sexuality. Lucas Everette apparently needs a lesson in just how nonexistent my embarrassment meter is around other men.

Sliding my hand down the front of his chest, I bring my mouth close to his ear just as the Hepperlys crest the hill. "I'm not embarrassed," I challenge in a low tone meant only for his ears. "I stroke my dick every morning. Yours just got in the way."

I swear his heart feels like it's about to beat out of his chest underneath my palm. He's as rigid as a post, but has enough sense not to move as our clients approach.

"Then why are you being an ass with all the body comments?"

Aw… Big man's embarrassed.

The thing about being embarrassed, though, is that it means you have to care about what the other person thinks. Why would Lucas care about what I think of his body? This isn't the first time his lips have parted like he's gasping for air when I'm touching him. Pretty sure he was doing it this morning, the way he just lay there, frozen and panting. I wonder…

Is the Chia wrangler in denial?

"What's wrong?" I purr, dragging my fingertips lightly across his chest. "Can't a man admire the way his lover's big, bushy tuft is packed into a child's size snack baggie?"

His throat undulates so hard I hear a *gulp* sound, and…he's fucking trembling.

"Stop it." I think he meant that to sound threatening, but it came out as a rasp.

Oh. My. God.

I think Lucas wants to climb underneath a coffee table. Is that why he looks all disgruntled every time I touch him?

His freak-out is not my problem. I didn't force him to come on this trip.

My fingertip touches something hard and puckered.

Shit. Pretty sure that's a nipple.

And…he just shuddered.

Yup. Definitely a nipple.

Screw it. He wants this commission as badly as I do.

Circling it with my fingertip, I leave him with one last parting order before the Hepperlys are upon us, remembering the way he complied the other day when I went off on him. "Why don't you just shut up and smile like a good boyfriend when I compliment you and your tuft?"

Smiling, I wave my other hand at the Hepperlys, who are busy cooing over the light breeze wafting in from the cay and the sunset that we're apparently missing. I've seen dozens of tropical sunsets. I can miss one to analyze this evolution of the world's angriest ranger.

Lucas sucks in a sharp intake of breath and his hand clenches over mine. I thread my fingers through his, but not to be cruel. Dario and Keenan are filing past us toward the water. Tufty needs to hold out for a few seconds longer, or this scene was all for naught.

Slinking my other hand around his waist, I hold him in place in case he gets any ideas about moving. I stroked a dick that wasn't mine this morning. My pride can't handle being publicly rejected by my fake boyfriend right now, so he can stand strong for two more freaking seconds.

"Ahh, yes," Mason hisses, bringing up the rear. "Water. Water that I can get in without being eaten by a shark." Just as he passes us, he calls out, "You blokes coming?"

"Be there in a minute," I assure him cheerfully.

There is no earthly reason why I haven't let Lucas go yet. There's no earthly reason why he couldn't have burst free from my arms now that all three men have likely reached the water. I think I'm just too enthralled over his ragged breathing and what it could mean. The guy's practically hyperventilating in my arms.

Sweat, I remind myself, when I catch a whiff of his potent, musky scent. Releasing him, I step back, all too aware of how our skin sticks to each other's for a second.

What the hell am I doing?

Chad always said I could never let anything go. This took things a little too far, even for me. I blame Lucas. He just pushes all my damn buttons.

Digging our room key out of my pocket, I toss it on the ground near Lucas' sandals and start toward the water. When I don't hear the sound of heavy, pouty footsteps following me, I glance back.

He's still standing in the exact same spot. His shoulders rise on an intake of breath that he lets out slowly. When he turns, his hand is covering his blue bulge, except…it's not able to cover all of it. It's not able to cover all of it because…there's more of it.

Holy shit. He's hard.

Whipping my gaze to the water, I move without thinking. It seems like the right thing to do. If I got caught getting hard over Lucas, I sure as shit wouldn't want him to see.

Except, I didn't. *He* did. And I did see.

A breathless laugh leaves my lips as my feet connect with the cool water. I didn't even do anything to make him hard! I wasn't even trying. All I did was give him a tip of foreplay and boss him around. How can…

Oh, man. No way.

I've had enough bed partners to know a kink when I see one. I can't hold back a chuckle. I am going to have so much fun with this.

Chapter 8

Usually, I find serenity in bonfires. Try as I might, however, I can't seem to get lost in the flickering golden flames in the fire pit on the patio. Not even the soft strumming of Mason's guitar and low humming along with the melody can distract me from the intrusive thoughts.

It's evening number two at the second resort we've shown them, and I think they've settled on it. The terrain is more conducive to building the stage Mason wants, so I think this one's a done deal. I should be happy. I should be checking to make sure all the arrangements are in place for the properties we're going to show them in Massachusetts. I could text my sisters back about my opinions on seating arrangements, but I can't bring myself to do any of those things without a clear head.

There's a hand on my knee.

Its fingers are softly kneading the meat on the inside of my leg, stirring butterflies in my belly with each brush of skin when they slip past the length of my shorts. It was bad enough that I woke up to another dick hug this morning, but now this?

I made it out of bed unscathed the last two nights. I woke up when I felt a hand on my hip and slipped away as quickly as possible. This morning, however, Andrew's hand woke up before I did.

'If you don't like it, put a pillow between us,' was all he said when I clamped my hand over his.

He should really go see someone about that. Is it like a sleepwalking thing? Sleep jerking?

As I try to sit still and appear relaxed in this patio chair, I know I'm the one who needs the most help. How could I get hard the other day when he was saying all that stuff about my tuft and stroking my nipple? What is going on with me?

I don't even like him. *He* doesn't like me.

It's getting difficult to believe both facts, though, the more he touches me, and my body reacts to those touches. And I swear he's amped up his touching game the last couple of days. We're always touching now in one form or another. If he's not holding my hand, he has his arm around me. He's even stroked my hair a few times. How is having my hair stroked a turn-on? And by Andrew, of all people?

Because that's what it is…a turn on. I thought maybe I was sick at first, dizzy. Short of breath. But I took enough First-Aid classes in the military to know my symptoms have nothing to do with heat exposure or food poisoning. My belly gets warm, and it spreads to my chest every time he pretends to say something nice about or to me. The most fucked up thing is that it's even worse when he gets bossy and commanding when we're alone. That's the part I really don't understand.

When we boarded the seaplane at Moonbeam Cay the other day to fly here, he slapped me on the ass as I was getting in and said, "Get that sexy ass moving, handsome."

It was like fireworks erupted across my cheek where his hand lit. I felt them all the way to my dick.

If I like guys, I can accept that. It's always been way easier for me to talk to and relate to men. I never thought I checked one out, but if I'm being honest with myself, I did admire the men in my unit. We worked out and would comment on each other's physiques all the time. I thought it was just part of our friendly motivation to stay in shape. Maybe it was…for *them*. But maybe for me it was more. When I got out of the service, I felt lost, like I didn't fit in anywhere. They say that's normal, but I've always suspected it was more than that. Something was missing. I'm starting to think it was that comfortable feeling of being around men who were close with each other.

I don't know, but I *can't* like Andrew. He's…annoying.

His hand leaves my leg, finally. Focusing on the knife in my hands, I continue carving the little piece of driftwood I picked up earlier, grateful to be able to function again. Just when I think I can let my guard down, though, his hand rests at the base of my neck. His thumb strokes my hairline, sending a shiver down my spine.

Ugh. Why? I really hate my body right now.

This is ridiculous. The Hepperlys aren't even looking at us. Dario and Keenan are murmuring softly on the other side of the fire pit, immersed in conversation. Mason is bent over his guitar in the zone. I'm pretty sure they all think we're a couple by now. None of them has said a thing to make me believe otherwise. I doubt they expect us to be on each other 24/7, anyway. We're supposed to be professionals. I've never seen Dario be intimate with anyone on his show, and I doubt Keenan makes out with either of his husbands when he's in his work office.

"Cold?" Andrew asks, but there's a coy hint in his tone like he knows I just shuddered.

"I'm fine," I mumble, moving his hand away. Just as I do, Keenan's gaze connects with mine. Shit.

Patting his knee, Andrew outstretches one of his arms and grins. "Come here and I'll warm you up."

Has he lost his fucking mind? I know his long, lanky legs look fit and all, but I've got like thirty pounds on him. There's no way he could take my weight for as much as he whines. He just said that to fuck with me. I'm sure of it, but instantly, I glance back at Keenan.

He's giving us a look that says he thinks we're sweet. Great. Dario just saw and heard, too, judging by the smile on his face.

Hunkering forward further over my carving, I want to disappear. Specifically, I want the tingling in my extremities at the thought of sitting on Andrew's lap to disappear. The only lap I've ever been excited to sit on was a mall Santa's when I was a kid, and it should stay that way. "Nah, I'm good."

"What's wrong? Are you mad at me?" I wonder if I'm the only one who can tell there is nothing genuine about the concern in his voice.

"No." I shake my head, trying to sound like a compassionate partner that doesn't want to kick their loved one in the balls and focus my gaze on my whittling.

"He's just shy, Andrew," Keenan laments. "It's okay, Lucas. We get it. We weren't big on PDA either when we all got together, but you don't have to worry about that around us."

Fuck. I'm fucking this up. It's only day four, and I've already brought notice to my display in this fake relationship. Why did Andrew have to say I was his *partner*? He could have just said co-worker. The idiot.

"No, I'm just…just tired is all," I babble, swiping up my empty beer bottle from the paver stones and rising.

The look in Andrew's eyes couldn't more clearly say, *'Have you lost your mind?'*

I know I have. I agreed to come on a trip with him.

"I think I'm going to turn in," I tell the guys. "I'll help you haul the bags down in the morning before we head to the airport."

"All right." Keenan nods, looking curious now, like even he and Dario wonder if something is up between Andrew and me.

Shit. I *am* fucking this up.

Turning toward Andrew, I hold my breath and pray to a higher power that my actions look natural. Leaning down, I brace a hand on the armrest of his chair, trying to avoid the questions in his eyes.

"I'll see you upstairs," I murmur, hoping I'm loud enough that the Hepperlys can hear and think it's some kind of affectionate goodnight.

It doesn't feel like enough, though. A couple…a *real* couple would probably kiss goodnight. A real boyfriend would probably press his lips to that bow-shaped mouth that's infuriatingly perfect for the cut of his jaw.

I aimed for his cheek.

I know I did.

When my lips land on the corner of his, I can't honestly say if I decided it at the last minute or if he moved, but I find mine covering his. For a mouth that can say the most foul of insults and lie with such ease, his lips are incredibly soft. They're not pinched shut tight like last time, but rather parted in surprise.

Did he think I didn't have the balls to fake it like he did? I only know one way to kiss, though, so the joke is on me. How do you fake something that's so simplistic?

Brushing my bottom lip over his, I end up capturing the top one momentarily. I can feel his breath on my lips. Smell the beer on it, mingled with his clean, soapy Andrew scent that always makes me scoff, imagining how hygienic and fussy he is.

Right now, he just smells good. Right now, it just feels like a kiss. A very *not* fake kiss, especially when I feel his hand on my cheek. God, it's been a long time since I've kissed anyone. A very long time.

When I pull back and find him staring at me, looking just as confused as I feel right now, I know I've fucked up yet again. "Goodnight," I blurt, straightening up and hurrying up the path to the resort.

I don't know if the Hepperlys believed that or not, but that's not the problem. *I* believed it. That was a kiss, a *real* kiss. I only meant to play my part so Andrew wouldn't say I'm slacking, but all I accomplished was the realization that I don't know how to fake anything. And that is incredibly terrifying considering how many days I have left until we're contingent.

A half an hour later, I hear the door to our newest shared room shut. The soft tread of footsteps stops at the end of the bed, and it's silent for a moment. Why is the thought of him watching me making me feel lightheaded?

My heart is in overdrive. I don't dare even exhale. Eyes pinched shut, I am more still than a sniper who has an eye on his mark.

There's a rustle of clothing dropping to the floor that ratchets my pulse up a notch. It's bizarre that I'm becoming accustomed to sleeping in the same bed as Andrew. I already know what it will feel like when the bed dips on his side, when his warmth permeates under the covers. I even know how his breathing sounds when he falls asleep.

My memories serve me well as each of those things happens in the next few minutes, except for his breathing going shallow. He rolls to his side, facing my back, and then it's quiet again. I can feel his eyes on me. Does he know I'm playing possum?

"What? No kiss goodnight?" he asks softly, teasing.

I blow my cover and tense, letting out the breath I was holding. Soft laughter floods the room as he flops onto his back and yanks the covers tighter against him.

"Goodnight, Lucas," he purrs.

I hate him. Truly, I do. I don't know what's going on with me, but my mind and body are clearly not on the same page. If they were, I wouldn't feel so disappointed as I whisper back, "Asshole."

Chapter 9

ANDREW BROADHOUSE
licensed agent

"Ugh, I hate you," Terry lets out wistfully as I turn my phone's camera to show him the view of the resort's beach.

"Why? You and Shaw do all right. You can go anywhere you want."

"We do all right because we both work all the time. It's not that simple," my cousin-in-law huffs. "Oh, my God! Is *that* Dario?" he whispers.

I spot said-Hepperly with Lucas down on the dock, fishing.

Why are they fishing? They already agreed to buy the place. Lucas doesn't need to hype up any more selling points. We've been here two extra days so they could decompress, part of the honeymoon aspect of it, I guess. Lucas must have missed the memo that we don't need to be involved in their alone time. The idiot.

"Yeah. The one and only," I concur, frowning at Lucas' bronzed bare back and the way his muscles glisten when he casts his line.

"And is that your *boyfriend*?" This amused query comes from Shaw.

They've seen enough, so I switch the camera back to face me. "Yup. Tell me what a lucky man I am."

My cousin snorts at my unenthused delivery. "Still sticking to your stupid plan, huh? How's that going?"

"I just sold an island. How do you think it's going?" I ask, taking a sip of my beer under the shade of one of the covered patios at the resort. "Why? Did you doubt me?"

"*I* didn't!" Terry pipes in. "Even though you're a terrible kisser."

I wondered when he'd bring that up. I'm sure it won't be the last I hear of it over the next thirty years or so. Glancing down the hill at the dock, I can see Lucas' plump lips from here. I used to think he was just bitter about his lot in life all the time, and his mouth was in a perpetual pout, but the man has some thick lips. Thick and…pliable. They're sur-prisingly soft. I'm not going to dwell much on how I know that. I mean, I've kissed two men in the past week, so what's the big deal? One to prove a point, the other to sell a lie.

I should be happy that he took the initiative the other night by the fire pit, but he had to make it all weird, like a real kiss. For a second, I forgot to half ass it. There shouldn't be anything thrilling about the way his eyes were drooped when he pulled away. I mean, I know I'm a good kisser, despite what Terry thinks, but I should have zero excitement over the thought of having an effect on the mouth-breather. He was panting like he'd just run a marathon.

So…I did what any curious, competitive man of the world would do. I've kissed him each day since then.

Yesterday, after breakfast with the Hepperlys, he came up with some bullshit excuse about calling his sisters and looking up a few more prop-erties for when we head to Massachusetts. We've already got enough planned that I'm sure the newlyweds will bite on one of them, and I doubt the babies really need big brother's help if they want a wedding that won't embarrass them. It was just an excuse to get away from me. I was sure of it, so I latched onto his neck and planted one on him for our clients.

I can still feel his little grunt against my lips. How I'm starting to get used to the feel of stubble against my face when I kiss someone, I don't know, but…it was weird. Lucas's lips shouldn't feel that good. I think I'm just fascinated by the way I can feel his body change under my touch. It's like his muscle tension melts the second my lips are on his. Maybe he has an oral fixation.

Last night, when we met up with the Hepperlys for dinner, he barely looked at me. Mason kept him busy talking about his army days, so at least the conversation flowed plausibly and didn't look like we were at odds. I had to stop myself from stroking the side of his neck with my thumb where I had my arm draped across the back of his shoulders because the dumbass got flustered a few times.

I really hate what this feud is doing to me. The more he does that heavy mouth-breathing when I touch him, the more I find myself wanting to touch him just to prove…to prove… I don't know. That I'm winning?

I sure as shit won last night when he was the first to excuse himself to go to bed again. He leaned in like he was about to steal a quick kiss, so I one-upped him. Latching my hand around the back of his neck, I put all my skills to good use, sucking on his lower lip and giving it a little lick with the tip of my tongue.

He…whimpered. I swear to God, he whimpered approximately ten seconds before he turned and bolted upstairs to our room. Terrible kiss-er, my ass. If I can make my enemy whimper, Terry can suck it.

"That's not what Lucas says," I mumble idly, watching Dario reach out and direct Lucas' wrist like he's showing him a casting tip.

"Wait…you actually kissed him?" Shaw squawks.

Shit. I said that out loud. Flipping the camera view back around, I sigh, like the topic is boring me, because it is. I don't want or need them thinking they're reading something on my face that isn't there. They watch way too much reality TV when they're not fucking in their living room. I blame Terry. His taste in the arts is shit.

"I told you. I'm going to make these sales happen. A man's gotta do what a man's gotta do. Not my fault you doubted my commitment *or* my abilities. But on that note, why don't you put a good word in with your dad for me the next time you see him?"

"And tell him you're duping his clients by making out with one of your co-workers? Yeah. He'll love that."

"If I were you, I think I'd wait until your honeymoon tour is over before you get too confident," Terry adds as I hear the side door to the pool open around the corner behind me. Mason and Keenan's voices float over the concrete, telling me they're headed for a swim in the pool.

Closing my eyes, I lean back in my lounger and take another sip of my beer. "Oh yeah? Why's that?"

"Because it looks like your man isn't as satisfied as you think," he says smugly.

What the fuck is he going on about? Opening my eyes, I peer down at the dock. Dario is standing behind the big furry monster truck enthusiast, chest nearly pressed to his back. The Aussie's hand is back on Lucas' wrist, guiding his arm back while his other hand is on his shoulder. And Lucas… Why the fuck are those big lips of his parted?

"Wouldn't it be funny if you faked it to make a sale and the guy you're faking it with ends up breaking up your clients?" Terry cackles.

Every muscle in my body locks up over the possibility. It shouldn't be a possibility. Nothing Terry ever says holds any merit, but damn it, I have eyes! What in the fuck does Lucas think he's doing getting cozy with the clients? On their honeymoon, nonetheless! And he thinks *I'm* dishonest? I'm not a homewrecker.

"Can it, Terry," I clip and end the call.

Scrambling out of the lounger, I nearly face-plant it on the patio and spill my beer. Freaking Lucas. Mason and Keenan are just around the side of the building. They have a view of the beach from over there. How in the hell is it going to look if they see him skin to skin with their husband?

Hustling down the path to the dock, I keep my eyes trained on my despicable boyfriend. Oh my God. He's laughing! Actually laughing. He doesn't laugh with me in front of them. How is that going to look?

"Shameless," I mutter. "Fucking shameless."

It only gets worse the closer I approach. The pole bends, and their faces light up. Clearly, Dario's tutelage has paid off. All I see when he grips Lucas' shoulder eagerly as Lucas reels in his catch is deceit. Lucas is just standing there, letting another man paw him right in front of me. No wonder his bride-to-be left his ass in the frozen section. The man can't be trusted.

Hands touch hands as they wrangle the fish into their grasp. This should not be the first time I see all of Lucas' freaking teeth. Boyfriends are supposed to smile at their boyfriends, not at other people's husbands. Have I ever gotten a smile like that from him? Fuck no. All I get is sass and indifference. Unless my mouth is…

"Drew! Check it out, mate. What do you reckon? Sixteen inches?" Dario enthuses over the fish flapping in his grip on the end of Lucas' line.

"Way to go, babe," my voice comes out low and possessive, although it was meant to be a warning.

Grabbing Lucas by the waist, my hand sinks into the soft flesh of his love handle as I yank him to me. His jaw parts, and I catch a shadow of his widened eyes behind his sunglasses before I grip his neck and slam my mouth down onto his.

This is his fault. Someone has to salvage his foolish display of grab-ass with Dario. We're just lucky that I have a superpower and am not afraid to use it.

Slanting my mouth against his, I tease the seam of his lips with the tip of my tongue, getting a whiff of his sweaty scent in the process. I thought he'd smell like a well-used gym, but he doesn't. There's something clean and sweet in his aroma that mingles with the salty breeze. It's heady and addictive, completely at odds with everything else about him.

On cue, his mouth-breathing activates and his lips part. Ha! I've still got it. I've still got it, and Lucas wants it. It's not enough, though, after the fuckery he just ensnared himself in.

I am a man on a mission. I *will* get another whimper out of this big lug so he can prove how much he loves his boyfriend, and isn't here to fuck up our clients' matrimony.

Slipping my tongue over that pillowy lower lip of his, a burst of flavor explodes in my mouth when his tongue meets mine. My breath hitches. He tastes like nothing and yet everything all at once—a chemical reaction like that stuff in food at buffets they say makes people unable to stop eating even after they're full. I'm suddenly starving, carving my tongue around his because no kiss has ever felt like this. There's got to be a catch. I'll hate it in about two seconds.

Thick fingers dig into the meat of my shoulder. I'm about to come to my senses and give up on my lesson about who this dickhead belongs to, expecting him to push me away, but he doesn't. Those fingers grip and pull me closer.

Closer.

Lucas Everette *wants* my mouth. That discovery alone has me pulling back to breathe.

I get only an inch away and a second of air. His parted, panting lips chase mine, letting out a needy little whimper.

Fucking hell. That sound.

If his taste is a food additive, that whimper is absinthe. When his mouth crashes into mine again, I shove my tongue as deep as I can into it. I don't know what in the hell is wrong with me, but I take it out on him with a punishing kiss that has him grunting and whining. Not fucking helping. Jesus. How is the best kiss I've ever had, an angry one with a grumpy, wood-whittling veteran who has a penis and more body hair than my front lawn?

A low whistle infringes on the feral noises Lucas is spilling down my throat. "Reckon I better talk to the fellas about rewarding me like that when I go fishing," Dario says behind me.

Shit. We have an audience.

What am I saying? Of course, we have an audience. That was the point. Why the hell else would I have let this happen?

Pulling back, I stare at Lucas' flushed face. The rosy tint above his beard isn't from his time in the sun. The way his chest is heaving isn't from pulling in that fish. He's a fuse, and I was the flame. His hand is still clutching my shoulder like he's still lost in our angry kiss. My God, the man is putty in my hands. I don't know what to do with this information, nor the tightening in my balls, but I'm still a professional, damn it.

Releasing my grip from his sweaty waist, I give his cheek a pat to smack him out of his fog. It might be a tad self-serving, given my peculiar fascination with the way it makes the flesh in his cheeks quiver.

"That's how I get him to bring the big ones home to his man," I tell our client, ignoring the breathiness in my voice.

Clearing my throat, I turn and flash Dario a smile. It's now that I notice the bucket by his feet, filled with water and several other fish.

"Looks like you two have earned your keep for the day," I joke, hoping it'll put an end to their bonding time. Lucas looks discombobulated, which is just completely offensive to me. He's the one who went back for seconds. Is he regretting it now? Giving him a slap on the ass jolts his attention back to me. "You going to go cook these up for our guests, sweetheart?"

It takes him ten awkward seconds to respond. "Um…y-yeah. I-I can do that."

"Great. Should we go tell the boys?" I ask Dario, not waiting, as I start back down the dock.

"Yeah. Let me just help with the poles."

"Ah. Leave it. Lucas loves to play with his tackle. Don't you, babe?"

If looks could kill. Luckily, he gets his shit together in time and manages a smile for Dario, waving him on.

After a cold shower and making drinks for the Hepperlys, I'm confident I've put the newest incident well enough behind me. That is until my boyfriend starts scuttling food out from the kitchen. Food that smells delicious. The bastard can actually cook?

The guys fawn over the delicious aromas, but I'm too stunned to care. My attention is snared by the professional-looking display of Lucas' handiwork. He literally caught, killed, cooked, and served this entire meal, and it looks like something I've paid for in a five-star restaurant. Maybe it's because I've never seen a man in an apron before that I can recall, but my gaze is fixated on how that white fabric is cinched around his waist each time he hurries back into the kitchen like his life depends on taking care of us. He seems to be good at that—taking care of people. No way would I have hauled all that luggage he's carted around if he'd thrown me under the bus the way I did to him.

Listen to me… One French kiss and I'm complimenting the guy. I'm such a man. Picking up my fork, I dig into the flaky seafood. It melts on my tongue, the flavor a perfect pairing with my beer.

Fine. So he has *one* tolerable quality. It was bound to happen sooner or later.

When he finally quits fussing over the Hepperlys and joins us, their praise flows for his culinary prowess. A mix of pride and possessiveness swirls inside me. Neither makes any sense. I have no right to be proud of someone complimenting him like he's an extension of me because he's not. And possessive, well, that's equally absurd. They're happily married. They're not Lucas hunting, no matter what my lapse in judgment made me think I saw on the dock today.

It's got to be all this pretending catching up to me. Maybe I'm like one of those method actors. I've gone so tits to the wall with trying to make us look believable that I've started to catch feelings. *Fake* feelings, of course. If there's a bisexual bone in my body, it sure as shit wouldn't have Lucas on its radar under any other circumstances.

Chapter 10

Tomorrow can't come soon enough. After we fly to Boston, we'll have three days to scope out properties before the Hepperlys meet back up with us after visiting Keenan's mother. That means three entire days away from Andrew. And Andrew's hands. And Andrew's mouth.

I shudder, tugging the sheets tighter around myself, and let out a calming breath.

I kissed him *again*. I swore I wouldn't after what happened on the dock today, but it felt like we've set a precedent for goodnight kisses in front of the Hepperlys. I'd just finished helping the caretaker clean up after dinner and found him and the guys at the bar. Andrew was filling them in on a few of the beachfront properties we found on the coast of Massachusetts, even including one I suggested that he previously turned his nose up at, most likely for the simple fact that I chose it.

I was honestly grateful he was stealing the real estate show again. I'd barely been able to form two sentences since he surprised me on the dock earlier. So, I just stood there, nursing a beer while I let him do his thing, that captivating energy bubbling off him. He could sell a cashew farm to a person with a nut allergy. He's…*good* at what he does. Why shouldn't he be?

The guy knows how to live and what people who have wealth look for, so of course, he picks up on selling points that I overlook. If it wasn't for Dario and my shared love of the outdoors, I doubt my expertise would hold any merit among the Hepperlys. They *did* like my cooking, though.

So did Andrew.

I shouldn't have looked over when he took that first bite, but my pride was on the defensive, waiting for some sign of disapproval. I don't know what a man's face looks like when he comes, but my entire body went warm seeing his when he tasted my cooking. It felt…personal. It was *my* food he put in his mouth. *My* cooking that painted his judgmental eyes with a sheen of bliss. I didn't dare look at him again after that throughout the entire meal. There's no way I could have, and survived it without embarrassing myself with the way he was stroking my neck again. Why is my body suddenly aware of everything that Andrew Broadhouse does?

When the Hepperlys started talking amongst themselves at the bar later, he turned to look at me, and I choked. All I could think about was his hand on my waist and how his more slender frame yanked me to him on the dock like I was a rag doll. It had lit me up inside, activating circuits I didn't know existed. Whatever sex life I've ever had never involved anything rough, certainly never being manhandled. I felt…alive. Alive and a strange kind of satisfying helplessness all at the same time.

I…*liked* it. Or at least my body did. How could anyone like Andrew manhandling them?

"Goodnight," I blurted before he could say anything to embarrass me. And then I leaned in…

Why the hell did I lean in? What was I thinking?

Pinching my eyes closed, I try to replay those few seconds over. No matter how many times I do, I find myself cringing. *I* went for his mouth, not the other way around.

"Crap," I huff into my pillow.

I was just going to give him a peck on the cheek, do my part for the screwed-up cause he got us mixed up in. My back was to the Hepperlys. They wouldn't have known the difference, but no. My mouth somehow gravitated right to his again at the last second, like that night by the firepit.

Maybe I miss kissing. But how can you miss a level of kissing you've never experienced before? Do all men kiss like him? Is that what my kisses felt like when I used to kiss Shannon?

I somehow doubt it, considering she broke it off with me.

Plus, I never nibbled.

Grunting, I shift my legs, nudging my cock in a different position. He…*nibbled* me. Nibbled me and then sucked on my lower lip before he stuck his tongue in my mouth.

Scrubbing my hand down my face, I let out a stream of breath and try to relax the tension in my body. Except, it's not the kind of tension that is alleviated with deep breathing or a massage. It's the kind that only gets worse the more a guy thinks about how good it felt having another man's tongue sweep around his mouth like he owned it.

The door opens and closes, chasing away every single thought in my head. I pinch my eyes shut again and try to ignore the unmistakable sounds and presence. It's an impossible task. Andrew, standing still by the doorway, watching me. Andrew, stalking slowly to his side of the bed. The *swish* of Andrew's clothes falling to the floor. The cool air hitting my skin when he raises the sheet and plops down unceremoniously on his side of the mattress. He's everywhere. Like a sex pheromone nightmare.

And then he rolls. Shit.

I can feel his hand reach out and inspect the pillow barrier I placed behind me. I suddenly feel like a kid who plugged in a nightlight to keep monsters away. How stupid. I'm a grown-ass adult. I have willpower. It's not like I'm going to roll over and kiss him again. No one's here who needs to see it.

Gross. I've become him—living a lie.

He snorts upon discovering my protective device, but seems to stay put. I know he did because I can feel his breathing, feel his heat, his gaze.

"I'm going to rent a car at the airport and drive down to Duxbury to catch a boat out to Clark's Island when we land tomorrow, so I can get eyes on the two properties there that Lou wants to show them. Why don't you do the same for the Harlow's Landing properties so we don't have any surprises when we get down there?"

It's a good plan, and I'm surprised he's actually putting effort into being proactive. Does he do that with all his listings? A sourness churns in my belly, though. Is he just looking for ways to get away from me?

I'm still debating on whether I want to answer, when he lets out an exasperated sound. "Don't act like you're asleep just because you're embarrassed you like kissing me."

I flinch, dropping any pretense of sleep I hoped to achieve. Blinking in the darkness, my mouth flounders for a solid rebuttal to his presumptuous claim.

"I wasn't. I-I *don't.*"

The force of his scoff gives me gooseflesh on the back of my neck. "For a guy who doesn't like it, you sure keep doing it a lot."

"That's what couples do. We're supposed to be a couple."

"And you know so much about being a couple? You kiss me more than the Hepperlys kiss each other."

"They…kiss in their room," I add lamely.

"You mean *fuck?*" he snorts.

He must regret saying that as much as I regret hearing it, because an awkward silence descends over the bed. To be fair, they've fucked a lot. We've heard them. They *do* kiss in front of us sometimes, though, I want to add, but he already knows that no matter what he says. He's just being…Andrew.

He might have a point about me not knowing much about being a couple. I only have one adult relationship to base my opinion on, but still, goodnight kisses are something I wouldn't mind doing if I were ever in a relationship again. Mom and Clark used to kiss goodnight. It always brought me a sense of comfort seeing them when I was younger, like all was right in our little world. Like he was a father that wouldn't leave.

"I used to kiss Shannon every night before I went to bed when I was home," I offer without thinking, but decide I want him to know my rationale. Anything is better than him thinking I kiss him because I like it. He doesn't deserve that kind of ego boost. "I did it because…you never know when it will be the last time you see someone."

"What? Like you knew she was going to leave you?"

"No. I meant you never know when it will be the last time you see someone," I repeat, trying not to let him rile me. "You never know…if your dad is going to walk out on you and your mom when you're seven. You never know if the great guy your mom meets years later is going to die on her in a car accident. You don't know if the two little blonde hellions you helped raise will come home safe at night. And you don't know when you'll get deployed again or if you'll see the hometown girl who's been patiently waiting for you…even if in the end she ran off with your best friend behind your back."

My wisdom starts to feel more like an uncomfortable confession the longer the following silence stretches. I didn't mean to share all of that with him.

"If this is you trying to get me to kiss you, try again," he says, sounding bored. Insensitive ass.

"If this is *you* gearing up to deny you like jerking me off every morning, try again."

Another gust of air hits my neck, this time with more force, before the sheet tugs against me as he rolls over to his other side. "In your dreams. If I *did* jerk you off, it'd only be to get you to shut up because you wouldn't stop begging for it."

I will *not* respond. I *won't*.

That's what he wants. I refuse to give Andrew Broadhouse anything he wants, even if what he just said is like a filthy-idea worm boring into my brain. How does he do that?

Chapter 11

ANDREW BROADHOUSE

licensed agent

Ugh. I can feel my bones. Waking up is like being sucked out of a black hole, your body fighting against the force to stay inside a cocoon of blissful weightless darkness.

There's that sound again…

Is someone talking? I must be dreaming because it's way too early to hear voices.

Stretching against the warm pillow in front of me, I point my toes, pulling the stiffness from my muscles and giving my cock a lazy stroke. It's hot and hard, but the friction brings me no relief or comfort. It's like my dick is numb and can't feel my hand.

Can a dick fall asleep like a foot can?

No. Then I'd have that strange sandy sensation in it.

"Andrew…" a hoarse voice calls, sounding desperate.

The pillow my face is squished against seems fleshy like skin suddenly. It's…beefy and smells clean, with a hint of something sweet. Not at all like Veronica's.

What am I saying? It can't be Veronica's. I'm in the Virgin Isles and she's in Brussels eyeballing around for Mr. Right.

Ugh.

That can only mean one thing.

Lucas…

Fuck him.

I'm not moving.

"Andrew…"

"*What?*" I murmur against his shoulder blade. "Sleep time. *Sleep.*"

I don't recall any of my past bed partners ever throwing off as much heat as he does. His *Chia-ness* must be good insulation. I bet he saves a ton of money on not having to buy winter weather gear.

The cool morning air from the coast breezes in, giving me a chill, further breaching that veil of precious slumber. Nuzzling closer to his back, I give myself another sympathetic stroke. It's strange, though. It produces no reaction in me other than frustration. I wish the rest of me was as asleep as my dick is right now.

Nudging my hips forward, I help it out by thrusting into my grip, but my cock arches against the downy feel of a pillow. *Not* my hand. What the fuck?

"Andrew," Lucas croaks more urgently. Something latches over my wrist, something that feels a lot like a hand. Again…*not* my hand.

One of mine is tucked under the pillow beneath my head. The other is on my dick. My dick that…can't feel my hand. My dick that feels extremely sweaty and…veiny. Has my dick always been this veiny?

Ah, shit…

Blinking my eyes open, I watch the solid back in front of my face rise and fall with a ragged breath. The biceps resting on Lucas' ribcage are flexed, and his arm disappears over his side…right next to where mine does, too.

Damn it.

I did it again.

I start to move my hand away, but there's something about the feel of the dick in it that has me lingering. I've never felt a dick other than my own.

Man, it's thick. It wasn't this thick the last time.

He's…hard. Fully hard.

Why is he just lying here and not bolting out of bed? How long has he been awake?

Oh-ho-ho!

Looks like the guy who doesn't like kissing me has erected a statue in Chia-ville for me. *Again*!

The twisted-idea fairy in my head arches a brow and nods at the devil on my shoulder. The devil knows exactly what to do.

Closing my eyes, I keep the smile on my face from pressing into his back and give the *Lucas log* another exploratory stroke. Weird, but whatever. We've practically made out already, and it's just a dick after all, one of two that I've had my hand on before. The entertainment value and vindication of the breath he sucks in far exceeds the weirdness. Someone *likes* my stroking.

"Mm," I groan, sleepily mumbling my next words for effect, "Go back to sleep."

"Y-your hand…"

What about my hand, Lucas? I want to ask. *The hand that you've not moved yet?*

Our conversation from last night comes back to me. He's the one who brought this up. Not me. I know now what his scent consists of—big horny hillbilly who likes my kisses and my hand. Suddenly, the idea of him begging seems like a highly satisfying challenge.

Tilting my head, I nuzzle the back of his neck with the tip of my nose and glide my thumb up one of his obscenely engorged dick veins. "What about it?"

And maybe because I'm a bit of a sadist and can't let shit go, I give him an experimental squeeze. His grunt is followed by a shiver that has his body vibrating against mine.

I have never felt more all-powerful. That's the only way I can describe the rush I just got from him making sex noises for me. It must be a divide-and-conquer thing, slaying the enemy…with his own dick.

"Y-you…you're jerking me off," he rasps.

Is he seriously going to play the Captain Obvious card? Like he's not stalling on purpose. The coward. I bet his favorite song is '*Linger*' by the Cranberries.

"The more interesting observation is that you're not stopping me," I whisper, moving my mouth to the back of his ear, no longer trying to sound like I'm sleep-stroking. I slide my hand down his length slowly, getting more acquainted with his veins, oddly high on how arousal-frozen and out of breath he is.

"Fuck," he gasps, and it's all I can do to hold back an evil laugh.

"How come you're not stopping me, Lucas? Is it because you *like* being my boyfriend?"

"What…I…what?"

When I slide my hand back up, I reach the bulbous head of his tip. I know I appreciate a good thumb graze, so it's second nature at this point. Except, the pad of my thumb comes back sticky and wet. So fucking sweaty.

Wait.

That's not sweat.

In the words of Dario…*crikey*.

This feels like some sort of sex leveling up. I've made women wet before, but never a man. At least, not that I know of or…*felt*. Typical Lucas to get some kind of fluid on me.

"I think my boyfriend *likes* my hand on his sweaty dick."

His grip kneads my wrist, but doesn't make any effort to stop me. He comes up with the awe-inspiring rebuttal of, "Shut up."

This time I don't hold back my snicker, scooting closer and nudging his stupid chastity pillow up higher toward his ass so I can shove my leg in between his. Time for another squeeze of the vein statue. He's ready to break. I can feel it.

"Just like you liked me talking bossy to you on the beach at the cay. Yeah. Don't think I didn't see the Chia Pet come to life after I brushed your nipple and told you to take it. You like your man being in charge."

"I…no! I d—don't."

He's panting so hard now, I want to ask him if he truly thinks anyone would believe that pathetic lie. Uncle Lou, we need a sign for where Lucas lives. Denial—population one.

The mattress shifts when I give him a faster stroke. His other arm moves to his pillow and grips it tight. My thigh is sandwiched in between his, where it's feeling heat it's never felt before.

It is the mecca of his Chia insulation. How can someone so confounding feel so damn cozy?

I'm basically angry-stroking him at this point, swirling his fluids over his tip and greasing them down his super vein to give me better traction. It's become personal.

Didn't like it? He's so full of shit. I saw the way his Speedo was tented and was gracious enough not to bring it up.

I've been turned down before. I can handle it, but not from Lucas. My pride couldn't take it. Given the way he's gone rigid as a post and is huffing like he ran a flight of stairs, I don't think I have to worry much longer. I've hit the nail on the head and he knows it.

"Yeah," I taunt at his ear. "My *big tough* army guy likes to let go and have his man take charge of him. Don't worry," I whisper with another squeeze. "I won't tell anyone your secret."

"You…you're an ass," he rasps.

Reaching out from under my pillow, I catch a grip on his hair. The second I tug, he groans. It's the sound of victory. I let my laughter flow right into his ear.

"But what you *really* mean is, '*Andrew, don't stop.*' Just say it, Lucas. Tell me you want me to get you off. Tell me that's why you're doing that mouth-breathing thing you do every time I touch you."

I swallow as soon as the words are out, realizing how obscene this has become, how obscene *I've* become, but then he shudders. Violently. Just from my suggestion.

Holy fuck. I'm right. He doesn't want me to stop.

I mean, I know I thought it, but thinking it and seeing this much confirmation of it are two different things.

I can only describe the haze that clouds my brain and vision as an overdose of smugness filtering over me from Lucas' needy pheromones. I own him. At this moment, I own him.

Rubbing my thumb over his slimy tip, I give his ear lobe a little nip with my teeth. "I bet I can make you come, Lucas. Do you want me to make you come?"

I didn't know my voice could sound like a sex villain, but it has Lucas gasping and his hips twitching. His shoulder flexes from squeezing his pillow in a vise grip.

"Shut…I…you…"

God. He can't even speak anymore. I've never rendered anyone speechless.

A soft moan filters in through the wall from next door. Keenan is my guess. And here I thought he was the quiet one. The added sensory effect has Lucas' cock flexing in my grip. Weird.

Weird that I'm still holding it. Weird that it doesn't feel weird anymore. Fucking rude as hell that he's flexing from another man's noises when his *boyfriend* is holding his cock. I give him another stroke to remind him who got him hard.

"Let me make you come, sweetheart. They don't have to be the only ones enjoying themselves on this trip. You've got your own man here to take care of you. Don't you?" *Stroke. Squeeze.* "Don't you?"

I didn't know a man's whimpers could be just as arousing as a woman's. The peculiar noise he makes, though, has my balls tingling. Power must be a turn on.

"Don't you?" I repeat, letting my lips brush against his ear.

"Y-yeah."

W-wait.

What?

I replay what I just said because I don't even know what in the hell I'm saying at this point. I think I just asked him if he wants me to make him come and…I think he just…begged.

My head has gone light. My cock bucks against his chastity pillow as I suck in a breath.

Holy shit. He'd actually let me make him come. *I'd* actually make him come. Wouldn't I?

Er…no! Of course not. Why would I do that?

I was just trying to get him to admit…

What was I trying to get him to admit?

Uh…his obvious attraction to my hand and my mouth.

Yeah. That was it. Fucking jerk, waking me up before I was ready to function.

Releasing the fleshy vein statue, I retrieve my hand, wiping the Lucas fluids on the sheet as I draw back. Gross, but there's always a price to pay for victory. That was the point, right?

Sitting up, I know I need to bring us back to reality, so I do the only thing I can think of. I slap him on the ass. It jiggles just like his face does.

"Good!" I chirp, bounding out of bed. "Glad to see you're finally getting with the program."

I rush to the bathroom without looking back. I don't need to see that stupid, confused face he gets. His vein statue is his problem to figure out. It's not my fault that I'm irresistible.

Something makes my boxers shift just as I reach the bathroom door. Glancing down, my thickened cock is tenting the fabric in the direction I need to go. I…grew my *own* statue. What the fuck is that about?

Chapter 12

Getting out of the *Uber* outside of the Duxbury Bakery, my stomach shouldn't feel like something is fluttering inside of it. I've had three days to prepare myself mentally for facing Andrew again. I told myself over and over to forget about that last morning in the Isles. That it meant nothing. That it was just him screwing with me again. The fact he acted like nothing happened the entire trip to Boston and even after we landed proves that it certainly meant nothing to him. He went and bought another Christmas ornament at the airport and then strolled on his merry way toward the car rental counter without so much as a backward glance at me.

However, seeing him through the window of the bakery now, biting into a croissant while he stares down at his phone, I'm finding it difficult to believe it meant nothing to me. Since when have I found the cut of his jaw and his high cheekbones alluring? Try as I might to have absorbed myself in prepping things for our showings down in Harlow's Landing the past few days, I found myself disturbingly distracted. Especially at night. I've slept alone for the last four years. It shouldn't have been so difficult to fall asleep without his obnoxious presence next to me in bed. Without his heat. His clean scent. His peaceful stream of breath. And without waking up to his wandering hand on my...

"Stop it," I scold myself.

Shaking my head, I wheel my suitcase toward the bakery door and inhale a deep breath. If I can't stop thinking about that morning or how I replayed an alternate extended version of it in my head the last few nights, he'll see right through me. I can act as indifferent and callous as him.

I can.

I should.

I shouldn't *be* affected by Andrew Broadhouse. In any way. I don't know why my body is having such a difficult time getting that message, but I'm determined to make sure it does. I mean, he's not even into me. Even if he does have one or two redeeming qualities, he's not into me. So, that's that. Besides, I can do better than a person whose only redeeming qualities are their command of sales and their good looks.

As I approach the table, I try to convince myself that he isn't even all that good-looking. What do I know about whether men are good-looking? Right? Except when those mischievous green eyes glance up at me, my breath catches in my throat. A lock of his sandy hair falls over the sun-kissed skin of his forehead. He brings his coffee cup to his bow-shaped mouth, the hint of a smirk at its corner that registers as one word in my addled brain—sexy.

Crap. I'm failing at this already. Failing and clearly have lost my mind.

He *is* sexy. For some unearthly reason, he is. No wonder women fall at his feet, and the Hepperlys have seemed charmed by him since day one. He's just got this charisma about him that makes you stupid in light of his bitchiness and immaturity.

"Wondered if you'd ever show up," he calls, averting his gaze back to his phone like he couldn't care less that I've arrived.

It shouldn't hurt. Why does it hurt?

It was just half a hand job, not a declaration of love. I'm too old-fashioned. The girls are always telling me that. Intimacy means something to me, I guess, even if I never intended on being intimate with him.

"I'm ten minutes early," I say without fanfare, just stating a fact, and take the seat opposite him.

There are two large pastry boxes stacked on the table. I can only guess they're either to pacify his high metabolism during our upcoming stay on Clark's Island, or he was thoughtful enough to acquire them for me and our clients. I really hate when I notice admirable things he does. I can't count how many times he's opened a door for me, which is completely mind-blowing after once getting stuck in one with him.

Reaching out, he nudges them toward me, again without eye contact. "Here. Eat something. They're heart-healthy and filling."

I'm sure that was a dig at my preference for granola bars, but my stupid heart skips a beat like a wistful teen at the thought of him remembering something I said. That's the thing that's so confusing. For someone who acts like he hates me so much, he actually pays a lot of attention to what I do and say.

As the box slides, I notice a smaller one beside it come into view. The front of it is clear, revealing a small ceramic croissant inside with a gold string attached to the top of it. The words Duxbury Bakery are inscribed over the golden finish.

"What's the deal with all the Christmas ornaments?" I ask.

His gaze flicks to mine, brow furrowed in confusion. My face heats. We've never actually had a real conversation about anything other than work or an argument.

"The ornament…you buy one every time we go to an airport or a new city," I elaborate, opening the pastry box to busy myself.

"They're for my tree. Why?"

Pulling a flaky roll out of the box, I shrug, at a loss for how to respond. I assumed they were a gift for someone special. Like maybe one of his women, his mother, or Aunt Vera. I wouldn't have thought he was so sentimental, nor that he cared about his work enough to commemorate each of his stops by buying an ornament. Will he think of the time he spent with me on this trip when he looks at them?

"Nothing. I just didn't peg you for a Christmas tree kind of guy."

It's true. I didn't. I always imagined he spent holidays at fancy parties where the drinks were flowing, not at home surrounded by knick-knacks.

Scoffing, he starts scrolling on his phone again, but says, "They're a giant sparkly night light that radiates the aura of childhood dreams. What kind of person wouldn't like that? I leave it plugged in day and night for an entire month and just sit under the glow, transfixed. It's… soothing."

An image of Andrew in stocking-clad feet on a couch, ogling a Christmas tree with all of his tacky ornaments flitters through my head. It's oddly endearing.

I tear a few pieces off my roll and eat them. I'm officially out of small talk. There are actually a million questions about Andrew that I'd like to know the answers to, but I'm not brave enough to ask. An exasperated sigh filters across the table, making me forget them.

"Are you going to be fucking weird from now on just because I know you have a crush on me?" he lets out.

"What?"

Throwing up a hand, he gestures to me. "You haven't argued with me or given me a dirty look since you got here. You're just sitting there like…"

"Like what?"

"Like some shy virgin who just received their first bouquet."

Where does he come up with these analogies? "I…What? I'm just being normal. My normal self. And I'm trying not to argue with you because we have to sell properties together, act like we're a couple, and maybe because I'm just tired of arguing. It's fucking exhausting."

He stares at me. Unnervingly. Maybe not unnervingly, but it feels like it because I do feel like a shy virgin who just got flowers. Fuck. I hope he doesn't see that too.

Quirking his brows, he looks impressed and then returns his attention to his phone. "About fucking time," he mumbles in agreement.

When he says nothing more, I start to relax. Embarrassment averted. It's not like he knows my skin feels taut underneath my clothes just from sitting this close to him. It's not like he knows how good I think he smells right now or how I kind of missed his scent.

"Good. Because I was worried you were going to be all needy after you begged me to jerk you off the other day."

My hand falls halfway to my mouth, and I drop the piece of roll from my fingers. *Begged?* I did not beg. Not exactly. He…antagonized me with…with the most blunt bedroom talk I've ever heard while he…

Shuddering right now is probably not a good way to convince either him or myself that I didn't want or initiate whatever happened that morning. I still can't believe how practiced his hand felt on my cock. Each slide, each squeeze, was confident and masterful. Sinfully breathtaking. I was helpless to the arousal he stirred in me.

Swallowing against the lump in my throat, I reclaim the morsel I dropped and school my features. Indifferent and callous, I remind myself and take a note from the Andrew Broadhouse school of behavior.

"I didn't beg," I murmur casually, shrugging. "Not even after you kept stroking my cock and grinding up against me like you couldn't get enough of me."

I hold my breath, knowing I probably don't have anything bolder than that to come at him with. He's always been better at the battles of wits than me. I think that's what aggravates me the most about him, and in some ways, I'm also kind of in awe of it. My phone rings, saving me from finding out just how loud the thunder is that I've called down, judging by the heated look he's shooting me from across the table.

"Hello?"

"Hey! You got a second to talk?" Julia's voice comes over the line.

"Uh, yeah. Yeah, sure. What's up?"

Instinct has me wanting to get up and find a private corner away from Andrew, but I fight the instinct. I've got nothing to hide and damn if I'm giving him the satisfaction of thinking I'm ever uncomfortable around him for any reason.

"Well, I wanted to talk to you about the bachelor party…"

"The bachelor party? You mean the bachelorette party?"

"No," she laughs. "We've got that covered. I don't think I need my brother's help to plan a bachelorette party."

Chuckling with her, I'm relieved to hear there's one less unpleasant task on my plate. "Good. Glad to hear it. I didn't feel like shopping for penis headbands or whatever it is women wear for those things. That might kind of ruin the memory of braiding your hair when you were little."

There are only so many places I can look in this little bakery. When I find my gaze crossing Andrew's, my cheeks burn at the sight of his amused and rapt attention. I'm not sure which is worse at the moment, that I said penis in front of him when we were just talking about mine or that he just learned I know how to braid hair.

"Uh, yeah! And don't worry. Mom already bought the penis headbands."

"Gross," I whisper, pinching my eyes shut. "So…what's up with the bachelor party?"

"Um…so, Tyler and Ricky were wondering if you'd want to go."

We hadn't discussed anything about bachelor or bachelorette parties, so it hadn't crossed my mind. I guess I didn't even contemplate if the boys were going to have one or even wanted one. Now I feel like a jerk for not suggesting it or planning one for them. Yet, I'm flattered that my future brothers-in-law want me to come.

"Uh, yeah. Sure. If they want me to. That was nice of them to invite me."

"You're our brother. Of course we want to include you in everything. The guys love you. You know that."

When she pauses, I can't help but get a sneaking suspicion that this call isn't just about an invite. "Is that why you called? Just to see if I want to go?"

There's a pause, and I hear her take a breath. "Well, Tyler wasn't sure…I mean, *we* weren't sure if you'd want to be there," she says, referencing her fiancé.

"Why wouldn't I want to be?" I laugh. "Is it at a mud wrestling place or something?"

"No," she laughs, but it sounds like her nervous laugh. Julia rarely gets nervous. What is the deal? "It's just that…Well, Mark will be there too," she lets out with a sigh. Her next words come in rapid fire. "Tyler doesn't know what to do. It's his brother, you know? He can't *not* invite his brother, but you're *my* brother and his future brother-in-law, and you're giving us away. So, he can't *not* invite you either."

"Oh…" I mumble, picking at the mangled roll in front of me, unsure of what to say. And here I assumed I'd thought of everything to make things go smoothly for the girls. I didn't want them to have a bad experience like I did, but I guess you can't prevent every awkward moment. I just didn't expect I'd be involved in one of those awkward moments.

"We just don't want you to be uncomfortable, you know? So…I thought I'd better warn you and see what you think." She sighs again, and I hate the sound of her distress. "I'm sorry. I don't know what to do."

"No. Hey. It's fine. I'll be fine going or not going. Tell Ty not to worry about it. And if he doesn't think it's a good idea for me to be there, I can miss it. It won't bother me. Mark and I…" I rub my eyes, remembering the first time I saw him and Shannon together after we broke up. My oldest friend and he just stared at me like I was an alien while he had his arm around the woman I once thought was going to be my future. I was more embarrassed that seeing them together made much more sense than Shannon and I ever did, except I pretty much lost a friend because of it. Some levels of awkwardness you just can't fix, I guess. "We're fine. I mean, I don't know if we're fine, but to me, it's fine. I'm over Shannon. Over…*it*. Seriously. I know they'll be at the wedding, so what's the difference if he's at the bachelor party, too? It's just part of it. Okay? Don't even worry about it."

"Seriously?"

"Yeah." I nod, even though I know she can't see me. "Jules…everything will be fine. It's about you and Ty. No one's going to ruin anything for you. If they do, I'll break their legs. Okay?"

That has her chuckling, making me smile. "You really deserve better than her," she adds. "Just so you know. Maybe you can bring a date to the wedding and make them both regret it."

Oh, brother. She's always been the feisty one of the two girls.

The bells to the shop chime, and I hear voices, three male voices with varying accents. Glancing over my shoulder, I see the Hepperlys streaming in, faces alight with curiosity as they take in the bakery.

"Uh, what part of '*I'm not going to let anything ruin your wedding*' did you miss?" I tease Julia.

"I'm just saying, Lucas! You're handsome, smart, kind—you're a good guy. You deserve to be happy."

"I am happy," I defend, and yet my words sound like a lie, even to my own ears.

"You know what I mean. Just…if you ever meet someone who makes you as stupidly giddy as I feel when I'm with Ty, I hope you know I'll welcome them with open arms. We all will. You deserve *that*, Lucas. That's what I mean. Okay?"

Her sentiment has my heart overflowing, and a tear forming in my eye. It's surreal sometimes to see her as a grown, responsible, compassionate woman when I often still think of her as a little girl. I sure never thought she'd be giving me well wishes and life advice.

"Yeah, okay," I laugh to hide my emotions. "I've got to go, though. Our clients are here. I'll talk to you later."

"All right. Knock 'em dead. Love you."

"Love you, too."

I exhale the weight of the conversation without thinking, momentarily forgetting where I am, or rather, who I'm with. When I look up from my phone, Andrew's gaze is fixed on me. I don't know what his peculiar expression means. It's not like he could hear Julia or possibly know the entirety of what we conversed about. Maybe he's just surprised to have heard what it's like not to argue with or lie to someone.

The longer I stare, something in his eyes changes. Something that looks a lot like that strange, heated look I still haven't quite figured out. The kind that means he's planning something or thinking something that will make me look like an ass. Or worse yet…needy.

I tear my gaze away and stand to face the Hepperlys. I will not be needy today.

Or awkward. Or made to look like an ass.

I won't. I can be a believable boyfriend without doing any of those things.

Chapter 13

ANDREW BROADHOUSE
licensed agent

What kind of boyfriend doesn't look at you once the entire day? Can you say insensitive?

I don't know what's up with him, but he's been laughing it up and smiling ever since we left the bakery for Clark's Island yesterday. He didn't even scowl or act weird when we dropped our bags in our room at the property we're staying at.

It's a double—two beds. When I tossed my suitcase on one of them, he did the same, like he didn't intend to try to sleep separately from me. Maybe he noticed that there's no lock on the door and knew not to try that shit since the Hepperlys were just down the hall in the primary suite. Since when has Lucas become compliant without having to be bossed around, though? Something is up.

This morning, I woke up as usual. Well, as per my new usual—with my hand on his dick again. I should start tying my wrist to my thigh or something at night. As for him being hard as iron again, it shouldn't make me feel so damn proud. Smug…maybe I'm just smug.

I *knew* he had a crush on me. At least, I think he does. He acted so unaffected yesterday, all through the showing, though, that I'm no longer entirely sure. So, I let him go as soon as I realized where my hand was, and neither of us has said a peep about it.

Right now, however, I'm even more confused. It's day two of our showings on Clark's Island, and he reached for my hand when we left the house to take the guys down the path to the beach. *He* reached. No tugging away. No grumpy face. Nothing typical Lucas-ish. But he's still not even looking at me. What the hell is up in Tuft Town? Am I just an asshole with a dick grabbing problem?

"Hey, Drew," Keenan calls, bringing up the rear where he was checking out some photos on his phone from their mini-break at his mother's house. "I've been meaning to ask you. There's a Broadhouse Publishing office in Boston. Any relation to you, by chance?"

Fuck.

"Uh, yeah. It's my grandparents' company. My parents run it now. They have five offices in the States. One in the UK, too, actually."

"You're kidding me!" Mason exclaims. "You and Lucas should pop over and see us at our apartment there if you ever come over."

Double fuck.

"Thanks, but I don't work in the business. Not anymore anyway." That sounds ominous, so I add, "I used to." Great. That sounds even worse.

"Really?" Keenan exclaims. "Oh, my word. You could be approving a Pulitzer-winning work or discovering the next epic fiction series. How come?"

Perfect. One of our clients just has to be a lover of literature.

Something heavy rests on my shoulder. My hand is suddenly empty, making me realize it's Lucas' giving me a squeeze and tugging me closer to him.

"Andrew left publishing to help his aunt and uncle. They own VeraLou. So, technically, he's still helping his family. He's the best agent they have, so I doubt they'd be willing to let him go back."

What the actual fuck? Did Lucas just…champion me?

And hello—someone knows things about me. I have to say, his version of my life course sounds much better than how I saw it play out. The way he tells it, I feel less like a failure or a disappointing son. I wonder if he'd be saying that if he knew my own father fired me.

"Well, Drew, I'd say you picked the better calling," Dario remarks, stopping when we reach the sand of the beach and staring out at the gulf.

A flock of birds swoop low in the sky and caw as the waves undulate far in front of us. It's hot as hell out here in the late morning sun, but it is a damn fine view. Far better than any I had in a Broadhouse office.

"Yeah. I think so," I concur absently, enjoying the smooth feel of the curve of Lucas' hip as I stroke my thumb over it.

Wait. When did I put my hand around his waist?

Glancing over, I see parted lips. Gaze fixed on the view, he looks like a man enjoying the scenery, except I realize I do know Lucas better than the average bear. He swallows like it took him some effort. I watch his throat undulate and his chest rise unsteadily. And then I smile the first genuine smile I've smiled all day.

Leaning in closer until our sides are flush against each other, I slide my hand a little lower down his hip and squeeze. "Who wants to be stuck in an office when you can stand on the beach with the man of your dreams?"

"Right on, mate," Mason concurs, slinging an arm around Keenan and planting a kiss on his head.

"Isn't that right, sweetheart?" I whisper for Lucas' ears only.

He mouth-breathes for a few seconds, that signature Lucas-arousal fog I'm starting to become acquainted with. I *knew* I was right. Why did I doubt my suspicions? Someone was just trying to put on a good face the last two days because he was embarrassed that I called him out on his crush. Ha!

Sucking in a breath, his nostrils flare and then his expression closes off. What is that? That's so unlike him. That's not what he's supposed to do. Usually, I say something flirty, and he gets all flustered or seems drugged, looking like he wants my mouth on his. Turning his gaze back to the gulf, he nods and squeezes my shoulder.

"Yeah, babe," he says loud enough for our clients to hear. "Nowhere else I'd rather be."

After that, my boyfriend turns into a robot for the rest of the day. Every minute that passes infuriates me even more. I want to reach into his back and rip out whatever circuit is giving him the audacity to pretend to override the giant hard-on I know he's carrying for me. It's one thing to lie to the Hepperlys, but isn't there supposed to be honor amongst thieves? Or is it no honor?

I don't know, but it's pissing me off that he's clearly straining his emotions and brain cells to hide the obvious. How do you get hard for a guy, admit you want him to jerk you off, stick up for him in front of your clients, and then pretend you're unaffected when acting like you're affected might actually help you sell some fucking real estate? I do not understand the hillbilly code of ethics.

And what in the hell was with that phone conversation yesterday with one of the babies? I didn't catch everything, but Lucas must have been too close to a few too many bombs in the war because his volume was up enough that I caught the gist of what his baby sister had laid down.

His freaking ex will be at their wedding…with his ex-best friend? The wedding he's paying for? And now he has to go to a bachelor party with the guy? Is he freaking paying for that, too?

Ugh. I can't with him! Can't he have some balls and less…heart?

'It's about you and Ty. No one's going to ruin anything for you. If they do, I'll break their legs.'

Staggering over a rock on the beach, I wipe the flop sweat out of my eyes and squint up ahead to where Lucas and Dario decided to stop and tinker with an old boat that comes with the property, while Mason, Keenan, and I trekked further down the beach to *Timbuk-fucking-tu*. He points to something on the motor, standing close to Dario. His drenched skin is shimmering under the sun, and try as I might to fabricate some nefarious assumption that he's flirting with the man, I can't. Somewhere deep down, I know he's just being helpful. Just being Lucas. Because that's who Lucas Everette is, isn't he? A helpful guy who gives a hundred percent of whatever little knowledge or even finances that he has. Except when it comes to *me*.

I only get a hundred percent of his bullshit. The bullshit that I, in some way, am responsible for by introducing us as partners. I get it—the furry Boy Scout doesn't like being involved in our scheme, but how come the babies and the Hepperlys get the honest side of him, and all I get are sass and denials? It's not like I'm a criminal. People have done worse things than fake date.

Yeah, the Hepperlys are nice, and I do feel bad about deceiving them. I did it to protect them and give them a pleasant buying experience, though. At least, that's what I've told myself. Was I really so wrong?

Shit. Listen to me. The heat must be messing with my conscience.

We've nearly made it back to where Lucas and Dario are when they get up and head to the house before we reach them. Where the fuck are they going? Is he going to ignore me all night now, too? This is some bullshit.

By the time I reach the house with Mason and Keenan, Mason is as red as a turnip and sounds like he's about to have an asthma attack. It helps my ego knowing I'm not the only one who's suffering from our beach tour under the sweltering sun. As we chug water from the bottles I stocked in the refrigerator, I hear the screech of the patio door down the hallway. Through the kitchen window, I see Lucas stepping outside with a towel and a bottle of shampoo in his hand.

Why is he headed toward the outdoor showers? I know he saw me coming up the beach. Is he avoiding running into me in our room?

"Excuse me, guys. I'm going to go get cleaned up," I inform them, starting toward the door to the hallway. When Dario walks into the room, I realize I'm still supposed to be playing host and not just disciplining Lucas for his shenanigans. "Uh, how about we cook up those steaks that I brought from town? Test out that grill on the patio?"

"Oh, that sounds good," Keenan agrees. "I brought some wine from this shop in Boston that I like."

"Yeah. I could use some cooling off first, too. Give us an hour or so?" Mason asks, still panting.

Dario slaps me on the shoulder as he saunters in. "Mighty nice of you, Drew. You handle the meat. We'll see what else we can rustle up. How's that grab ya?"

"Sounds good."

As I rush to my room and snag a towel and change of clothes, I can feel a smile creep across my face. Dario's advice sounds like just the remedy for Lucas' attitude problem.

"Fucking ignore me," I mutter, shoving through the patio door and rounding the side of the house.

No one's in more need of some grabbing than Lucas. As soon as he sees me naked, I bet he'll be the one wanting to handle meat.

I clear a turn in the path around an Umbrella Magnolia tree that Lucas had babbled on about to the Hepperlys earlier. It leads to the outdoor showers at the back of the house. Certainly not a necessity, but we used the fact that they overlook the beach and are next to a hot tub on the property as a selling point for their convenient, quick access to wash off chlorine or salt from the bay. *Not* for boyfriends to hide from their man. Upon finding said boyfriend, I stop in my tracks.

That really *is* one big bubble butt. Damn. Meaty. Very meaty.

Swallowing, I canvas its circumference, noting the shadowed crease that ends at one tufty sac nestled snugly at the base of his cheeks. I always just shrug my shorts down my hips and kick them off. Not Lucas. He apparently has to bend over and delicately slip his feet from each leg hole, exposing his ass to the world. How in the hell did he disrobe like that in the Army and not come out with a boyfriend? The guy is like a walking invitation.

When he straightens up, I give my head a shake and move toward the picnic table next to him, tossing my things down to make my presence known. That gets his attention.

Frowning, he covers his junk with his hands and glances down at my change of clothes and towel, then back to me. Gracing him with my most pleasant and innocent boyfriend look, I slowly peel my sweaty tank top over my head.

That's right, big fella. You like what you see, don't you?

When his gaze returns top side, I watch him try to snuff out the spark of lust kindling in his eyes.

Swallowing, his lower lip pouts for a second. "Can I have some privacy?"

Really? How can a person ogle their incredibly irresistible boyfriend's chest and then ask for privacy? Sighing, I trail my hand slowly down between my pecs, watching the way his gaze follows.

"You weren't saying that this morning."

He tries to scowl at me, but it mostly looks like panic—panic that he knows he doesn't look *scowly* at all.

"It's not my fault you have a dick-grabbing problem," he blusters.

"It's not my fault you have a getting-hard-for-me problem." Wriggling my brows, I dart a glance at his hands and add, "Or is it?"

His jaw drops, but then his mouth snaps shut. "Fuck you," he mutters, spinning on his heels.

Kicking my shorts off my feet, I snicker, watching his meaty globes jiggle when he stomps up the two steps to the first shower bay. So angry. So in denial.

A commotion to my left pulls my attention away from the furry manchild. I tense for a second, seeing our merry trio filing down the path to the showers. It's just like an outdoor locker room, though. What do I care if they see what God gave me?

"Ah, shit. Sorry. We thought we'd make less of a mess outside. Are we interrupting?" Mason asks.

Lucas looks like he wants to crawl in on himself, practically cowering with his shoulders hunkered forward, only flashing a brief glance over his shoulder. I should be a good boyfriend and put him at ease. That's what a good boyfriend would do. Wouldn't they?

Surveying the open stall on the other side of the waist-high partition, I grin. "No! Not at all. Go ahead. There's one still open."

"Nice," Mason sighs. "I'm sweating my bollocks off. They're sticking to my leg."

Gross. TMI.

Walking toward Lucas' stall like a man confident and proud of his nudity, my feet slap against the wooden planks of the steps. Lucas whips his head around, eyes going wide. Just as quickly, he looks back to the wooden shower wall when he catches sight of the Hepperlys disrobing behind me.

Shit. Maybe this is too much for him.

Sidling up behind him, the cool water from the reservoir tank rains down on my sweaty hair. I brush the droplets off my face and run my fingers through my locks, oddly fascinated with the way the water is trickling down Lucas' rigid back.

"What are you doing?" he whispers over his shoulder.

And here we go.

"Showering. Pass the soap, will you, lover?"

Nostrils flaring, I can't see any of the lust in his eyes anymore, just pure, unadulterated, hillbilly rage. That's so impolite.

"It's okay." I smile. "I'll get it."

Leaning forward, I slap a hand on the wall over his shoulder and reach around his other side, effectively caging him in when my hand lands on the bar of soap he set on the wall mount. A gasp leaves his lips, lighting me up with joy. *There* he is…

Glancing to our right, he sneaks a peek at the Hepperlys, who I can hear stepping under the other showerhead just five feet away. His lips part and…is he fucking mouth-breathing right now? Because of *them*? Rude!

Moving my mouth to the side of his face, I murmur, "You like what you see? Shame. Shame. Gawking right in front of me."

His shoulder rotates backward, bashing into the front of mine as he looks the other way. "Hurry up and get this over with," he mutters.

Hmm. So he wants it quick, huh? Quick and dirty, perhaps? Is that his style?

Bringing the bar to his chest, I bite my lip when I feel him flinch. The vein in his neck pulses like a big juicy target, a siren's call in physical form. So, I scrub in circular motions across his pecs, clumsily rubbing the bar over each of his nipples as I watch.

One of his hands goes to the wall, and he inches forward, letting out a puff of breath. Confirmed—Lucas likes nipple action. That vein in his neck is getting bigger from the way his breathing has become so erratic already.

Crap. He's not a premature ejaculator, is he?

We only need to sell that we're a happy couple enjoying a shower, not porn. I'd better slow it down.

Grabbing his other hand, I slap the bar into his palm. "Get my back for me, babe?" I ask sweetly, with enough volume that even the fish in the bay can probably hear me.

Fuming, his shoulders tense. That's what you fucking get for ignoring and lying to me, I want to tell him as I turn around and lean my head back, letting the water sluice over my hair.

I start massaging my scalp, so we still look *showerific* in case the guys catch sight of us. He won't do it. He's too chicken. He'd better at least be soaping himself up so he doesn't look like a Freshman on his first day in a locker room.

Something waxy and wet touches my shoulder blade. It's rectangular and hard. There's barely any force behind it, but I know it's the soap. I let out a quiet snort, impressed. It's probably more of that stubbornness he's been living with these past few days, him trying to fly on my level of cool, calm, and collected. The bar moves slowly across my back, and then I feel something else.

Lucas' hand.

My smug smile falters at the touch. It's beefy and warm, flattened against my wet flesh. It glides over my shoulders with a hint of pressure, almost like a massage, spreading the sudsy water across my skin. Lucas is washing me…with his bare hands.

My mouth is suddenly dry for some reason, and my heartbeat feels quicker than its usual rhythm. As his hands move lower to the middle of my back and make slow sweeps over the edges of my ribcage, my abs go taut. My abs and then…lower. Everything seems to be tightening. The air feels thicker, too.

I don't have to look down to know Andrew Junior is starting to stand at attention. That's twice now. I thought maybe last time had to do with some kind of power kink I didn't know I had when I was trying to get Lucas to admit he wanted me to make him come. Except, he really doesn't have to be washing my back right now. Definitely not with his bare hands. Slowly. Adoringly. Curious. It feels like he's making a map, studying me more closely than any romp I've ever had, and I've certainly had my share.

And the thing about mouth-breathing…you can feel that shit on your skin when it's wet. He's panting heavily behind me, like he's in a trance over the lines of my body. What will he do when he runs out of back?

He hesitates at my hips and then starts a slow trek back up, his fingers softly kneading the flesh as they go. I shudder like I'm as wanton as he is, and shit, maybe I am. Terry is never going to find out about this if I have any say in it, but hell, I'm starting to see why he and Shaw are such sluts for each other.

Shifting my gaze, I catch a glimpse of the Hepperlys. They're all in the same state of undress as we are. Keenan is lathering up Mason's back while Mason and Dario are grinning, laughing over something.

But Dario's just scrubbing the water across his own chest. It's definitely more PG-rated over there than here. Regardless, it's doing nothing for me. They're all singularly attractive in their own way. Three good-looking men. I can easily admit that. But I don't want their hands on me the way Lucas' are right now. It doesn't make a bit of sense, considering I never thought I'd want Lucas' hands on me, period.

Maybe it's so fascinating to me because I know these hands have gone to war, can whittle the most intricate little knick-knacks out of driftwood, and know how to fix boats, fish, and braid little girls' hair. They can do all those wholesome, noble things, and yet, right now, they're choosing to caress my body. *Me*—a *very* not wholesome, not noble man.

When he reaches my waist again, I know this strange blip in time is nearly up. Feeling greedy, I reach back and slide his hand around to my stomach, curious how he'll treat my front or if his pampering of my back was just a fluke.

His flattened palm stays frozen just above my belly button. Another gust of air hits my spine just below my neck. This time it's thicker, with more force behind it. I'm holding my breath—something I don't remember doing from someone's touch since I was a teenager, first discovering sex. His thumb moves first, shifting slowly upward. And then his palm makes a slow circle over my stomach, spreading wildfire through my insides.

Jesus. It's like he has magic hands. Big, magic, country-boy hands that have me going harder than I've ever been in my life. When his fingers graze the sensitive flesh just above my cock, my dick bobs in the air like it knows he's close and is begging for him to move his hand lower. He doesn't, though. He freezes, like maybe he felt the vibration.

Shit. He'll probably turn around and act like a mannequin the way he does in bed every morning when my hand wanders over to his side. I need to know, though. Need to know what effect his touching me has on him. Because...well, because I just do.

Reaching back, I find his hip and pull him closer. A warm piece of flesh pokes the back of my thigh. It's thick and veiny. The statue.

"You... you're good," he blurts, pulling away. "You're done."

I feel the bar of soap slap into my palm. I turn around and find him leaning against the shower stall, both hands on the wall, head down. His back is rising and falling.

It's the most erotic statement I've ever witnessed, a piece of modern art, a conversation piece. Anyone standing around a gallery viewing his pose would be whispering, '*Lucas likes touching him.*' I shudder so hard, my knees nearly buckle.

I think I used to hate him because, while physically he portrayed this big, tough image on the outside, he always looked kind of pathetic. Like a man who never got what he wanted, nor knew how to. Fuck me three ways to Sunday for discovering that is somehow a turn on for me now.

He made me feel ashamed that I always get what I want, like it some-how meant I hadn't earned it because I didn't suffer in silence like him.

I refuse to feel ashamed, though, for not being such a pushover that I'd pay for a wedding that never happened and pretend to chum it up with an ex-best friend who stole my girl. I refuse to feel bad that I don't have the kind of relationship with my family that involves braiding any-one's hair. And right now, as I catch the way his eyes are pinched shut tight—the way his lungs are expanding like he's willing his cock to stand down—I refuse to neglect the other superpower that life granted me. I *do* always get what I want. Like hell I'm stopping now. It doesn't matter that what I happen to want this time is a first for me.

Stepping up flush behind him, I reach underneath his arms and press the bar of soap to his stomach. It flexes underneath my touch when I scrub it in a circle to form a lather.

"No. I'm not done," I whisper at the back of his ear. "I missed a few spots."

When I feel a good froth of bubbles, I lower a hand to his happy trail and run my fingers through the wet hair there. It's a foreign sensation, but it's familiar too. It might not be a woman's smooth navel, but it's taut flesh that's registering the desire I've stoked there with my touch.

"I…I can do it," he rasps, cupping my wrist.

His grip is so lackluster, it feels like I just won an award. "It's okay. I don't mind helping my boyfriend out," I assure him, inching my fingers closer to one side of the hot V at his hip juncture.

The hair gets coarser the lower I go. I reach a patch near the side of his cock, and he lets out a strangled noise. His fingers dig into my wrist, but don't pull me back. I know it's just petting in the grand scheme of foreplay, but there's something so carnal about it. The hair, his reac-tion—and mine. My balls are drawn up so tight, it feels like I'm going to choke on them.

"*Sooo* tufty," I murmur, running my index and middle fingertips through his jungle, weirdly enamored with how soft it is. "Gotta wash my tuft good."

My two-inch height difference gives me one hell of a view. His cock jolts upward in the air and he sputters. If he runs on me out of fear of the unknown right now, I might kick his ass. I didn't know a vein statue in an uncharted tuft jungle could make my mouth water this much.

"Listen to you…fucking mouth breathing just from me soaping you up. You love it, don't you?

Leaning my hips forward, I press my thickened cock against the back of his thigh. It's a helpful suggestion. A white flag, if you will, to help him overcome any embarrassment over his current state. "*Love* me touching your tuft," I repeat nonsensically with my lips against that pulsing cord in his neck.

"Andrew…" The breathy croak of my name on his lips is a liquid injection of arousal that goes straight to my dick, making it kick against his thigh.

The soap falls from my grasp, so I replace it with something else solid, wrapping my hand around his cock. I'm winging it here, having only ever specialized in teasing breasts and clits, but so far, determination and instinct don't seem to be letting me down.

"What?" I rasp in his ear, giving him a squeeze. "Is *this* what you want? Is that why you've been pissy all day? Because I didn't finish what we started this morning?"

Maybe he meant to say a word, but all that comes out is a garbled, desperate noise. He shudders again, making his cock slip forward in my grip. It's slick from the soap and water, and I can feel his pulse in it under my touch.

As far as I know, hands don't have erogenous zones, so why is the feel of his flesh in my grip so thrilling? I want to stroke him and see what other noises I can pull from him. He's *good* and thinks I'm *bad*, and the thought of Lucas being enamored with a bad man is a fantasy I can't seem to eject from my brain. I want to feel what his cock is like from root to tip while it's soaked, but his little wiggle gives me a better idea.

"Then *move*, Lucas," I whisper, holding my grip in place. "Show me what you want."

His hips jerk forward with a full-body spasm. "Fuck," he gasps.

I say the word with him, completely in awe of the effect my sexy talk is having on him. He's helpless to it. Totally helpless. And apparently, so am I, because I give him a languid stroke from base to tip.

"That's it, Tufty. Use my hand."

I wait. And then I wait some more, suspended in anticipation of him answering my plea. I can feel every rigid muscle in his back pressed against my chest. Feel the way his body is coiled in need as much as my own. The flash of ideas going through my mind about what I want to do to him is astounding. As much as I want to act on them right now, I don't.

An invisible wall of restraint is stepping on the neck of the greedy voice inside of me. More than I want to listen and give in to that voice, I want him to take what he wants.

Come on, Lucas, I growl inside my head. *For once in your life, do something for yourself. Be as bad as me.*

Chapter 14

'Use my hand.'

He wants me to fuck myself with his fist. *I* want to fuck myself with his fist.

But…I can't.

What if it's just another trick, and he makes fun of me for it later? Worse yet, what if the hard cock stabbing the back of my thigh means he actually does want it as much as I think he does? Because if he does, I don't think I could stop myself, and something tells me there would be no coming back from this. It cannot be humanly possible to feel this lost in someone and not have it change the way you see them afterward. I know now that he's right—I do have a crush. The pin-hair trigger holding me back is the only thing keeping a crush from turning into a complete pulverization by the life force that is Andrew Broadhouse.

For a guy who teases me about breathing heavily around him, his own is ragged against my ear. It's a miracle I haven't already come just from the thought of me having that effect on him. Andrew—with his razor-sharp tongue, an intellect he tries to hide, and a fearlessness I never even saw in battle—is panting in my ear over how much he wants me. No one has ever wanted me like this.

"Fuck my hand, Lucas," he rasps in my ear like he's the one who's begging. "Show me how bad you want my hand."

It's the most messed-up request I've ever heard, and the phrase is as bossy as he is, but it's the delivery in his tone that gets me. The way he speaks it… Well, it's the nicest he's ever spoken to me. Or maybe I just can't take it anymore, because I do exactly what he asked. I move.

Rocking my hips forward, I thrust my cock through the ring he made with his thumb and fingers around my tip. Every inch of me plunges through that slick hold like it's a sleeve of relief until the side of his hand hits my navel. A groan rips from my throat at the burst of static it sends to my nuts and down my legs. It was the right thing to do because it feels so damn good, but it was also the wrong thing to do. There is no way once is enough.

Especially not after he whispers into my cheek, "Fuck, yes."

My hips punch backward instinctively, drawing me through his cuff. He tightens it along the way, making my eyes nearly cross. The head of his cock stabs the back of my thigh, sending gooseflesh across my skin. I'm the cleanest I've been all day, and yet I feel incredibly filthy. Yet, it's a kind of filth I want to live and die in.

How many times have I jerked off and had my release held up by the awareness of it being my own hand, the straining and cramping of my fist taking away from the pleasure? He's giving me the answer to all those frustrations, and I'm suddenly terrified he's ruining masturbating for me for the rest of my life.

"That's it," he whispers encouragingly.

His palm moves up my chest, and his thumb circles my nipple, sending electricity across my pecs. I moan and punch my hips forward again.

The slip of my cockhead through that steadfast ring he's created feels like heaven as it glides over my glans. I want more of it. I draw my hips back just a fraction and do it again. And then again, teasing the tip of my cock.

His grip tightens and on one pass, he slides the pad of his thumb up my slit as I pass through. "Andrew," I let out on a strained breath, overwhelmed by the pressure it's causing in my balls.

"You like that, huh?" he asks, dropping his lips to the base of my neck. "Get it, Lucas. Get it," he urges, and then I feel teeth against my flesh.

His lips suction against my skin there, and his hand falls from my chest. It settles on my hip, gripping me tight, and then I feel him press his thighs against my ass. He thrusts with me, connecting us with each of my little nudges so there's not an inch separating us.

"Oh, God," I croak, lost in the sight and the sensations.

It feels like he's fucking me. Like we're fucking. My ring spasms at the thought, and I now know for certain that he's ruined masturbating for me. Ruined it and opened Pandora's box, because as I watch the shape of my cockhead morph each time I jerk it through his grip, I imagine what it might be like to actually have him fuck me.

"Andrew," I beg again, gripping the wrist that's holding my cock, although I don't know what I'm begging for.

"Fucking hell," his hoarse voice floats over my shoulder. His tongue draws a stripe up the side of my neck over my jugular, telling me that if it was mercy I was asking for, there will be none. His mouth captures my ear, and he twirls the tip of his tongue around the inside of the shell of it.

I let out a cry, learning that my ear is somehow connected to my nuts, as a thrill runs from it down the center of my body. When his hand snakes back up to my chest and pinches my other nipple, the ungodly pressure in my nuts bursts and my cock spasms, flexing against his grip. Andrew sucks in a breath and a low growl rumbles next to my ear.

"Yesss," he hisses, his hand moving into action, sliding down my length to stroke it furiously.

All I can do is make noises that sound like I'm in pain as I watch my release spurt out of me. I'm leaning my weight against him, afraid I'll fall to the shower floor if I don't. I might pass out. Is this what sex is supposed to feel like?

I don't even realize I closed my eyes until I feel his hand grabbing mine. The hand that was on my cock guides my wrist behind me. I start to turn my head, wondering if he wants to spin me around for a kiss, but then I feel something against my fingers. Something wet and slick and hard. His hands wrap mine around it and my foggy brain realizes it's *his* cock, stealing my already short supply of air. Draping an arm over my shoulder, he leans his head against the back of mine and starts to guide my fist. Absently, I realize the Hepperlys are long gone. My God, I'd completely forgotten about them. Did they see anything? That concern is quashed when I feel friction against my palm.

He's…using my hand to jerk himself off. I didn't think this could get any hotter than it already was. The feel of his flesh sliding through my grip and the way he's panting against my shoulder, though, have my spent cock twitching against its recent death. God, it feels right. I know there is no reason why it should, given our past, but it feels so freaking right.

Resting my hand on the shower wall for support, I pinch my eyes closed and dig deep for energy that I don't have. I want him to feel the way I do, to experience the level of release that I just did. Giving his cock a stroke, I stop at the tip to give it a squeeze. The grunt he huffs onto my skin has it prickling with gooseflesh. He's thrusting so fast, I can barely keep up, clenching his hand around mine. I want to tell him I'd gladly take over, but he seems lost, like a man possessed. All I can do is squeeze tighter to let him know I'm here with him, a willing participant.

As soon as I do, he freezes and lets out a groan. His cock flexes under my touch, making my eyes go wide. I can feel it pulse, feel the blood rushing through it, the release. Something warm runs down the back of my thigh. I shiver. Tendrils of possessiveness and pride wind their way around my heart, knowing he came because of me. Languidly, I stroke him through his release. His hand falls away, letting me take over. I find myself smiling with each uncontrollable jerk of his body against my back, my chest filled with warmth.

Through his ragged breathing, his hand settles over my wrist, squeezing gently. He's gone soft, and I imagine it's a signal to let me know he's become too sensitive. His forehead is still resting against the back of my shoulder as he catches his breath. When he lifts it, I swallow against a flurry of butterflies in my stomach.

What happens now? The urge to turn into him and seal these sensations with his mouth on mine is strong, but so is my apprehension. Except, Andrew always knows what to do, always takes the lead. So, trembling, I slowly turn and face him.

Nothing could have prepared me for what I see. Cheeks tinted pink, lips parted, chest rising and falling, Andrew stares back at me with his pupils eclipsed. I've never been a jealous man, but I'm suddenly envious of anyone who's gotten to see this look on him. But right now, I remind myself that it's *for* me and *because* of me. I'm oddly proud of myself for doing something so out of my norm. Flashing him a little smile, I can't help but get snared at the sight of his mouth. I wet my lips, wishing the droplet of water I licked away was a taste of him.

He swallows, and I'm pretty sure his gaze is fixed on the tip of my tongue when it peeks out. His gaze darts downward, and the next thing I know, he's bending down. I tense in anticipation, wondering what else he has in store for us, but he rises with the bar of soap in his hand. I'd forgotten he dropped it.

I watch him slather some suds onto his cock and as the water rinses them away. When he hands the bar to me, I reach for it hesitantly.

"I think I smell the grill," he says. "We'd better go."

It's now that I notice the rapture in his gaze has been infected by something that looks a lot like fear. Nodding dumbly, I accept the bar from him. He turns and shuffles down the two steps to the picnic table and wraps his towel around his waist, not even bothering to dry himself off. The high I've been floating on crashes, bringing me back to earth. I'm not going to get a kiss. Nor a comment. No more heady words. Not even his usual snark. Nothing.

That can't be it, a voice inside me cries. Except, another brutally honest one tells me it is. Picking up both his clean and dirty clothes, he starts toward the path to the house. A wanton ache in my chest knows it means he doesn't even want to stay long enough to get dressed in front of me. He stops, though, making my breath catch in my throat.

Half-turning his head toward me, he asks, "I'll see you on the patio?"

He can't even look at me. Andrew—effervescent Andrew, the man who drew me into a game I didn't even know I wanted to play, can't look at me. I already knew I wasn't built for casual encounters, but the sinking feeling in my gut signifies that truth as I nod again.

"Yeah," I call, but it sounds barely like a whisper.

The speed at which he pads away produces another pain in my chest. I tell myself it's stupid to be feeling like some betrayed lover. I keep telling myself that as I stand under the water, hoping it will rinse away the sensation of his touch.

After I dry off and go around the back of the house to our empty room and change, I'm still trying to tell myself that, but it's difficult. My body still wants to revel in the feelings of what occurred under the water. And the damnedest thing is, I know what betrayal feels like. I've been there because of Shannon and Mark. Andrew pretending nothing earth-shattering just happened shouldn't hurt as badly as that did.

When I step out onto the patio, silently hoping for some reprieve, he's immersed in tending to the food on the grill. That means I'm going to be stuck in this hellish limbo like a starry-eyed teen until whenever we're alone again.

I find Keenan at my side, asking about the next property we're going to see in Harlow's Landing tomorrow. I've gauged that he has the most say in deciding on what will be the throuple's US family home, since it's so near his mother's place. The topic is just the distraction I need, and I find I can't contain my excitement over what I hope will be the best we've shown him thus far. Except, as I elaborate on the upcoming property, a niggle of insecurity worms its way under my skin, remembering we started our shower with an audience.

"Um…about the showers earlier," I preface, unsure how to finish the sentence. "I'm sorry if…uh, if you saw anything that…"

I don't get to finish, as he chuckles and puts his hand on my shoulder. "Lucas, you're good. I'm guessing we left before it got too heated."

Jesus. What does that mean? How much did they see or hear?

"Don't worry." He laughs. "We've been trying to be on our best behavior, so honestly, it put us at ease."

God. Now I feel even worse in a different way. More deception. But is it really deception if I enjoyed what I was doing and was a very willing participant?

"Still, um, we should be more professional around you. You're our clients."

"Oh, my God. No! We think of you two like friends after all of this, hauling us all over the world, arranging for us to have extended stays at listings, lugging our baggage around." He gestures to Andrew, who still hasn't looked at me once. "Even cooking us meals." Gripping both of my shoulders, he centers himself in front of me, his expression somber. "You guys are head over heels for each other," he says softly. "Don't think you have to put a lid on it for us. Enjoy your time together now for when you have to go back to showing listings separately. You'll thank me later. I know what it's like to be apart from the people you want."

Head over heels? Why does it feel more like *ass over tea kettle*?

"Um, yeah." I let out a nervous laugh. "Okay. Thanks."

I take a seat at the patio table, wallowing in the bizarre irony that I have permission to want a man who doesn't seem to want me other than past a few heated words each time his hand is on my cock. As I stare at his profile, I notice his laughter and smiles don't quite reach his eyes tonight. Am I being too hard on him? This is all as new to him as it is to me, at least, I assume so. Maybe he just doesn't know how to proceed, either.

When our food is ready and we plate it, Andrew takes the seat next to me. I have to force myself to stop sneaking glances at him. And then

I have to force my steak down my throat when it becomes apparent that I'm the only one sneaking glances. He really is avoiding me.

Keenan starts talking about his childhood in Massachusetts, including stories about his father, which only worsens the misery in my gut. I must be hitting a new low because the question comes to mind—am I ever going to be good enough for anyone?

I wasn't for my father. I wasn't for Shannon, although I ended up eventually not minding that I wasn't. But now I'm not good enough for Andrew. I don't know if I'll be able to fulfill Julia's wish for me: ending up with someone who makes me as giddy as she feels with Ty. Any time I'm faced with the possibility, they leave me or want nothing to do with me.

Andrew lets out a yawn the second his food is gone and excuses himself. My head jostles when he ruffles my hair and wishes me a hurried, "Goodnight."

No kiss.

No more kisses—it's a painful verdict I know to be true.

Despite the hurt, I still want him. Why? Am I as fucking stupid as he once insinuated I am?

I shouldn't be hurt because Andrew sucks as a human being. Except, there are parts of him that don't suck. A lot of parts I've gotten glimpses of. The cynicism and indifference still feel like a smoke screen, concealing a completely different human being. Or is that just wishful thinking?

The steam from my shower filters out into the empty bedroom as I pack up my toiletries bag to head out to Harlow's Landing tomorrow. I thought the hot water would wash away the memory of Lucas' body pressed against mine from earlier, but it's official. The Hepperlys shouldn't buy this place; the water pressure is shit.

He was giving me puppy-dog eyes all night. I could feel it. I saw them even before I left him at the outdoor showers earlier. What the fuck am I supposed to do with puppy-dog eyes? We barely get along. Did he forget that?

He sure looked like he wanted to get along when he turned around and faced me, though. Grunting, I adjust my cock roughly behind my boxers. *We went to Tuft Town once, you hear me?* I silently admonish it. Once was enough. You saw the way he looked at us.

What business did he have looking at me like that, anyway? We were both just getting off. What does he expect will happen next? That I fuck him?

I can't fuck him. I mean…I probably could. It can't be that difficult to figure out. I've done anal before. Men's and women's bodies aren't entirely different.

"Shut the hell up, Andrew," I grit to my reflection in the mirror. "What are you even saying?"

My phone resounds with a familiar ring tone, making me groan, but I answer it. There can be no better way to cleanse my brain of my current debacle than a chat with my mother.

"I stopped by yesterday and you weren't home," comes her veiled scolding, and any hello is forgotten.

"If you'd called first, I could have told you that so you didn't waste a trip."

"I was in the area doing some shopping."

Wow. Way to be blunt. She didn't come to see me at all.

"I'm in Massachusetts showing some properties."

"The miles you probably put on that car of yours," she tsks. "Lou should give you a company vehicle."

"I flew. First class on his dime. Don't worry." Rolling my eyes, I toss my toothbrush into my bag. Her disdain for all things Uncle Lou is astounding. "Although, I guess I could have picked this last one up as a get-well present for him," I add, just to push her buttons.

"*Get-well* present?"

"Yeah. He had surgery yesterday."

"For what?"

Is that actually alarm in her voice? Loretta Broadhouse has never shown an ounce of alarm over her brother in my life. "Hernia repair. Aunt Vera said he's sore, but he's all right. He has to take it easy for a few days, so I guess he'll be laid up at home if you want to go visit him," I venture, curious about how deep her unexpected sympathy runs.

"Oh?" There's a pause, and then her unconcerned tone returns. "I'll send him a card."

Yup. I knew it was a fluke. Whatever falling out they had years ago—that no one has ever elaborated on—has me shaking my head. At least, I assume there must have been a falling out. Her repeated claims of him being the black sheep of the family whenever I used to ask why he was rarely ever invited to family functions never seemed to add up to that kind of isolation. And by family functions, I mean only Christmas.

"That is *very* generous of you, Mother Dearest," I deadpan.

"Don't call me that," she scolds. "I know what movie you're talking about, and I am nothing like that." I bite my lip on a snicker, mentally picturing her spine stiffen over the jab. "Did he send me anything when I had back surgery five years ago? No. I don't think so."

Sighing when I zip up my bag, I realize I don't even care about whatever their age-old feud is right now. I need to slip into bed before my bearded cock interest decides to come to bed. Two can play possum, and I plan to play the Lucas Everette card tonight, closing my baby greens before he even gets here.

"How's Dad?" I ask, deflecting and trying to be a good son.

"Busy…"

Fuck. Why did I even ask? That's the most loaded statement I've ever heard. "He could use your help if you're finally tired of being a house salesman."

"*Real estate agent*, and no. I'm working on the deal of a lifetime right now. Also, I think his exact words on my last day at Broadhouse Publishing were, '*You're fired.*' I highly doubt he asked for my help."

I want to tell her the scoff she makes is unladylike, but why poke the bear more than I already have? "He was just upset. If you'd told him you were dating that intern and explained all those charges on the company card, he might have been more reasonable."

"One—It is not my fault he didn't elaborate on what types of purchases could be made over the workday. And two—which intern?"

There's a grumbling noise on the other end of the line that makes me smile. "I'm not discussing this with you if you can't be serious."

Leaning against the doorframe, I inspect my cuticles. "Maybe I'm being perfectly serious."

"You're just like him, you know?" she huffs.

"Who?"

"Your father."

How in the hell does sleeping with a few employees who had just as much of a blast as I did make me just like my stalwart father? Am I missing something?

She elaborates without me having to ask. "Never appreciating one thing, always thinking something better is out there."

Pinching my eyes shut, I stifle a groan and run my hand down my face. I am in no mood if she's gearing up on one of her tangents where she claims Dad doesn't love her.

"Mom…he dotes on you. You've got him so wrapped around your finger that he wouldn't take a shit unless you said it was okay."

"Vulgar," she warns, but then her tone turns more subdued. "And I don't know about that."

Sighing, I let my forehead thump against the drywall over the towel rod. "Is this why you called?"

"No. We're getting off track."

I'll say. No shit, Loretta. Was there even a track when we started?

"We're having a party for the Fourth of July on Saturday the fifth."

"So, you mean you're having a fifth of July party?"

"Hardy-har-har. Yes. Whatever. Will you be home from…wherever?"

She knows damn well where I am. The woman has a memory like a steel trap. "Yes," I grumble before I can think better of it, so I add, "Maybe."

"Good," she clips, seeing right through me. "It's been a while since you've come to visit. Your father and Chad will be happy to see you."

My eyes are going to be damaged by how many times I've rolled them during this conversation. "Yeah. I bet."

"You can invite Shaw and Terry if you like," she says off-handedly. "I haven't seen them since Easter."

I will never understand why Lou's kid is welcome, but he isn't. "Yeah. Sure. The fourth on the fifth."

"Noon. Don't be late."

"I wouldn't dream of it."

She hangs up, and as I stare at the phone, I want to know why it's the first time I'm pondering why we never say '*I love you*' back and forth the way Lucas does so freely each time he talks to the babies. Does that make my family dysfunctional or his?

Turning off the light, I decide it's not worth burning the brain cells over and step into the room. I stop the second I do, seeing a lump in the bed. A very large, Lucas-shaped lump.

How long ago did he get here? I didn't even hear him come in. And is that…a fucking pillow shoved behind his ass underneath the covers?

Snorting, I shake my head at his fuckery. There is no way he's worried about me reaching over in the morning. Someone's pouting already because I didn't tell him he was the best double jerk session I've ever had, no matter that he was the only one. He's making me as needy as him because I have to step on the lightness that brings to my chest like squashing a bug. He was just drunk from coming. I'm not special. The idiot. He's too old to have a crush. I bet he drove around Podunk in his pickup for months, blaring '*Friends In Low Places*' after his woman ditched him.

I toss my toiletry bag next to my suitcase, telling myself he did me a favor with his chastity pillow. I honestly have no idea how to extricate myself from…whatever the hell is happening between us, short of turning down the boyfriend signals around the Hepperlys tonight.

The closer I pad to the bed, the angrier I get watching his still frame and that fucking bulge from his extra pillow. Fucking Lucas. We've still got almost two weeks left with the Hepperlys. I can't afford for him to piss me off, along with his pouting. Every time he aggravates me, I end up putting my hands or mouth on him.

Damn it. I need some advice.

Huffing, I head out into the hallway with my phone and keep going until I reach the patio door. The night air has a chill in the breeze, but I'll take all the cooling off I can.

I hit the video icon on my favorites, and after three rings, Terry's face appears with the backdrop of their kitchen in view. "Where's Shaw?" I ask, not wasting any time.

"Hello to you, too."

"It's important. I need some advice."

His sourpuss brightens, his face lighting up. "Ooh, about the '*boyfriend situation?*'"

"No, about the mouth fungus you gave me."

His head twists around, straining the cords in his neck. "Shaw! Your dickhead cousin's on the phone. Want me to hang up?" he yells at the top of his lungs.

Drama king. I glance out over the bay when the view on the camera starts wobbling with his angry steps through the house.

I catch his muffled voice as my cousin comes into view, looking half asleep on the couch. "There's trouble in paradise. He wants the keys to Prostate City."

"What?" Shaw asks, flipping the phone around to face him.

"Hey, I have a question."

"I was just going to head to bed. I have to be up early. Can you make this quick and not weird, please?"

"What do I do if my boyfriend has a crush on me?"

"Oh, my God! He *actually* likes you?" Terry squawks somewhere in the background.

"Why is that so difficult to imagine? I'm a total catch."

Shaw shakes his head, fortunately dismissing his husband as easily as I do. "Um…remind him you're just playing pretend boyfriends," he ventures. "Seriously, is this why you called?"

"Yeah, but he looks at me like…" I don't even know how to go there, so I just rapid fire off the other list of crimes, "and gets hard for me, and jerked me off in the shower, and I don't know how to end it without his pouting fucking up our deal. We still have two more properties to sell."

"*Holyfuckingshit.* Go the fuck back, right now," Terry interrupts, his head appearing in the shot behind the couch like a jack-in-the-box.

Doesn't he have his own cousins? "Why can I still hear you? This is *your* phone, isn't it, Shaw?"

Shaw sits up, looking slightly more attentive now, at least. "Dude… did you just say he jerked you off in the shower?"

"Yeah. Keep up." I bat my hand in front of my screen, waving off his attempt to get hung up on details. "So, how do I tell him it can't happen again?"

"Uh…maybe, I don't know—don't fucking shower with him," he says, sounding amused.

Terry throws his hands up behind Shaw and glances at the ceiling. "*Seriously?* You *showered* with him? How do you not see that you're attracted to men?"

"Being attracted to men and trading hand jobs with *one* guy are not the same thing."

"Whoa! *Trading?* Did you say *trading?*" he shrieks, his eyes bugging out.

Oh my God. I don't have time for this. My nipples are getting hard out here.

"Um…cuz, I think you have more than one problem here," Shaw says sagely, with a hint of amusement.

Great. Terry's infected him with his cockamamie theories.

Now I'm the one looking skyward. "He was begging for it. I was proving a point, and getting me back was the least he could do for all the effort I put into that shit. Quit making such a big deal out of it."

"A big deal?" Shaw scoffs.

Terry's hands slap the sides of his head as he leans over the couch. "Are you listening to yourself? Oh, my God, you're freaking out big time. It's okay," he soothes, but then shakes his head and adds, "I can't believe I'm actually consoling you, but it's okay."

Oh, for fuck's sake. Now Terry wants to braid my hair right along with Lucas.

"I'm not having a fucking freak out. I was hard and turned on. He… pisses me the fuck off. Apparently, I have an anger kink or something when it comes to him. I'm not bringing him to a Pride parade with you. He's just... Help me out here, will you, Shaw?"

"Your John Stamos?" he suggests, referencing one of our favorite movies, '*Stepbrothers*,' where two guys agree on the one guy they'd sleep with if they were women.

"No! I don't want to fuck him. I just let him fuck *my hand*."

Terry snorts and rolls his eyes.

"Snorting? What's the snorting for?"

"You're an idiot." He sighs, shaking his head as he straightens up. Patting Shaw's shoulder, he tells him confidentially like I can't hear, "Don't help him," and then disappears from the frame, but not before I hear his enthusiastic comment of, "Let him fuck it up and figure it out on his own."

"Goodnight!" I call. "Shaw will tuck you in under the coffee table in just a few."

Resting my forearm on the retaining wall off the patio, I close my eyes and sigh. I need another gay cousin. One who's not married.

"Drew...what's going on with you?" Shaw asks.

"I told you. I had a one-night hand job, but I need it to end there. What should I do?"

Sighing, he scrubs his hand down his face. "I don't know. What do you normally do?"

"I leave and never call, but I can't do that, can I?"

"Then... I don't know what to tell you. Stage a breakup, but tell the clients you still want to work together to show them the properties."

"No way. They love Team *Drewcus*. They'll try to play matchmaker and get us back together."

It's true. Me and my freaking method acting are what got me so deep into this madness.

"Then tell Lucas it was great, but you're not interested in anything more."

Ew. Has living with Terry turned him into a schmuck?

"Why do I have to compliment him?"

"Because you're still stuck cohabitating with him for the next week and a half?"

"God, you give the worst advice. You know that?" It's true. Why did I think calling him would help? "Honestly. Your advice is what got me into this mess."

"*My* advice?"

"Yeah, it all started when I kissed him. He went all doe-eyed and started mouth-breathing whenever we were close, like the sun shines out my ass."

He snickers at that and covers his mouth.

"I'm glad this is so funny to you."

"I'm not laughing at your situation. I'm laughing at you."

"How the fuck is that supposed to make me feel better? And what does that even mean?"

Now he's rolling his eyes like I'm the one who's not understanding the situation. "Drew, most people *want* to find someone who thinks the sun shines out of their ass. I'm laughing because you've got one and you're annoyed about it."

"Well, yeah, because he's…he's…"

"What?"

Good. Patient. An open book. Devoted. Stirs my blood in all the right places.

"Nothing. Forget it. *Thank you again* for absolutely nothing."

He lets out an amused huff and smirks. "My pleasure."

"Oh, and my parents are having a fifth of July party at their house and asked if you and a plus one want to come."

"You mean Fourth of July and Terry?" he asks, his face scrunching up.

"No. *Fifth* of July, noon, and bring someone who's not obnoxious."

"I'll see if we're free."

"*Be* free, so I have someone to talk to."

"Lucky me." He yawns. "That it?"

"Yeah. Bye."

"Goodnight."

He may give shit advice, but at least he's a good listener and never lets emotions get in the way. There aren't many people in my life like that.

"Shaw?" I call just as he starts to lower his phone.

"Huh?"

I try the salutation out to see how it feels. "I love you."

His head rears back, and you'd think I just shot him with a stun gun. "Oh, my God." He cracks up, shaking his head. "You need help."

The call ends, telling me what he thinks of how much I value our *cousinhood*. What the fuck am I doing? Trying to be like Lucas?

No. That's stupid. I'm trying to be the opposite of Lucas right now. I remind myself of that on my way back to our room.

As I get into bed and brush up against his Andrew-don't-jerk-me pillow, I see red again and jam a pillow of my own up next to it. Two can play this game.

Lying back, I close my eyes and sigh, suddenly exhausted. I'm tired of playing games. It feels like my entire life has been a game to some degree or another. Doing just enough of what my parents expected of me without pulling my hair out. Being the messenger boy between them and Uncle Lou's side of the family. Charming women over and over until I found one who didn't expect anything from me. Trying to convince her she'd never have to expect anything from me only to find out she's foolishly dreaming about expectations. This game, however, the one between Lucas and me, needs to end. I'm not about to wake up with my hand on his dick again and then have to be an asshole when he starts breathing heavy like he was dreaming about it all night. He needs to step up to the plate and take a turn because it's getting exhausting being one all the time.

Chapter 16

LUCAS EVERETTE

licensed agent

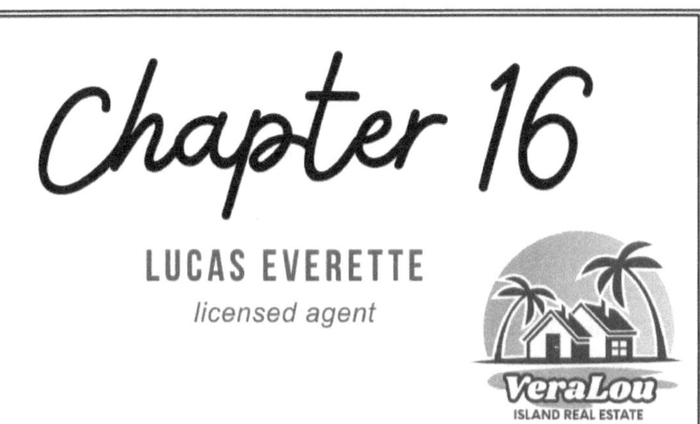

Nothing has gone right for my half of the Massachusetts showings. It's been raining all damn day, and the first house had a leak in the roof. A full-on leak that collapsed in the kitchen above all the appliances, so Lord knows how long it was dripping down inside the walls. We got back in the rental car and took the guys out for lunch, hoping that would help salvage the shitshow and then headed to this property, but not before it became an apocalyptic thunderstorm.

Everyone was soaked to the bone by the time we hauled our bags inside. And because fate hates me, as I was changing into dry clothes in my room, the fucking power went out.

At least we're dry and under a roof that isn't leaking for the day, but this is not a good start to my goal of selling them their dream home. I think it's the best property we've shown them in Massachusetts, and I haven't even gotten the chance to show it off. It has a four-car garage, a guest house, a pool, and ample acreage within walking distance of the beach. Their first view of the primary bedroom, though, was using their phone flashlights just to find clothes in their suitcases.

"I'm so sorry," I apologize again as we all congregate in the kitchen, freshly dressed.

As though fate hasn't screwed with me enough, a loud crack of thunder resounds, shaking the house and lightning brightens everyone's faces momentarily.

"Ah, no worries. Better luck tomorrow, mate," Dario assures me.

"Yeah. Lazy day in the dark." Mason shrugs. "We'll be grand."

"I still feel horrible. Again, I'm sorry about that leak at the last place. This property is amazing, though. It has everything you want and more. I just…wish I could show it to you."

"Really, Lucas. It's fine," Keenan says. "We can wait until the storm is over. We'll be roughing it soon once we head to Australia. A day off is fine by us. Why don't you and Andrew do the same?"

I think that's Keenan's way of ensuring I know he meant what he said at dinner last night. I glance at Andrew, who's leaning against the counter, arms folded across his chest, staring at his feet. Of course, he lets me take the lead when it's a total fuck up of a day. I nod at Keenan and smile, however, even though I'd rather have anything else to do than kill time with my boyfriend.

The Hepperlys head to their room. Maybe to unpack, but probably to fuck because I was just considering that a nap might be a good way to pass the time. Andrew starts down the hallway after them toward our room, and I silently hope he has to hear their mating calls as punishment for being a ginormous jerk.

I meander to the living room and plop down on the couch. The view out the wall of windows overlooking the backyard is completely obscured by the tsunami-like conditions. It reminds me of when I take my truck through the carwash, but it provides the most natural light out of any room in the house. I stare out of them, grimacing over the rest of the events from this morning.

I woke up feeling warm and at peace, an arm hugging my chest. No hand on my dick. Andrew was spooning me, and for a brief moment, it was just as nice as our intimacy yesterday, but in a different, less chaotic way. It was…*really* nice.

There was something about being held by someone so commanding and sure of themselves, as though I was getting a special view of a tender side he keeps locked away. I wish he would show that side more often, if it even is a side of him. Maybe he's only gentle in his sleep.

I got caught up in the sentimental vibe of it and stroked my thumb over the soft hair on his forearm. "Good morning," I whispered when I felt him stir.

He went tense, and I bit my lip, waiting for him to melt back into me. I thought maybe he'd had time to process everything, to get comfortable with the idea of…me.

"Morning," he grunted, taking his arm back and climbing out of bed.

I'm so confused. Confused over why he's pretending nothing happened. Confused over why I want so badly for something more to happen. Confused over the jealousy I felt when I heard him talking to a woman on the phone last night before I realized it was his mother. I'm even confused over the pity I felt for him from what I picked up from their conversation. It was so businesslike, nowhere near as easy and open as the way my chats are with Mom and the girls. I'm starting to see the root of his sarcasm. It's like a shield he carries to protect himself.

Closing my eyes, I lean my head back on the couch and focus on a wind-whipped tree outside. I stare at it until my lids begin to droop and the dozens of questions in my brain downshift from incessant to murmurs. A loud crack of thunder has me bolting awake much later, judging by the absence of light in the room. The rain is still pouring, albeit with a bit less force. There's not a light on in the house, and it sounds void of life, except for...*moaning* coming from down the hall. Great.

I hear footsteps a moment later and turn to see Andrew padding into the kitchen, looking like he was just rudely awoken, too. Small graces.

Wonderful—I'm becoming as negative as him, if I'm wishing him unpleasantness.

I pull my phone out of my pocket and see that it's been three hours since our meeting of the minds earlier. I have no signal, which doesn't really matter. Mom and the girls are still at work, so I have no one I can call.

There's commotion in the kitchen, and then Andrew saunters through the doorway to the living room with an open bottle of wine in his hand. Glancing down the hallway in the opposite direction of our room, he takes a draw straight from the bottle.

"What are you doing?" I ask, forgetting we've taken a vow of silence.

"Checking out the rest of the house."

"With wine?"

"You heard them—lazy day." He shrugs and starts down the hall, disappearing from my view. I see a dome of illumination on the wall and hear a door open that I suspect is the hallway closet. It closes, and his footsteps move on.

I don't care what he's doing or that he's still avoiding me, but a hundred bucks says he's trying to find fault with the house, since it's one I picked out. There's nothing wrong with it. As I listen to the rain coming down, I hear more doors opening and closing. Try as I might to ignore it, I can practically feel his judgment from here.

Grinding my teeth, I push off the couch and head to the kitchen, retrieving a beer from the fridge. If he's got criticism, I'd rather hear it now to give myself time to cool down before we have to interact with the Hepperlys again.

Hedging my way down the hall, I listen for sounds to locate him. The pantry, home office, and laundry room doors are closed. A dim pool of light is spilling out onto the floor at the end of the hallway, where I hear music. Did he walk all the way down here to listen to his phone just to make sure I saw that he wanted to get away from me? And, go figure, *he* has a signal, but I don't.

Pushing open the door to the sunroom, the sound of a piano surrounds me. I never would've expected what I'm looking at.

Sitting in the corner of the room is an old piano I'd forgotten was here when I did my pre-checks a few days ago. Sitting at the piano, fingers flying effortlessly over the keys, the bottle of wine on top of it, is Andrew. It sounds like '*The Day I Tried To Live*' by Soundgarden, but it's exceptionally beautiful and haunting in this classic-sounding rendition. I stare in disbelief, half-expecting it to be one of those pianos that plays by itself.

Andrew's gaze flicks up, a moment of surprise in his features. It shutters, though, shifting back to indifference and questioning, like he wants to know why I'm here.

"You play the piano?" I ask rhetorically, still in awe.

"No. I'm tuning it." He doesn't miss a note, his body still moving with the ebb and flow of the song. "Why? Any requests?"

Averting my gaze, I walk to the windows, trying not to let his complete lack of sincerity ruffle me. "I just can't imagine you taking piano lessons."

"Nothing but the finest for Jacob and Loretta's baby boy," he quips, ending the song. "Just one of her and my father's many attempts to make a gentleman out of me." Toasting the air with his wine bottle, he adds before taking a gulp, "As you can see, they wasted their money."

It's surreal to me that someone who's bragged to me so much isn't making every effort to capitalize on his obvious talent. "It's a skill not everyone has," I say off-handedly. "You should be proud of it."

"Maybe I'd be proud of it if they'd asked me my opinion about taking lessons." He fingers a few notes of a dark melody, which sound a lot like the basement music in the Mario Brothers video game, then adds, "Or which degree I should get." More basement music notes. "Or whether I want to work in publishing." The dark notes resound again, painting a mood to his narrative. "Or get married and have five babies."

He ends it with the merry tune that's played when Mario starts above ground. It completely solidifies my theory about his sarcasm. The wound I scratched must be deep. I never figured he had any expectations placed on him.

"Is that why you work for Lou? Because it pisses them off?"

"Are you trying to psychoanalyze me?"

"No. You just seem like someone who does whatever he wants."

Snorting, he picks up his bottle and takes a healthy drink. Studying the label, he lets out a tired stream of breath. "Not without a price."

Is he saying he has regrets over the debonair way he flies through life? Shooting me a look, he must notice my confused frown because he rolls his eyes.

His hands move again, but what I hear next isn't a sarcastic choice, at least not to my ears. Elton John's 'Sorry Seems To Be The Hardest Word' flows out of the piano like a wave of regret.

"Put it this way. We didn't braid each other's hair in the Broadhouse family. And no one consults me on my opinions about weddings, other family functions, or anything, for that matter."

He remembered I used to braid the girls' hair? Shit. I need to stop taking phone calls in front of him.

"Because you slept with all their interns on purpose?" I ask, genuinely curious if I've hit the mark.

A derisive laugh cuts the song short. "Jealous?"

The jerk. He's so conceited. Correct, but conceited.

"No. I'm just trying to understand why you could fuck up so badly at publishing and then become the best agent Lou has." If he overheard my phone conversations, I no longer care if he knows I overheard his, too.

"Because I'm good at what I do, sweetheart. I hope you've been taking notes."

I stare at him, equal parts frustrated and baffled. "Why do you do that?"

"What?"

"Avoid saying what you really mean."

His cackle barks across the distance between us. "Uh, I really *am* good at selling properties. Scout's honor." Holding up his index and middle finger, he feigns a solemn expression, but then frowns. "Or have you been in a coma for the last four years?"

As I watch his brow wrinkle in laughter, it's like seeing numbers appear in one of those color blindness tests. It's clear he thinks he's a comedian, but his method is all sarcasm. He can't even answer a simple question. It's not like I'm being antagonistic. I know we started off on two wrong feet, but he should know me well enough by now to know that I don't kick people when they're down.

"You're such a coward." I shake my head, saying it mostly for my own ears.

"What?" He laughs. "Oh, please. Do tell."

When we first started this trip, my annoyance kept me from speaking to him. Then, when *things* happened, it was my nerves. I'm annoyed with him right now, but for new reasons, and while some stupid part of me still wants him, I'm grateful my nerves have taken a back seat.

"Anytime someone wants to talk about anything remotely serious or uncomfortable for you, you make jokes or get insulting."

"Yeeeah. It is *extremely* uncomfortable for me to talk about how amazing I am at being a real estate agent," he drawls.

"And playing the piano. And talking about how your family is disappointed in you," I add, because he needs to look in a damn mirror if no one's ever held one up for him.

"Wow," he deadpans with a slow clap of his hands. "Well done. You got me."

He's so fucking stubborn. All he's doing is proving my point, so I hold out my hand and gesture to him. "Exactly."

"Okay, what else?" He chuckles, waggling his fingers in the air for me to lay it on him.

I've only got one other major example. It's as difficult for me to fathom voicing as I assume it will be for him to admit, but I'm sick of not seeing who the real Andrew Broadhouse is.

"And...trying to pretend you're not attracted to me."

The amused sound he lets out seems overdramatized. It means I'm right, but the sound still hurts.

"Ah, there it is! Ladies and gentlemen, we have a request!"

It takes me a second to make out the melody he plays next. When I do, I want to march over there and slam the lid down on his fingers.

When '*I Touch Myself*' by the Divines stops, he meets my glare with a thoughtful look. "I can try a country version of it if you prefer."

"You're fucking hilarious."

Glancing up in thought, he sighs. "I like to think so, yes."

I don't even care anymore if I won't make a dent. He can hide behind whatever ten-foot-thick wall of fears he has. I want this off my chest.

"At least I'm honest."

"What the hell is that supposed to mean?"

"It means, I know I don't know what's going on with me, but I turn you on too! So, quit acting like I'm the only one, like it's something I should be ashamed about. At least I can fucking own it."

Shaking his head, an amused puff of air leaves his lips as he glances down at the piano. It's like he can't even look the truth in the face.

The opening notes of '*I Hope That I Don't Fall In Love With You*' filter out of the instrument. I'm certain they're meant to mock me, but it's such an obvious picture of denial. All I see is a dark cloud of conflict circling around him, and it stirs a longing deep in my chest that I know I shouldn't have right now.

"We jerked off because we've been playing boyfriend for too long," he says matter-of-factly, but I don't miss the humbled tone he can't seem to conceal. "All guys have like one percent of their brain that thinks about peen on peen. That's all. Don't write it in your diary or act like you know me. I fuck interns, remember? I'm not real boyfriend material. My interest doesn't hold for that long."

"You're scared." The realization tumbles from my lips as I stare at him like an unraveling riddle.

"Of what?" he scoffs, but his cheeks go pink. "That I want a season pass to Tuft Town? I told you, the boyfriend Kool-Aid just got to us. Besides, even if I wanted to try more Kool-Aid, we don't even get along."

Turning toward the window, I fold my arms and shake my head at his newest insult. They aggravate me for different reasons now. I've realized each of his digs is actually something he likes about me. Like my... tuft. God, I hate that word, but he certainly enjoys running his fingers through it as much as I like him doing it.

"Because you're antagonistic on purpose," I counter, so he knows he's the one who needs to take the blame for us being at each other's throats.

"Because you bring out the worst in me."

"No, because I've seen the worst in you and know it's all bullshit."

"Aw, what's the matter, sweetheart? You can't even look at me during your heart-to-heart?"

A somber repetition of notes plays. He doesn't even have to get to the beginning of the verse for me to recognize it as Bonnie Tyler's '*Total Eclipse Of The Heart*.' I love that song. Now he's going to ruin it for me by using it as a weapon—the jerk.

I will not fucking turn around now, especially not after he adds, "Is this the part of the Hallmark film where you tell the bad man you experimented with, after your fiancée ran off, all his redeeming qualities, and then he throws you over his shoulder and makes sweet love to you?"

Closing my eyes, I let out a humorless laugh. I don't know what happened in his life to send him down a path where he has zero faith in anyone, but without a doubt, his well-practiced defense has most certainly been what's prevented him from being able to alter his course.

"No." I shake my head. "Because you don't deserve to hear them."

Chapter 17

What the hell is that supposed to mean? And what redeeming qualities?

"I told you I heard music," Mason declares, stepping through the door with his husbands.

Flashing them my practiced smile, I put more zeal into my playing as Mason starts singing the words. He *is* a musician, after all, and I'm supposed to be here to impress him. Plus, there is the added benefit of my song choice pissing Lucas off. That's what he deserves after all that personal shit he brought up.

Sulking over, he takes a seat on the piano bench next to me. I suppress the urge to roll my eyes. What's the point in moving closer to me when he looks that agitated right now? We're not going to fool anyone.

Dario and Keenan seem to be distracted by the performance, enjoying it, so I chime in with backup vocals to accompany Mason. Flashing Lucas a cheery smile, I can't help but gloat that the song is basically his anthem. Crushed dreams later in life—it is the perfect saga for a thirty-seven-year-old man with a misplaced crush. He must know it, too, because his nostrils flare.

"Lucas, let's hear what you've got," Mason encourages.

I cackle at the request as Lucas looks up at him, wide-eyed. The piano keys are sticky under my fingers from the humidity in the unpowered room as I approach the next verse. The discomfort, however, is worth the payback value for Lucas' tantrum earlier.

"No. He can't carry a tune," I assure Mason sadly.

A belted, growly timbre startles the shit out of me, making me miss a note. I whip my gaze at Lucas. Those chocolate eyes of his have murder in them with my name on it, but that's not the cause of my surprise.

Holy shit. The grumpy bastard can sing! His voice is low and sexy as he holds my gaze and stands up to me in song form.

I know he still wants to kill me, but the eerie resolve behind the hostility in his eyes makes it seem like he's singing about me as he enunciates each word. The room suddenly feels overcrowded and warm. My pulse skips a beat as I mumble the harmony and stare at the steadfast conviction in his eyes. I feel…seen. Seen like no one else has ever seen me, nor even bothered to try.

He basically said that earlier, but I was too busy trying to brush him off. His exact words were, *'Because I've seen the worst in you and know it's all bullshit.'* They make my stomach flip hard as they sink in deeper.

I *am* kind of full of shit most of the time, if I'm being honest. And apparently, he knows it. And…he still thinks I'm redeeming?

Why am I staring at his mouth? It's getting…harder to breathe, and I'm warm. All over.

Oh, God…

No…

Lucas Everette *cannot* be my *John Stamos*. Bonnie Tyler, what have you done to me?

Something in his expression changes, softening his features as his gaze canvases my face. It looks like recognition and opens a cavern in my chest, a giant, Lucas-sized cavern that feels like it can only be filled by him.

Mason starts singing again, and I realize we've trailed off. Tearing my gaze away, I laugh airily and focus on the notes. When we finish, the guys applaud. Dario leaves and returns with more beverages from the kitchen, turning this into a makeshift karaoke party. As I field requests, I do everything I can to put on a good show and not sneak a glance at Lucas.

I've never been self-conscious about my playing. Probably because I rarely ever play for anyone. The average Joe might be intent on impressing Mason right now and getting him to put in a good word for them in the music industry, but my curiosity is focused solely on wondering if the man beside me, who's kicking off body heat and smelling way too intoxicating, is enjoying it.

I'm thirsty for Lucas Kool-Aid. Not in a way that I wonder how many flavors of his I could taste. That's the damnedest thing about it. I just want to drink in the fact a hair-braiding warrior with morals I've never known, maybe sees something good in me, like the sun shines out of my ass.

In my years of gallivanting, it was never outside my understanding that I was both using and being used by the company I'd link up with for the night. It never bothered me or them. That was the arrangement up front. There's something about the idea of being appreciated instead, however, that is so shiny and new, I couldn't make myself stop wanting it if I tried.

I was wrong. I don't think it's a power kink luring me to Lucas, after all. I think it might be awe.

Lucas and I finish off the bottle of wine I brought in over the course of the longest hour of my life as the Hepperlys laugh, sing, and tell stories. I can feel the tension between us, a thick blanket of heat and mutual need as the minutes drag on. Is he feeling it, too?

The power flickers back on, and our trio erupts in cheers. Thank fuck that seems to make them give up on karaoke, and they gather up their empties.

We all walk back down the hallway. My hand bumps into the back of Lucas'. The rush of heat it sends across my skin has me feeling light-headed. The Hepperlys stop in the kitchen, leaving Lucas and me both standing dumbly awaiting their next move. Why aren't they going back to bed? It's evening now.

"You guys hungry?" Keenan asks. "We were thinking of getting food delivered."

"No, thanks," Lucas and I say in unison.

I smile at them, hoping it alleviates the awkwardness of how we sound like twins. Reaching down, I take his hand in mine, silently praising Bonnie Tyler when he doesn't pull his away.

"I think we'll call it a night. We've got a house to show you tomorrow," I joke.

My pulse flutters as Lucas moves when I do, accompanying me down the hall to our room. He doesn't throat punch me or drop his hand from my grasp the entire way, not even once we step inside. It gives me hope. Maybe he's willing to extend some of those good graces of his. I sure hope so, because I need to know…

My nerves are the equivalent of a tightly coiled spring as I drop his hand and close the door.

Although the power is back on, I'm grateful that our room lights are off, the space only illuminated by the moon. I stare at him, and he stares back, cautious and questioning. The silence is as thick as pillow filling. It's clear he's said all he has to say. I know I'm up, but nothing comes.

Clearing my throat, I'm sure there are more delicate ways to ask, but I don't know how to be delicate or ask for things. "Tell me," I blurt.

"What?"

"The redeeming shit I don't deserve to hear."

His posture tenses, and he looks away. His answer comes after a beat, barely audible. "No."

Stepping closer, I watch his lips part. His tongue comes out to wet them, making me want to groan. He'd kiss me, but he's hoarding his secret compliments like treasure. Fucking cruel. I'm only human here.

I don't think I've ever felt more helpless. Whispering, I hope my request sounds more humble this time. "Tell me."

I watch him stare at my lips as he swallows. He takes a step back as though he has to fight giving in to the urge my mouth presents. Did not need to see that right now. Fortunately, the wall blocks his retreat.

Inching forward, I place my palm on the drywall next to his head. "Please," I add, testing the foreign word out on my lips.

His gaze flicks up to mine in surprise. Yeah, yeah, let's not make it a habit, my snarky internal voice wants to say. I hold back, though, and wait.

"You're…good looking," he stammers.

I've actually heard that before, plenty of times, so it shouldn't surprise me. I've never heard it from Lucas, though. It makes me grateful for my face for the first time in my life. Bringing my hand up, I stroke his beard with my thumb, wondering if he knows how much I don't hate his face anymore.

"And…" I press, greedy for more confessions.

"And you work for your uncle because you want to do something you weren't forced to do…but you'd be good at anything you tried."

It feels like time is interrupted as I gape at him. Reaching down, I grip his hip to steady myself and remember to breathe.

"Like playing the piano," he adds, "but you can't enjoy it because they made you."

Something is squeezing my throat. The pressure feels a lot like it starts around my heart. I lean in and rest my forehead against his shoulder, inhaling his scent against the burning in my lungs. Can he just shut up already?

"And…you don't even know just how good you are."

Swallowing against the thickness, I tilt my head and taste the cord in his neck. "What else?" I rasp, a glutton for his punishment.

His head falls back into the wall with a thump, and he grips my elbow. "You know…"

"No, I don't." I kiss his neck. "Tell me."

"*You know*," he repeats, "just how to touch me. Just what to say…like you know more about me than I know about myself."

Finally, a compliment that doesn't gut me. Shifting my hips forward, I press them into his, smiling when his hardness meets mine. I move my mouth to his ear and whisper, "I'm listening."

His voice comes out breathy. "You're bossy and yet somehow… sensual in a way that…that makes it hard to breathe. And…you always know what to do or say, so I…so that I…"

"So you don't have to?"

Turning his head, he blinks at me. The surprise on his face is the redemption my battered pride needed. I nip his lower lip. "So you don't have to fucking take care of someone for a change?" I wager.

You'd think I just doused him with a bucket of water. Two fists grab handfuls of my shirt and yank me forward. His mouth slams against mine. Whining like he's in pain, he reaches around and grips my back until there isn't an inch separating us. He's carnivorous with want. It makes me question if I've ever actually witnessed desire.

I give back as good as he's giving, keeping up with each sweep of his tongue. It's like drowning on dry land. I don't know the playbook for this, but I know I want him naked, so I tug at his shirt, dragging it over his head. His fingers fumble with mine. I lift my arms to let him get the same experience. When it passes over my head, the vision before me is too much to bear.

I grip the back of his neck and tug him to me. Tracing his reddened lips, I tremble at the feel of his chest rising and falling against mine.

"This fucking mouth. Every time you part your lips like that, I want them around my dick."

He drops like the floor fell out from under him before I can lean in for another kiss. What the hell is he doing?

The question dies a quick death when his fingers unfasten my shorts like there's a fire inside them he needs to extinguish. Aw, fuck. I have no problem with how literal he took that.

The soft fabric of my shorts slides down my legs. My cock twitches behind my boxers. He reaches for the waistband, but then hesitates, glancing up like he needs permission. He had my permission ten seconds ago. Maybe even two weeks ago.

"Do it," I croak. "Pull me out."

The way he wets his lips makes it look like he's anticipating something delicious. He's fucking killing me. Lowering my waistband, his fingers wrap around my cock and draw it above the elastic. His wet lips enclose my tip and then draw back like he's kissing an ice cream cone. He pauses, his hot breath ghosting my damp head, and stares at it in wonder. Glancing up at me with his lips parted, I couldn't dream of a more enticing sight. His face says I'm officially his favorite flavor.

The next thing I know, he swallows half of my cock and starts bobbing his head, taking the wind out of me. His tongue wriggles around my circumference while he attempts to take me to my base several times, as though he's trying to test out every technique all at once. It's sloppy, with lots of suction noises, a few grunts, and even some gagging. A bead of slobber dribbles down my balls. It's the worst blowjob I've ever received. It's also now my favorite. Fucking hell, I want to devour him.

"Get up here," I growl, hooking my hands under his armpits.

Hoisting his heavy frame up off the floor is enticing in its own right. The feel of his weight, the hair underneath his arms, the way his cock bobs as he moves—he no longer looks like someone I have to fake it with. He just looks like a lover.

His lips are pliant underneath mine as I capture his mouth once he's on his feet. They open and move at my every unspoken command, trying to keep up with what I give them, what I take. I don't let him up for air until I can't breathe myself.

I take in the sight he makes, chest and stomach heaving. He's like a furnace, and I'm stoking a fire he can't keep up with. Running my hand across his pecs, they twitch under my touch. I snake downward, grazing my palm down his belly, through the thick trail of soft hair there. His jeans are obscenely tented, and I almost don't want to take them off just so I can see him like this a little longer. Reaching down, I cup his bulge and squeeze. He grunts, and I feel it on my lips as I murmur, "Get on the bed."

He absorbs that and then nods, moving around me. I watch him bring a knee up to the mattress and give him a swift little swat on that bubble butt of his.

"No clothes," I warn when he glances back at me.

Turning around slowly, he looks down at himself, but then his fingers move to the button on his jeans. His gaze stays fixed there like it's taking all his concentration, so I slide my boxers down over my hips and watch his face when he sees them hit the floor. He stares at my cock for so long, I have to give myself a squeeze and clear my throat.

He does his usual de-pantsing routine, bending over and slipping them off each leg. My chuckle must be louder than I thought.

"What?"

"Nothing."

He does the same thing with his briefs. It's a bizarre yet unintentional foreplay, and I want to know if anyone else ever took notice and appreciated that he does it. When he straightens, I wonder for a moment if he's going to cover himself with his hands. His gaze takes me in again, though, and his posture straightens like his want bolstered his bravery. Turning, he steps around the bed and sits down in front of his pillow. His movements might be awkward, but the look on his face is a gift I've never been given. I'm the only thing in Lucas' world right now. I don't know why he thinks there's anything good about me because all I can think is how he'll be sorry if he ever stops looking at me like that.

Chapter 18

The sight of Andrew prowling across the bed with that determined expression is both terrifying and arousing. The odd thing is that the terrifying part is just as enjoyable as the arousal. I have no idea what to do or what he wants to do, but I feel free. I didn't even know I felt fettered before. But now, with both of us stripped bare, seeing the hunger in his eyes, and his hard cock pointing to the ceiling like a twin to mine, all my worries seem weightless. They're all still there in the back of my mind, but yet, none of them have their claws in me at the moment. No more feeling insecure about my ability to help sell these properties. No more worrying over my bills. No more discomfort about whether seeing Mark and Shannon at the wedding together will be awkward, even though I assured Julia it won't. And no doubts over Andrew pretending later that whatever happens tonight didn't happen. Because right here, right now—he and I? It feels right. Seeing on his face that he thinks so too is the answer I didn't know I needed.

Slipping one knee between my legs, he inches forward, towering over me. "Good looking, huh?" he smirks, leaning down to cage his hands on either side of my shoulders.

"You know you are."

Just as I think he's leaning in to give me another one of those breath-stealing kisses, his head lowers. My nipple is enveloped by his mouth, and I gasp. His weight lowers onto me. I can feel his cock pressed up against my thigh, and he damn sure can probably feel mine pressed into his abdomen. The pressure there and the static electricity that zips from my nipple down to my balls have me fighting to hold still.

My fingers are in his hair before I even realize it. It's so soft and feels like a privilege to be able to touch what always looks so wild and unruly, as though I tamed an animal.

He murmurs something that sounds like, "Those fucking noises you make for me," and moves on to my other nipple while squeezing my thigh. The combination has me making more noises I'm sure I've never made in my life.

I'm leaking against his stomach. I don't know if that's going to weird him out since he's made comments about fluids on more than one occasion, but when a streak of wetness paints my thigh, I'm not mad about it. Not at all. His taste…it was like a drug hitting my tongue when I took him in. I don't know why he stopped me, but I feel a sense of pride knowing that the precum smearing against my skin may have, in part, been from my doing.

I desperately want to pull him up for more kisses, but he moves lower, his breath ghosting down my abdomen. I watch his hand trail over the line of hair on my stomach, down to my groin. He pauses, staring at my dick.

Is he having a change of heart? Is there something wrong with my dick? I can count on one hand how many partners I've had, and while I don't regret the low number, I wish I were more versed in sexual cues so I could have some idea of what he's thinking.

"I got tested after Shannon…" I hesitate, drawing his gaze up to mine. "Everything came back negative."

His brows quirk, telling me my health test results probably weren't part of his concern. "How long ago was that?"

"Four years." I don't know why it makes my face heat. There's nothing wrong with abstaining. "But…I should still be good."

He blinks at me, and now I know why I'm slightly mortified. In the Andrew Broadhouse logbook of sexual activity, you'd have to be completely incapacitated to go four years with no human contact. His palm glides down the underside of my cock as an almost-delicate caress.

"I'm good too," he says, looking entranced and moving his hand over my pubic hair. "I got tested before our trip."

Was he planning on hooking up with someone while we were trying to sell properties? I'm torn between a flicker of unfounded jealousy and feeling like I snagged the prom king.

He whispers something reverently, distracting me. It sounds a lot like, '*So fluffy*,' as he blows a stream of breath over the hair around my cock.

I shudder and have to inch my legs apart when he slips his other knee in between them. His palms run down the tops of my thighs and then back up, warming them with a touch that's surprisingly gentle. With his lips hovering over the tip of my cock, it's all I can do to hold still. I pray it doesn't twitch and slap him in the mouth.

What is he doing? Also, what is he waiting for?

"*Four* years?" He arches a brow, looking concerned and maybe even angry.

I avert my gaze to the ceiling and shrug like it's no big deal—because it's not. Each of my brain cells is more focused on whether I'm going to get to experience what I hope I'm about to. A hand wraps around the base of my cock, angling it up. I look back down, but his attention is fixed on my dick again.

"Well, fuck you, Shannon," he mutters and draws a stripe up the slit of my cockhead.

My cock does twitch now, bucking against his grip. I don't know what his hostility toward my ex is about, but it was worth waiting four years for that little lick. And it's worth waiting the three seconds following until he takes my cockhead into his hot, wet mouth.

For the love of monster trucks, the sight of Andrew's sassy mouth with my cock in it is the only thing I need to see before I die. His cheeks go concave, increasing the suction around it, making me cry out a warbled noise.

He hums as though he approves and draws off for a breath before taking me in again. His tongue swirls around my glans, teasing it. My hips buck involuntarily, making the roof of his mouth crash into my tip. Grunting, he pops off and wipes the slobber off his chin with the back of his wrist.

"This isn't working," he says breathlessly at the same time I murmur, "Sorry."

My first blow job in forever, and I fucked it up. Damn it.

Glaring at my dick like it committed a crime, he mumbles, "I don't know what I'm doing."

The confession quashes my embarrassment and makes me sympathize with him until he adds, "But I have another idea," and barrels off the bed.

Where is he going? I rise onto my elbows as he rummages through his discarded shorts and pulls out his phone. If he thinks taking sexy nudes is a good alternative to exchanging our first blow jobs, I'm going to have to say something.

I watch his bare ass trot to the bathroom, feeling my heart sink with each step, even as I admire the dimples in his cheeks. When he returns a second later with a bottle of lube in his other hand, I lean back, trying to pretend I wasn't momentarily terrified he was calling it quits. Climbing back on the bed, he resumes his place between my legs, but his thumb flies over the keys on his phone. It seems like an odd time to be on the phone.

"What are you doing?"

"Calling in a lifeline."

"A what?"

"Have you ever been with a man?"

He's asking me that now? "No… Have you?"

"No, hence the lifeline." Patting the outside of my thigh, he assures me, "Don't worry. They're professionals."

Wait a minute. Is he…texting someone for gay sex advice?

"They? Who are *they?*"

Chapter 19

How far in is the prostate gland?

I wait impatiently for a response to my message in the group chat I have with Shaw and Terry. I seldom use it as I mostly just text Shaw, but this is time sensitive. I'll take whatever help I can get.

TERRY: Oh no. That poor man.

"What are you doing?" Lucas asks.
"Calling in a lifeline."
"A what?"
"Have you ever been with a man?"
He hesitates even though I'm fairly certain of the answer. "No… Have you?"
"No, hence the lifeline." Patting the outside of his thigh, I reassure him, "Don't worry. They're professionals."
So to speak. He doesn't need to know my cousin and his husband aren't sex therapists.
"They? Who is 'they?'"
"My cousin, Shaw, and his husband," I mumble absently, reading Shaw's message that pops up.

Not all men are created equal, but the middle knuckle is a safe bet. Why???

ME: No time to explain.

TERRY: Why do you think?! Seriously, Shaw, you did not just help him!

Fucking Terry. I don't have time for this. The man has no respect for emergencies or the rules of not monopolizing a chat.

ME: How do I stimulate one?

TERRY: For the love of baby Jesus! STOP! Do not proceed!

"Your Uncle Lou's son?" Lucas squawks.

Great. Now Lucas is about to freak out. It's not like Shaw is going to tell his dad what his employees get up to.

"It's fine. He doesn't gossip with his dad." Bending down, I flick my tongue over the tip of his cock again, producing a gasp from him. I can't believe I have the urge to gobble it down my throat—that's a new one for me—but I think we're beyond questioning how we got to where we are.

"Just relax. I'm going to make you feel good," I murmur, slipping my knees underneath his thighs so I'm seated with his legs straddling mine. He looks positively scandalous like this, and I will now see this image every time I look at him. It's taking everything in me not to just toss my phone over my shoulder and go in blind. But I've always been good in the bedroom, and it's imperative that I shine more than ever this time. If I'm going to boldly go where no man has gone before, I'm damn well going to make sure I do it right. The guy hasn't been touched in four years—he's not getting mediocrity from me.

SHAW: I can't believe I'm saying this, but…just massage it. Slow, gentle circles.

TERRY: And LUBE!! Lots of lube! Jesus, Shaw. You're going to send a man to the hospital and scar him emotionally for life in the process.

ME: Message received. Going in. Talk later.

Dropping my phone on the mattress, I glance down at Lucas. He looks sufficiently horrified—not the kind of look I want to see on a lover's face.

"You ready?" I ask him, flashing him a reassuring smile to let him know Shaw and Satan are no longer in the room.

"For what?"

"To come for me again."

My words and bedroom voice are enough to take the edge off his expression. He swallows and glances down at himself on display for me. Drizzling lube onto my hand, I'm liberal with the pour. I don't fucking need Terry to tell me to use lube. I've done anal before. I'm not a fucking idiot. Heart hammering, I'd be lying if I said I wasn't nervous, though. I have no idea if he'll like anal play the way the women I've done it with did. The determined part of me that wants to make him fall apart, however, isn't ready to give up yet. He freaking carved out my soul with his redeeming qualities list. I can't live like this unless he's as big a mess as I am right now.

Reaching between his cheeks, I whisper, "Tell me to stop if you don't like it. Okay?"

When my slickened fingertips connect with his ring, he flinches and sucks in a breath. There's something inherently adorable in how he clearly did not expect that to be my intention, and his reaction to the touch. His mouth falls open as if he's about to say something, but nothing comes out. His asshole is apparently another one of his speechlessness buttons—noted.

I glide my hand up and down through his seam, lubricating the mess of soft, dark hair to his silky flesh. He's so freaking warm there. Maybe it's his natural body temperature, but I like the idea that it's for me. Do people get hotter the more turned on they are?

My cock twitches, feeling how tight his pucker feels against the pad of my finger, knowing no one's ever been there before. I don't know where these possessive thoughts are coming from, but they make me want to brand his entire furry body with my mouth.

Later, Andrew. Focus.

Holy shit, pleasing someone has never required this much thought. If he says anything about the way my hand is trembling, I don't think my pride will recover.

I rub his thigh, and his muscles relax beneath my touch. His breathing turns more labored as he stares, gaze flicking back and forth from my hand to my eyes.

"You like that?" I venture, tracing my fingertip around his entrance.

His reply is a garbled noise. He reaches one hand above him and grips his pillow in his fist. Mouth floundering for words, he looks positively flabbergasted, caught between disbelief and arousal. I want to tip the scale to full arousal. I want to see the Lucas I saw in the outdoor shower, the one who was helpless to the passion I stoked in him. I want to hear my name on his lips and know that it's the answer to who he thinks has sunshine coming out of their ass.

My phone dings, making his gaze ping to it in alarm. I don't even have to open the message to read it. The preview is still showing on my home screen.

TERRY: For the love of God, don't prod! It's not a dartboard. And LUBE. I cannot stress that enough!

Snagging it up, I hit the power button and then fling it over my shoulder. The coffee table cockblocker will not ruin this for us.

"Hey," I call down to Lucas, getting his eyes back on me. "Do you trust me?"

The length of the pause before he answers is discouraging. "I...don't know."

Okay. I can't fault him for his perpetual honesty.

"Can you *try* to trust me?" I digress, running my palm up his cock and twisting my closed grip over his cockhead.

A puff of breath leaves his lips. "Y-yeah," he concedes, panting from that small tease.

Fucking hell. He's like a keyboard full of buttons that all have my name on them.

Keeping his gaze, I press my fingertip forward, holding my breath that my magic spell doesn't fade from his eyes. He's hot, hugging the tip of my finger like a snug, terrified inferno. His brows knit together, and his mouth drops open even further, as his gaze flicks to the ceiling. He looks like he's searching for an answer, but I want it to be the right one.

"Breathe, Lucas," I soothe, giving his cock a stroke.

Closing his eyes, he listens, his stomach falling on a slow stream of air. I give his cock another stroke, and the tension in his ring eases around my finger. I don't feel anything yet, but my hands are too occupied to send a complaint text to Shaw. Plus, I'm not about to kill the mood by fetching my phone. I can't see my second knuckle, but then again, a sphincter isn't exactly a paper-thin muscle. Did he mean the middle knuckle once it's *past* the sphincter? And in which direction do I aim once I'm further inside?

Fuck. I should have asked him to send me a map.

Offering up a silent plea to the sex gods, I slip deeper into his heat, searching for any change in the texture inside his channel. My fingertip connects with something soft and spongy, a nub, if you will. Interesting. This is truly not how a person should get an anatomy lesson, and I honestly feel sorry for Lucas right now for *trying* to trust me. But for fuck's sake, if I've ever done anything good in my life, now would be a great time for the universe to pay me back for it by cutting me some slack.

An unholy noise peels out of Lucas. It sounds like a bear taking a satisfying stretch after a long winter hibernating, and it startles me so much that I retreat a fraction.

His chest is arched, head thrown back, and if I thought his mouth was open wide before, he's at risk of catching flies now more than ever. The groan dies on his lips, and he lets out a breath, along with a little whimper. His eyes unroll from his head and look at me. They're completely bottomless.

Hell. I actually found it. Who needs a fucking map?

"You like that, big man?"

His bewildered gaze flicks to where my hand disappears below his junk like he's expecting to see a magic wand rather than just my finger. I want to tell him there's more where that came from, but I decide it doesn't sound sexy at all. It's just a fucking finger, and more isn't necessarily better, according to Shaw.

"You like it when I tell you what to do?" I remind him instead. "Here's what I want you to do now—nothing."

He blinks, confused, until I slip my finger deeper again, connecting with that bundle of nerves. His chest expands on a gasp, and his eyes slam shut. The way his cock flexes in my hand tells me everything I need to know. I hope his prostate isn't shy, because I'm officially making it my new best friend if he looks like that when I give it some love.

"*Nothing*," I repeat, circling my fingertip over it while I start working his cock. "I want you to do nothing but lie there and let me hear how good you feel."

The moan he emits as he raises his other arm to clutch his pillow is music to my ears. Quiet, restrained Lucas, who looks like he never indulges in anything, not even an overabundance of granola bars, looks good fighting not to let go. Maybe revelations don't often come from having your finger inside someone else, but this puts something into perspective. As I tease his cockhead and his gland, I see a guy who always has to have it together. A guy who needs to be strong for two little sisters and his mom, and probably has for a long time. He's the opposite of me in every way. I think I've exploited being the weak one in my family for so long that it became comfortable. Let them think of me what they will. Never try because they don't expect me to try. I'm aware I should probably analyze that some other time, but right now, I can't fix myself. Lucas doesn't need fixing in my opinion, but he damn well needs to stop fucking trying for everyone else so much. He should look like this at least three times a week. Who the hell can live like he has, silently swallowing every serving of misery I assume he's been dealt?

"Drew…" he pants, his head thrashing between his arms.

My cock is in pain at this point from being untouched. It's a welcome agony, though, snuffing out that sickening vulnerability his words in the sunroom exploded in my chest.

"Let go, Lucas. Let go," I urge, bending down to capture one of his nipples. I have to release him from my grip to brace myself on the mattress. The feel of my cock bumping into his sends a rush of electricity down my legs. To hell with going untouched any longer. I can't take it.

"Give me your hand," I demand, even as I reach up and capture his wrist. I bring it between us as I straddle his thigh for a better angle to line us up without having to let up on his ass. The second I get his palm wrapped around both of us underneath mine, my body jolts from the sensation. I didn't know a dick could do that to another dick.

"Shit, that feels good," I slur over the groan he lets out.

His strokes are timid and shy, even though he sounds like he could go over at any moment. It's both endearing and frustrating. I realize I told him to do nothing, but I reserve the right to change my mind.

"Show me how you stroke it, sweetheart."

His gaze flicks to mine, and a hint of rose paints his cheeks. He sputters out a breath, but then looks at our joined hands, jaw clenched. His hand moves down our lengths and picks up fervor.

"Fuck," he grits, eyes slamming shut, bucking his hips up into our grip as I tag his prostate again and again. "Fuck."

"I'm going to come all over you and mark you up, and you can't wash it away this time," I growl, surprising even myself when his eyes flare open. The damndest thing is that I want it to be true. Badly. Lucas, marked by me.

He keens, his grip going slack, but I can feel his rigidity as my hand slips over the top of his. Body frozen, tense, his cry echoes throughout the room, and he spills over onto my hand.

Fucking hell. I just talked him into an orgasm. Talked him into an orgasm by talking about owning him. And that…just did it for me.

Squeezing us as tightly as I can, my arm is about ready to fall off from working us so hard through my own release. I don't know if I've violated Terry's advice about whether I'm prodding, but as I pulse and endure full-body spasms, I keep my finger pressed firmly to that magic button inside Lucas' warmth, desperate to hold him in this state of euphoria for as long as I can.

His neck is twisted, the cords in it strained from turning his head to bury his face in his pillow. I'm disappointed he's muffling the feral noises he's making, but it's probably best. My head is so light I think I might pass out if I hear any more of his sounds. When my cock is spent, I slip my finger out and release him.

Falling onto my elbows, I cage him in with my hands in the air like a surgeon who just scrubbed up. I'm not used to this many fluids during sex, but I'm not complaining. It's just another pleasant wonder. A welcome newness to an activity I thought could never surprise me anymore. I have half a mind to run my hands all over him and mark him even further. However, that might require us to leave the bed next. Lucas isn't going anywhere if I have any say in it.

Covering his jugular, I suck hard against his labored breaths. I don't know why. I don't even like love bites. He tilts his head back as though it's instinct to yield to my touch. If he does one more thing that makes me want him, I don't know if I'll be able to handle it.

Whimpering, he pulls away, so I release him and drop my head to his shoulder to catch my breath. The skin on his neck has a red spot the shape of my mouth that makes me smile.

I did it. I wrecked him. That strange, exposed sensation has been quieted.

As I lie here on top of this living, breathing moment, his warm, satisfied body beneath me, a sliver of dread embeds itself in me. I know he said he thinks there's good in me, but what happens if I don't have enough sunshine for him? I really want to have enough.

I think…I like having a fake boyfriend. Fuck me, though, if I know how to keep one.

Chapter 20

LUCAS EVERETTE
licensed agent

As Andrew peels himself off me, our skin sticking together, I add it to the list of new and surprising sensations I never imagined existed. My body is still tingling from his touch, and the loss of contact stirs a need in me I didn't know was possible to feel while being this spent. Is this the part where he goes back to Andrew-the-asshole? I was really hoping for something different this time, especially after the way he reacted to our verbal throwdown in the sunroom.

'*Sweetheart*.' When he said the word this time, it didn't feel like he was mocking me. It felt like… well, kind of like he thinks of me as a sweetheart. Watching his naked body flex as he steps off the end of the mattress, I'm embarrassed by how much lust it stirs in me. This can't be real. No matter how good it felt, no matter how surprisingly thoughtful and attentive he was, it's Andrew—it can't be real.

He disappears, dropping to the floor in a flash, landing with a thud and an *oof* noise. Shit. Did he trip? I lean up on my elbows, but he pops up just as quickly.

"I'm fine!" he calls out, heading toward the bathroom, but glancing back and pointing at me in warning. "Stay there."

This is all so confusing. I can't say I minded discovering a part of my body could make me feel such bliss, but it's still tender. I can still feel the sensation of his finger in my channel and little aftershocks. I really hate that he was the one to show me that reality, and yet, part of me is celebrating that it was he who did. I don't think I could imagine letting anyone else be that intimate with me.

What are we? How did we get here? And why do I want someone so unpredictable?

Lying back, I close my eyes and let out a long breath. I feel…good. Physically. Amazing, really. Knowing I might have to prepare for another emotional war in a matter of minutes, though, is not the kind of dynamic I'm looking for.

Listen to me… I wasn't even looking for any kind of dynamic. I was perfectly content thinking that a relationship wasn't in the cards for me. I'm thirty-seven, for crying out loud. Marriage, babies, the common path that people expect—well, I'm getting a little too old to think it was ever going to happen. Honestly, call me selfish, but the thought of taking care of someone else's needs is a bit exhausting. I've been doing it my whole life. I'd do it again in a heartbeat for Mom and the girls, but I don't know that I have it in me to be a doting boyfriend, fiancé, or husband again. I sure as shit got it wrong when I tried. Andrew was right about that—it is nice not having to make decisions for once. When I'm with him, I don't have to think. Maybe in some strange way, I do trust him.

Something warm and wet touches my stomach, making me flinch. I open my eyes and gape at the sight—Andrew, wiping off my stomach with a wet cloth. He's cleaning me up?

"I… I can do it," I babble, taking the rag from him.

It's probably just his fluids hang-up and the thought of sleeping next to me while I'm a mess. Andrew doesn't strike me as the kind of person who's thoughtful after sex, except then I remember what else he said. He told me he wanted to mark me up and didn't want me to wash it away. As I swipe the rag over my dick, my face heats at the memory. Why is just the thought making me hard again?

Setting the rag on the nightstand, I lean back. My neck touches an arm as my head hits the pillow. When did he reach over? I start lifting my head back up, so he doesn't think I'm trying to force him to cuddle with me, but his hand grips my shoulder, tugging me closer to his side, almost like he wants me to stay put. This is…unexpected.

I blink at his profile. Eyes closed, his sigh sounds contented from where he's resting on his own pillow. I have no idea what this means. Is he really not going to freak out?

"You, uh, okay?" he asks, motioning to my lower half with his chin.

Jesus. "Uh…yeah. Yeah, I'm good."

I'm *so not* good. I have no idea what just happened. One moment, we wanted to rip each other's throats out, and the next, he was looking at me like I'd cracked the code to his soul, and it showed me the sensitive little boy who lives inside the prickly man. And then he turned me into a puddle with a few words and kisses that made my toes curl. The worst part is that I still feel like a puddle and want more of those kisses, but he's trained me to be afraid to want those things with him.

"So…" I preface to fill the silence, having no idea how to. I remember something from our sparring in the sunroom, though, and now that I have, I can't get it out of my brain. He said he fucks interns. Am I just like another intern? Does he get some kick out of having dalliances with people in his family's employ? "What's with the intern kink?" I venture, holding my breath for a bitter truth I don't want to hear.

He snorts and glances over at me. "*That's* what you're thinking about right now?"

I keep my gaze fixed on the ceiling and shrug. "I just wondered…did you do it on purpose to piss your family off or…do you have a thing for messing around with co-workers?"

"Interns aren't exactly co-workers. It'd be pretty shitty of me to be the son of the owner of the company and take advantage of someone who's trying to get their foot in the door."

"Wait…so, you didn't sleep with any interns?"

Sighing, he retrieves his arm and reaches for the comforter, tucking his long legs underneath it. I scramble to do the same when he holds it aloft for me, baffled on so many levels. When I lean back again, he slips his arm behind my shoulders for a second time, and I realize this feels a lot like we're about to go to bed naked. Together.

"I took one of the board members out one night, and the chief of editing a few months later. There was one intern who asked me on a date—that I declined—but she wouldn't give up, bless her." Flashing me a smirk, he adds, "Can't say that hurt my ego, but apparently my dad and brother noticed and assumed the worst."

"So…you let them think so?"

Grimacing, he shifts lower, nestling himself deeper into his pillow. Deeper and closer to me. "It may have coincidentally been the same week that the bill from my company card came in, and they saw charges from the Super Bowl on there. In my defense, I took two of their best-selling authors to the game with me. I still don't see how that's not a valid corporate expense, but they didn't exactly give me a chance to explain."

I don't understand him. How does he not see he's the orchestrator of his own misery?

"Why would you let them think the worst?"

Scoffing, he rolls to his side and tugs for me to do the same. It's awkward and perfect all at the same time, even though I'm not sure where to put my hands, so just leave them squished between us. He's so warm and smooth, strong and…real. God, I didn't know how much I missed having a body next to mine.

"They were going to think it anyway," he mumbles, eyes closed. "What's the point?"

There are so many arguments I could make against that, but I find myself at a loss on how to address them. I'm too baffled. He possessed enough morals to know it would be wrong to fraternize with an intern, and yet he has no qualms letting his family think otherwise because they assume he's capable of that behavior? Why bear a cross you don't actually own?

"Get some sleep. You've got a house to sell tomorrow," he murmurs, brushing his nose over the hair at my peak and running his open palm up and down my back.

As I lie here mystified, everything seems to fade away except one glaring fact. There's no pillow between us, and that was a cognizant decision on Andrew's part.

In the morning, the dream I'm having turns out not to be a dream at all. The damp lips on my neck, placing kisses there. The hot, hard flesh rubbing back and forth against mine. The firm grip on my ass cheek, urging my thigh to slink over the top of his. Andrew is ravenous, and I'm helpless to follow in his footsteps, gripping his back to press him more tightly to me for more of that satisfying friction between us.

"G-good morning," I pant awkwardly, not knowing how long I've been fondling him.

"Mm, morning," he purrs, nipping my earlobe and jerking his hips hard into mine. "Thanks for the unexpected wake-up."

"Wh-what?"

"Looks like I'm not the only one with a dick-grabbing problem in his sleep. Zero complaints from me, by the way."

Shit. I did not. Did I?

A chuckle resounds in my ear. "You did," he whispers, as though reading my thoughts.

Crap. I've been around him so long, I'm adopting his habits. I'm about to apologize, but he said he has zero complaints. Plus, it's getting difficult to concentrate on a clear thought. He smells so good, and I'm enamored of the way his muscles flex beneath my touch. I've never felt this light during sex, as though my body could float away. I've also never wanted to crawl inside someone the way I feel like doing right now. I can't get close enough. With each slip of his glans over mine, a flurry of sparks plumes inside my navel, amplifying that need. How has someone I couldn't stand become so addictive?

"I never sleep naked," I rationalize, remembering I should explain my new wake-up behavior.

His grip on my ass cheek shifts. A fingertip traces through the seam between my cheeks, and he nips my lower lip. "That's a shame."

When his fingertip taps my ring like he's knocking on a door, I gasp at the twitching sensation his touch invokes there. Closing my eyes, I dig my fingers into his shoulder, hoping it's the equivalent of becoming invisible. Except, typical Andrew doesn't miss a thing. His hot breath floods over my lips.

"Fuck, you kill me when you react like this," he practically growls.

His hand disappears, and his hips stop grinding into mine. I flare my eyes open, wondering what I did wrong. Does he like how wanton he makes me or not? I don't get it. When I spot the bottle of lube in his hand as he brings it back down behind me, I think I have my answer.

Shit. Round two. I think I'm about to get what I didn't realize I just asked for.

"Why can't you look at me when you mouth-breathe like that?" I hear him ask and realize I'm staring at his lips. "Or do you just prefer staring at my mouth?"

Said mouth ticks up at the corner just before it captures mine, and I hear the lube bottle cap flick open. A rush of butterflies flips inside my chest at the sound. When my tongue connects with his, I'm no longer feather-light. I'm a thousand pounds of melting man, incinerated by the connection. How has kissing never felt this good before?

My morning grogginess evaporates, and a message becomes clear. This is really happening.

Me.

Andrew.

Atomic passion.

Right here. Again. And…I can't think of a single reason to fight it.

Slipping my fingers into the back of his hair, I pour myself into the kiss and hike my knee higher up his thigh, unsure if he needs more access. He seemed to do all right last night, although he said he'd never been with a man. Oddly, and despite that, I *do* trust him. When his fingertip returns, it's slick and cool this time, lighting up my entrance in anticipation.

Entrance… I've always thought of my asshole as an '*exit*,' but I want nothing more than to feel a part of him expanding me again. Andrew may be careless in all things, but I'm starting to realize not when it comes to pleasuring me.

He must appreciate my eagerness because he groans right along with me when he inserts that wicked fingertip of his. It still feels strange and kind of foreign, but only for a second. Then it just feels like home, like I'm home with him. Bizarre, I know, but I'm too far gone to analyze it. He connects with my prostate and circles it, making my eyes cross and my head fall back on a throaty moan. His mouth envelops my Adam's apple, and his hips buck into mine.

"Damn, Tufty," he rasps against my throat. "Goddamn."

His mouth sucks on my neck again, probably leaving a mark. It's vicious and almost painful, but sinfully exquisite all at once. I writhe uncontrollably, mad for more friction where our cocks are rubbing between us. I don't even know if this is considered any kind of sex or foreplay, but it damn well should be.

"Yeah," he pants, "grind that cock against me."

I want to. Lord, do I ever, but want and ability are two different things. I find my hand on his ass and realize it's the first time I've ever felt it. It's firm and bulky, so unlike any other I've touched. I press him into me to help eradicate any semblance of space that may be left between us. All I know right now is that I've never felt this incredible, that he wants me, and that I think most of my feeling incredible is because of how much he seems to want me.

My gaze connects with his, and I can't decide whether it was the worst or best idea in the history of unplanned ideas. It's like being shown the true definition of passion. Whatever I thought I knew before wasn't it. I crash my mouth into his and give over any amount of restraint I was hanging onto. Hot, wet heat erupts between us. My cock is pulsing. My body is convulsing. Andrew cries out into my mouth, and the heat amplifies between us, telling me he's coming with me. I'm clawing at him and clinging to him. His finger at some point turned into two without me even realizing, and it's the most comforting sensation of fullness I didn't know I needed. Sore, but comforting all the same. It feels like I earned it. Earned something more than a dalliance from Andrew Broadhouse.

My grip slackens as I come down, and he slips free of my hole. His hand stays there, though, kneading slow circles across the globe of my ass. I can barely breathe, but drunkenly accept each surprising little kiss he gives me. One after another.

We're kissing, and we don't have to. No one's watching. Which means we're really kissing. Someone is kissing me because they want to kiss me. Vaguely, I'm aware of a distracting sound, but I try to blot it out. It's not until I hear a voice that I realize it was likely knocking.

"Hey, fellas. We're up and about whenever you're ready," Mason's voice calls from the doorway.

Oh shit! Catching sight of him over Andrew's shoulder, I stiffen and follow my instinct—burying my head under Andrew's chin.

"Sorry, I thought maybe you didn't get to set an alarm with the power outage last night. It's half-past nine already, but take your time. We're in no hurry. Just wanted to let you know we saved you some breakfast."

Andrew's arms tighten around me, but he cants his head backward toward Mason. "Thanks. Give us a bit to shower and we'll be out. Sorry, we must have lost track of time."

"No apologies needed, but you were right, Lucas; the place is brilliant."

The door closes, and I release a breath. "Fuck," I mutter and swipe my hand down my face.

I completely forgot about showing the Hepperlys the rest of the property today. I wonder how much of it they've snooped on their own without me to upsell the features.

"Hey," Andrew chimes in, drawing my hand away, "it'll be fine. Come on. Let's get cleaned up, and then you can work your magic."

My magic? Who is he?

He pats me on the cheek and climbs out of bed. I'm left looking down at the mess covering my stomach and the morning light streaming in to illuminate it.

"You coming?" a cheerful voice calls. I glance up and find him waggling his eyebrows at me by the bathroom door. "We can play army."

I think that's supposed to be a joke to put me at ease about co-showering, but I'm not used to jokes from him putting me at ease. The sight of his full-frontal nudity is also something I'm not used to. And while I wouldn't say it puts me at ease, it ruffles me for another reason. If I go into that shower with him, I don't know if it will be as quick as we need it to be.

"Come on, Tufty. I've already soaped you up before." He grins. "Don't deprive your man on your big day."

And so begins the most surreal day of my life. I wait at every turn for the bottom to drop out, but it doesn't.

When I show the Hepperlys all the rooms, Andrew stands by with what looks like a proud smile while I do all the talking. When I take them outside to view the outbuildings and guest house, he's Johnny-on-the-spot, opening blinds and exterior doors that help accent the spaces with natural lighting. Stranger still are the occasional squeezes he gives me and whispers of "You got this" and "Good job."

After we've shown all there is to show and agreed to give the Hepperlys an hour before we meet up for dinner in town, he grabs my hand and heads toward the beach. Stopping by a retaining wall, he motions for me to take a seat. I didn't peg him for the type to watch sunsets, but it seems like a peaceful way to pass the time while we're in limbo for our clients' decision.

What I don't expect is when he climbs up on the wall and takes a seat behind me, effectively straddling his legs around me. His fingers settle on my shoulders and work the muscles there.

"It'll be good. I have a good feeling," he comments off-handedly.

"You're awfully optimistic today."

"I have to be." He laughs. "Because you're freaking out."

"I am not."

Scoffing, his fingers dig deeper into the knots in my shoulders. "Look at you. Arms crossed, tense as shit. I bet you want to eat a comfort granola bar right now."

Shaking my head, I let my arms fall to my sides. "And there's the Andrew I know," I murmur, although I feel a smirk playing on my lips.

"What are you going to do with your commission?"

I don't know why he's so sure I've made a sale. I know we're splitting it regardless of who sells the three properties, but I'd really like to be the one to make this deal. Also, I don't exactly feel like rehashing my current state of financial affairs. It makes me tense under his touch just when I was starting to give in to the unexpected pampering.

"I already told you," I mumble, kicking at a rock in the sand. "I saved up for the girls' wedding, so I haven't been able to pay extra on my loans for a while. I'll use the commission to knock out what's left from my wedding loan, my truck, and then probably put a chunk down on my house to get ahead."

"Seriously, you're not going to do anything nice for yourself?"

"Being financially responsible is nice," I counter.

"Such a wild man."

I don't *have to* pay ahead on my house. My interest rate is stable, and I'm healthy. I'll probably live long enough to pay it off. If not, I've got enough life insurance for Mom and the girls that they can pay it off and still have some left over for themselves.

"My mom could use a new bathroom remodel," I venture, trying to prove to him that I can be reckless.

His sigh gusts against the back of my ear. That must mean I've disappointed him. His hands move to my lower back and begin to knead at the small of my spine.

"Tufty, Tufty, Tufty…" he murmurs. "Okay. Tell me this—if there was one thing you could have or do and money wasn't an option, what would it be?" Before I can even think of a response, he adds, "For *you.* Not anyone else. Just for you."

His thumbs dig into the tight muscles along my spine where my arthritis always kills me, making me grunt. I drop my head and close my eyes, trying to humor his ridiculous request.

"Army injury?" he asks softly.

"I slipped a disc when I was loading my gear onto a flight one day," I admit. "I don't know why. I'd done it dozens of times before."

He works the spot for a while. It doesn't escape my attention how careful he is. I think I may have broken him when I had that come-to-Jesus moment with him in the sunroom yesterday. This Andrew is…

Uhn, that feels so good.

"Well? I'm waiting?" he interrupts.

"I don't know! I don't need anything."

"It's not about whether you *need* anything. It's about what you *want*. What your heart's wildest desire is. That's what hypotheticals are for."

Try as I might, nothing that might inspire Andrew comes to mind. "I don't know. I don't want anything."

His hands leave my back. I feel two fingers pressed against my jugular.

"What are you doing?"

"Checking for a pulse. Seriously, are you human?" he laughs.

I no sooner smack his hand away than Mason pops around the corner of the wall, scaring the shit out of me. Man, the guy just appears out of nowhere all the damn time.

"Are we doing dinner or what?" he asks.

"Yeah. Ready whenever you are," Andrew doesn't miss a beat, sliding down from the wall. "Did you guys get to talk it over about the property?" he asks, flashing me a smirk like he knows I'm itching for an answer.

"Well, we were going to wait to tell you over dinner, but if you promise to act surprised," Mason says conspiratorially, slinging an arm over each of our shoulders, "Welcome to the Hepperly US home, mates!"

I'm nearly clotheslined by Mason's arm when he continues walking, and I stop in my tracks. I did it. I actually fucking did it. I sold them their dream home.

Andrew's widened eyes meet mine. He turns in Mason's hold and grips both sides of the man's face. "You're fucking kidding me."

"No," Mason laughs. "We love it."

Andrew pulls him into a hug and slaps him on the back. I'm so damn ecstatic I can't stop a giddy laugh. It only grows louder when he practically shoves Mason out of the way to pick me up in a bear hug and spin me around. It's my face that he grabs next, but this time he plants a kiss.

"I fucking told you," he enthuses, coming up grinning. Flashing a smile at Mason, he adds, "Can my man pick a winner or what?"

I think I float for the rest of the evening. And I think it has everything to do with the fact that Andrew didn't react anywhere near this way to selling the cay property in the Isles to them. Shannon wasn't unsupportive, but she sure as hell never championed me with this level of enthusiasm. You'd think our dinner would be to celebrate the Hepperlys finding their forever family home in the US, but within the first few minutes, Andrew set the precedent that I'm the one to be celebrated. Or maybe it just feels that way with how close he sits to me. His arm never leaves the back of my chair. His hand never stops stroking my shoulder. I lose count of how many times he leans in to steal a kiss or murmur something silly in my ear or the crook of my neck.

The drinks flow liberally, and at one point, I can't tell whether the warmth in me is from the alcohol or the overpowering presence of the life force that is the proud boyfriend at my side. It all becomes a bit cloudy, but I think I actually sat on his lap when we squished into the Uber on the ride back to the house at the end of the night.

What wasn't cloudy was the repeat of this morning once we hit the privacy of our room. The speed at which we got naked. The feel of his skin against mine. And the words he said to me.

So fucking hot.

Like a giant teddy bear with a big ol' cock.

Say my name, Lucas. Say it loud enough so that everyone can hear it.

They were as ridiculous as he was. Yet, I'm pretty sure I did as he asked. It's the last thing I remember saying, repeating it like a drunken prayer as I drifted off to sleep, sated, happy, and full of my heart's desire. There is one thing I want, after all—to feel like that all the time.

Chapter 21

A man can be supportive of another when he sells a house. He can give him a hand job in the dark under the privacy of a blanket on a first-class flight to Australia. He can book a suite for an overnight stay and work on blowjob techniques to pass the time the night before a property showing. He can do *all of that*, but apparently, paying top dollar for designer outdoor wear is where he goes wrong. I am out of my element, and Dario can suck a big fat one for dragging us to this god-forsaken place.

Survivalist expeditions—who the fuck considers buying four hundred acres with coastal access in the Northern Territory for survivalist expeditions? I literally know people who can't fend for themselves in civilization without their assistants. And furthermore, do we really need to canvass every damn inch of this place on foot? That seems to make it lose its wonder, if you ask me.

"Fuck! Fucking bugs!"

"You all right?" Lucas glances back at me from further up ahead in the brush.

I am the weak link on this adventure, and I hate it. My foot is killing me. I've been bitten by probably twenty different species of insects, and I'm fairly certain at least three of us will be eaten by a wild animal before this bullshit is over.

"Yeah, I just…need to sit down for a second. Go ahead. I'll catch up." Hobbling over to a rock, I ease my ass onto it and hike my foot up onto my knee. The spot of blood on my worthless 'trail shoes' hasn't gotten any bigger. That's a good sign, but my toe is screaming at me.

"You don't look so good." Lucas' voice sounds close and yet far away at the same time.

Wiping the sweat from my brow, I refuse to admit how lightheaded I feel.

"I'm fine. I just want to get a look at my foot. I think that thorn is still in there."

"A thorn? When did that happen?"

"Like three hours ago," I grump, no longer able to maintain my Don Juan attitude of the last few days. Romancing Tufty has had to take a backseat for survival and dignity preservation. Tugging at my shoe, it's aggravating how weak I feel. I don't work out on a schedule, but I'm in decent shape. I shouldn't be this sapped. Hell, I haven't heard Mason complain once. I can't even keep up with a pampered pop star.

When I fumble with my shoe a second time, Lucas takes over, gingerly prying it off. I wince at the stab of pain that shoots through my foot. I cannot be taken down by a damn toe.

"Have you been hydrating?" he asks.

"If I drink anything else, I'll be pissing more than Uncle Lou."

"You're bleeding," he remarks.

Ten points to Captain Obvious. He is now five percent less sexy than I thought he was. Why couldn't we just rent a drone and camp out at the bunkhouse where we parked our safari-looking wagon? We could be viewing this roughage from a laptop screen and the luxury of the sparsely converted shipping container that someone with more sense than Dario had placed at the entry point of the property.

Lucas peels my sock over my foot, making me wince when the fabric brushes my injury. "Shit," I hear him whisper.

"It's purple! Why is it purple?" I demand, looking at my toe that's now two sizes larger than it should be.

"The thornhead must still be in there."

"Ah, bugger, mate. That's a nasty one," comes Dario's obnoxious commentary.

I possessed a natural-looking toe before we got here. I am not nasty. I'm just pissed off.

"What kind of thorn was it?" Lucas asks, rotating my foot to inspect the damage.

"I don't know! I wasn't cataloguing flora and fauna."

"Steel-toe boots, mate. Always steel-toe," Dario adds.

If I punch him in the throat, he might not buy this place. Besides, I think there are two of him as I blink through the sweat dripping into my eyes. Why am I sweating? It's the cold season in Australia.

"I think it's infected already," Lucas remarks. At least someone sounds concerned.

"Yeah. We need to get that thornhead out of there," Dario suggests.

If he pulls out a Crocodile Dundee knife, I will miraculously reacquire my ability to run. Lucas drops to a knee and rests my foot on top of his thigh. The next thing I know, pain blooms through my toe. I yelp.

His mouth is covering it. He's…sucking on my toe.

I shut my yap when I realize that's better than a knife. He surfaces with a bitter expression. Reaching in between his pursed lips, he pulls something out. Placing it on his fingertip, he shows it to me—a tiny curved thornhead that makes me feel like less of a man for how much pain I'm in, given its size.

"Got it."

"Burn in hell," I tell it. "Thanks."

Sighing, I sit back on the rock and close my eyes. The stabbing sensation has at least subsided, but the thought of opening my eyes again feels like it would take too much effort.

"Let me get this jacket off, and I'll be good to go," I tell my audience.

"I don't think he should go on," Lucas says. "I'm sorry. Maybe we can postpone for a day or two?"

"What?" I chirp. I am not doing a repeat of this. "No. We're going. It's just hot as hell. Get this thing off me." I start undoing my backpack to rid myself of my jacket, but I feel hands steadying me.

"Whoa, Drew. Easy. I think Lucas is right. You look like you should head back to the bunkhouse," this from Keenan, I think.

"There's a med kit there. A shot of antibiotics should get you right in no time," Dario enthuses. "We can circle back as long as you guys have time. Our schedules still have room. Don't want a man down."

Oh, God. I do not want to do this again. They want to camp out for the night in the wilderness, probably so Dario can show off his caveman skills to his husbands. "No," I protest. "Just…go on without us. You're the wilderness guy anyway, right? We can't show you anything you don't already know."

"No, mate. We don't mind."

Fuck. Why does he have to have that happy-go-lucky Aussie air about him? "The babies!" I blurt, feeling woozy.

"Come again?"

"Lucas' babies are getting married next week. He needs to be back in time for it."

"You have kids?" That was definitely Keenan.

"Um…two little sisters. It's a double wedding. They're both getting married on the same day."

There's talk, a swarm of murmured voices as I fumble with my sweaty sock and blink through a throbbing headache. Lucas can be mad that I threw him under the bus, and he missed out on roasting marshmallows with his idol. I'll deal with his hostility when I'm well again. Right now, I am just a man on the verge of tears because I can barely don my own useless footwear.

Suddenly, there's silence and big hands steadying me. Glancing up, there's no sign of the Hepperlys, just inhospitable brush intended to kill me and besmirch my good name. My shoe is back on, and a solid arm slinks around my ribs, hoisting me to my feet.

"Come on. Let's get you out of here."

I lean into his softness with a sigh. Lucas Everette is no longer just the best person I know. He is, without a doubt, the best person on the planet.

146

Chapter 22

LUCAS EVERETTE
licensed agent

I haven't been this stressed out since the twins got food poisoning when they were nine. I know it was just a thorn and that the antibiotic shot I stuck in Andrew's ass should be working its magic soon, but it's troubling to see such a vivacious man brought so low. Low and delirious.

His demonic tone has me nearly jumping out of my skin as he rolls over on the cot and latches onto my wrist. "Snuggle me!"

"But you're burning up."

His fingertips dig deeper into my flesh, showing a surprising amount of strength for someone I practically had to drag all the way back to the bunkhouse. "Snuggle! Me!"

Jesus. Is his head going to spin around next?

"Fine, just…give me a second."

Stripping down to my underwear, I watch him shiver, clutching the sheet around his body. First, he said he was hot. Now he says he's freezing. I'm pretty sure his fever is coming to a head, but damn it, he's going to give me a heart attack in the process. If I had a helicopter here, I'd fly his ass to a hospital like a protective mother hen. Watching someone you don't hate being so miserable is hell on the nerves. What the heck does he do when he's unwell at home, with no family or partner to take care of him?

My heart practically pulls me under the thin cover with him. Wrapping an arm around him is the only thing I can do to bring him comfort. I've never felt more helpless. Reaching around me, he latches onto me like a baby koala. He lets out a contented sigh through his shuddering, like just my touch brought him some peace.

It's strange to feel needed. I don't think Shannon relied on me emotionally for anything. Maybe that was part of the problem, or at least a red flag. I can't begrudge her looking for what she needed elsewhere.

I've never felt like I was Andrew's equal. Knowing I can provide him with something makes me feel like I have worth and a little less helpless to the addiction to him that's taken hold of me.

His head burrows underneath my beard, and he murmurs, "Soft. Warm."

Running my hand down his back, I try to soothe him. I want to give in to my instincts to place tender kisses on his sweaty brow, but I'm wary. Does he have it as bad as I feel like I do, or is it all just lust and the high of our success on this trip? Because right now, this feels like the kind of thing you do with someone you want to grow old with. Tending to them when they're ill, even if all you can do is hold them. I really like holding Andrew when he's not prickly. Just as much as I like the way he held me the last few nights when we fell asleep. God, I want to let go.

I want to laugh at his jokes without having to hold back the way I did the night we celebrated in Harlow's Landing. Is there a chance of that ever being possible without ending up looking like the fool Shannon and Mark made of me?

How far does this go? What happens when he's done exploring, like the way we experimented in pleasuring each other with our mouths last night?

I shudder now right along with him, remembering the feel of him in my mouth. The feel of me in his. His sultry, encouraging instructions removed any insecurity I might have had about being bad at it. He's quickly become my shadow—an extension of myself that I look for each second of the day. But, like he said, I have the girls' wedding next week. Our lives are back there waiting for us. What happens then?

Everyone back home thinks I've stayed single because I've been moping over Shannon for the last four years. It hurt. Don't get me wrong, but I wasn't moping. The thought of disconnecting myself from whatever this is with Andrew, however, feels like it would be an amputation of a vital organ. I'm starting to wish I hadn't discovered he isn't an asshole.

I laugh a bitter sound, shaking my head. It's absurd, I know. We could barely tolerate each other a few weeks ago. And now I can't imagine life without the guy.

"Shh," he mumbles against my chest. "Sleep time. Sleep."

I laugh again, but this time it's a soft, earnest sound. Everything he does has become endearing. I give in, placing a kiss on his mop of golden hair, telling myself fate will sort everything out sooner or later.

"Goodnight, Andrew."

Chapter 23

ANDREW BROADHOUSE
licensed agent

He took care of me. No one's taken care of me since I was a little kid, and my mother was so beside herself with what to do over a fever that she practically needed to be sedated. Clutching my new most-favorite possession in the world inside my pocket, I am counting the seconds until the driver drops us off at the hotel in Darwin.

"What is that?" I asked, waking up with my face plastered to Lucas' chest late this morning. I thought maybe I was still hallucinating when I saw a miniature baby grand piano sitting on the table next to our cot.

"Uh…I carved it while you were out of it yesterday," he said, reaching for the rustic little wooden figurine and presenting it to me.

There was a tiny hole in the open lid of the piano, and I knew in an instant it was meant to allow it to be used as an ornament. My parched mouth went drier staring at the detail. He even carved all the keys into it.

"It could use a little more work," he said, fidgeting with it.

I snatched it out of his hand so fast I was worried I'd broken it. "No! It's perfect! I mean…it's fine. Just the way it is."

And then the fucking door opened and the goddamn Hepperlys returned, unscathed by nature. Where is a crocodile when you need one? Worst clients ever. I don't give a fuck that they announced they want to buy that stretch of no-man's-land.

"How's the foot, Drew?" Mason asks, pulling my attention from the back of Lucas' head, which is way too far away up in the front seat of the van.

"Better." Sore as shit, but better, I don't say. "I had a good nurse," I quip, selfishly hoping Lucas may hear my praise.

Turning around in his seat in front of us, Keenan smiles. "He's a keeper. Have you two ever thought about tying the knot?"

Shit. Where did that come from?

"Uh, we don't want to rush anything. We're happy with the way things are."

"Rush? Haven't you been together for like four years?" Keenan laughs.

"More or less." I squirm, acting like my seat belt needs adjusting. Was four years the lie that I spun? I honestly don't even remember. "What about you guys?" I deflect. "Is the honeymoon over after this?"

Mason blows out a breath. "Afraid so. I kick off a PR campaign next week in the States, but I'll get to see Keen for a few days. Dario starts shooting at the end of next week for a month and a half, though, so it'll be a minute before we're all together again."

I realize now this really was their honeymoon. Certainly not one I would have picked. I silently take back any complaints I made about their after-hours bedroom noises. Being apart for so long has to be hell on a relationship. At least, I assume so. I've never had the desire to be with one person for long enough to know.

"How do you do it?" I ask without thinking and realize I'm staring at Lucas again.

Soon, we'll each be off showing properties on our own. Me, going home to my big empty house each night, and him, making that thirty-minute commute to his place in the sticks.

Keenan's hand pats my arm. "The same way the two of you do." Smiling, he motions his head toward Lucas and adds, "When every time you look at someone is like the first time you fell in love with them, it's not as hard as it seems."

I let out a breathless laugh at his romantic assumption, but then find myself choking on it. My gaze returns to the beefcake, who's curiously watching the passing countryside out the front passenger window, with a faint love bite on his neck, and I feel warm all over. Is that how I look at him? That seems a bit far-fetched to me. We've just graduated from fake to…something casual.

Recovering, I chuckle and nod in agreement to pacify Keenan's whimsy. For the rest of the ride, however, I can't help but feel that the fake part of my fake relationship doesn't exactly feel fake anymore. And I kind of like that it doesn't.

When we finally reach the hotel, Mason pulls me aside and shows me a screenshot of the purchase of two tickets. Two tickets to a monster truck rally up in Lancaster back home for Wednesday when we get back.

"Just a heads up, I'm going to send these to you. We felt bad about Lucas missing that show you said he wanted to see and wanted to make up for it, but maybe it'd be a nicer surprise if you spring it on him."

I stare at the image dumbly, unable to move. I can't with these guys anymore. Yeah, I know they have enough money to buy twenty monster trucks, but something about them being supportive of my big fat lie from day one is like a sucker punch right now. Or maybe it's because they just did Lucas a solid, though not a solid he actually may enjoy—I was just fucking with him about the monster truck thing, after all. Anyone who recognizes that Lucas deserves kindness, however, is golden in my book.

Reaching out, I shake his hand. "Thanks, Mason. I appreciate that." And because I'm still me, I tell him one more lie. "He'll love it."

"No, thank *you*. I've been all over the world, but you guys gave us the trip of a lifetime and made us feel at home wherever we went. We were grateful to have two good blokes like you handling all of this for us. If you guys ever need anything, give us a ring."

Two good blokes…

He got it half right. After I assure them Lou will send over the contracts soon, they pile into their vehicle and drive away, and my gaze connects with Lucas'. I want Mason's decree to be fully accurate. I want to go to a monster truck rally with the guy in front of me and hold his sweaty-ass hand while I'm there. I don't care that he's a guy or that it'd be a date, well past a twenty-something-night stand. Because when I'm with him, I feel like maybe I am good or can be.

Nodding at me, he motions to my foot. "You doing okay?"

Does he know how cute he looks when he tries to act like he doesn't want to braid my hair? Braid it all you want, I want to tell him.

"Yeah. Right as rain." It's not. It still fucking hurts, and I want to whine the whine of the whiniest little bitch in Whine Town, but not tonight. He snuggled me and whittled me a tiny piano ornament. Whatever this is, it isn't fake. At least, not if I have anything to say about it.

"I'll go get us checked in. How about you take a load off in the bar? I'll meet you there when I'm done."

Ever the Boy Scout, he tries to argue, offering to help with the bags, but I shut it down. "I'm gonna need you to find two of the biggest and best entrees on the menu. Can you do that?"

Chuckling, he nods. "Sure."

I thank heaven for his compliance kink, and head to the reception desk. Tossing down my platinum card, I book the nicest room available and arrange for our bags to be brought up for us. Trying not to limp, I make my way into the lounge, anxiously rubbing the little wooden piano in my pocket. Sidling up to the bar, I take advantage of his distracted state, where he's studying a menu.

"You come here often, sweetheart?"

Head whipping toward me, he pauses and lets out a little snort. His hand moves, sliding a beer toward me—the brand I drink. Color me flattered. Familiarity is starting to look less suffocating and more like a soft, warm blanket.

"Ah…I see you're expecting company." Swiping it up, I take the stool next to him, angling my body toward his, and yet it doesn't feel close enough. "Do you think he'll mind if I drink his beer and keep you company for a while?"

A smirk plays at the corner of his mouth. "It's a free country." Frowning, he mumbles, "I think."

Lucas… I want to put him in a preservation case and label it, *'protect at all costs.'*

Slinking my arm across the back of his stool, I assure him, "It is. But even if it wasn't, he's going to have to fuck off because I'm not letting you out of my sight for the rest of the evening."

Staring at my mouth, he swallows, but then his gaze flicks to the bartender, who approaches at the most inopportune moment. Is he… ashamed to be seen with me in public?

"Did you decide?" the man asks.

"Uh, this looked good," Lucas says, turning the menu toward me and pointing to a dish.

Every entrée has a niche name, a play on words after some Australian animal. The kind of marketing that makes you uncertain of what you're actually getting. He's clearly playing it safe with what looks like a hamburger.

"We'll take two kangaroo skewers, two wallaby burgers with potato bites, two slices of devil's cake, and two more beers each. Can you send all of that up to room five-oh-four?" I ask the server.

The man takes our order down and leaves to dispatch it to the kitchen. Lucas blinks over at me in surprise. "You want to eat in the room?"

"I thought you might be more comfortable up there."

I retrieve my arm from his chair and turn my waist so I'm no longer caging him in. This is going downhill. I never stopped to consider that he might be apprehensive about his newfound explorations or that we're no longer in our party of five bubble. I get it—he hasn't spent endless hours with *'The Shaw and Terry Show'* like I have. This is new for both of us, but it's probably more uncharted territory for him than for me. We're in a foreign country, though, so what does he care if anyone sees him? It's not like he knows anyone here.

Picking at his beer label, he shrugs, his cheeks pink. "We were just seen outside with the most famous throuple in Australia. I don't think we'd shock anybody."

I think that might be his way of giving me a green light. Bravo Lucas. Grinning, I lean in and give him a peck on his lips.

"Yeah, but we wouldn't want to steal their thunder," I say huskily. "Why don't we head up and relax? I'll find us a flight for tomorrow while you get a shower. I'll never forgive myself if I don't get you home for all the babies' activities on time after you saved my favorite toe."

Chuckling, he blushes again, but doesn't survey to see if we have an audience. This man surprises me at every turn. I don't see a gender in front of me I've never been interested in before. I just see the person I want. Seeing that he might see the same is a vibe that has me floating on air.

I suppress the urge to pin him against the wall of the elevator and settle for brushing his pinky finger with mine. He brushes mine back, mouth-breathing like nobody's business. Validation has never come in such subdued actions.

I have a point to prove tonight. I'm not sure exactly what it is, but know it involves me and Lucas being as close as possible for as long as possible. If I thought I was out of my element in the bush yesterday, I'm well out of the zone tonight. Something profound needs to happen; that much seems evident. Toe-saving, piano-whittling, soul-seeing…a lush suite with room service doesn't seem like it's enough. What the hell do romantic people do?

He stops ahead of me inside the room and glances at the bed. It's a king-size with a plush white comforter and a view overlooking the city. I can already picture him naked in it, underneath me, panting, calling my name, and writhing against me when I tag that place inside of him. God, I wish I could fuck him. Typical greedy me. Jerking and rubbing cocks together is enough, but I still want more.

Unassumingly, he tugs his shirt over his head and starts toward his suitcase, sitting by the closet where the staff left it. I watch like a voyeur as he opens it and takes out a clean pair of his snug-fitting briefs. And then I watch as he unbuttons his pants and bends over, his bubble butt straining against his drawers. I don't think the answer to a search for profound ideas is supposed to be sex, but that's the lightbulb illuminating in my brain as I stare at his round ass. Like a magnetic pull, I want to draw closer to it. I *can* fuck him.

Theoretically.

Physically.

Realistically…

And maybe even momentarily.

I *can.*

I mean, what's the difference between two fingers and a dick, really?

"Everything all right?"

Shit. I feel like I should be wiping drool from my mouth, and yet, it's so dry, I have to peel my tongue off the roof of my mouth. "Ye-yeah." Hoisting my phone up, I scurry to the table by the window. "Just looking for an outlet to plug my phone in while I search for flights."

When the bathroom door closes behind him, a voice whispers to me. Ironically, it sounds a lot like Terry's, which is disturbing as shit. Since when has my conscience adopted his tone?

'If you do this, you know there's no coming back from it.'

'*Well, no shit,*' I tell fake Terry. But I pause as I bring up the airline website. It's a valid warning. This isn't some one-night stand with a woman who has no intention of being called or calling me again. This is Lucas. Lucas, whom I'll see at the office whenever we run into each other there. Lucas, whom I could see *more frequently* at the office if I actually made more of an effort to show up there. My smile turns into a laugh.

Clicking on a late afternoon flight that will give us plenty of time to sleep in tomorrow, but get us back to Wilmington by dinnertime the next day, a sense of rightness washes over me. A sense of rightness that makes me a little less sad about going back home.

"Maybe I don't want to come back from it," I murmur.

Chapter 24

Andrew is acting peculiar, even more so than usual. He's been smiling at me strangely ever since I stepped out of the shower to find him setting up our room service delivery on the table. He told me not to wait for him when he went to shower, but that seemed rude, so I held off and checked some messages from the girls and Mom, and sent off my replies. Doing the polite thing, however, meant I sealed my fate of having dinner for two with him. I suppose I expected that was the plan when I walked into the bar earlier, but it feels different now that he's sitting across from me in only his towel, smiling that strange smile. It's…sweet and makes my stomach flip each time I catch it. I think it's because I keep picturing what it would be like to see him like this in my kitchen back home. Is this the giddy feeling Julia was talking about?

There's something in his expression, though. I swear he looks nervous, which can't be right. Andrew doesn't get nervous.

Setting my beer back down, my breath catches when his fingertip brushes against mine. It's like the third time he's done it throughout what feels like a romantic meal for two with the backdrop of the king-size bed next to us. That's the other thing…

The Hepperlys are gone. Maybe he didn't plan a romantic dinner for two, but we don't have to sleep in the same bed any longer. Did he forget, or did he book a single on purpose?

"Not hungry?" He gestures to my half-eaten sandwich.

I can't think about my stomach when I'm around him. I'm hungry, but only for Andrew. Maybe it's this overpowering infatuation, but most of me believes this *is* a romantic dinner for two. The way he sighed when

I held him last night, his flirting in the bar, and how he brushed my hand in the elevator… He doesn't even need to try. I've fully accepted that I'm a goner whenever he's in the same room. Plain and simple.

Either it all ends after tonight, or it doesn't. Either way, we still have tonight. I'm done questioning and fighting why he has this effect on me. I've been cautious and responsible my entire life. He's always insinuating that I need to let go. Staring at where our hands are touching, I swallow against the lump of nerves in my throat.

Weaving my fingers into his, my voice comes out hoarse. "Just…distracted."

When our gazes lock, the anxiety in his expression fades. It's replaced with a smoldering look.

His fingers tighten around mine. "You're distracting too." His gaze canvases down my chest. "And so is that T-shirt."

I was going to put pants on before he came out of the bathroom, but I like to air-dry. Tuft…and all that. When he strolled out in his towel and went right for the table, I thought about it for a moment but decided I'd look more foolish if I made a scene of covering up further. So, I joined him in just my underwear and this old Tractor Supply Company shirt. I didn't think it was possible to make an old T-shirt feel sexy, but he just did with that husky delivery.

The air feels thick as I inhale and rise. Holding his gaze, I draw the hem up and over my head. I'm still in awe that he can look at me the way he does. I'm a man—I have all the same parts that he does. I don't know how I'm fascinating to him, but that's exactly what I see in his eyes. And it's exactly what I think of him when he gets up with purpose and steps toward me.

His fingertips slide along my jaw. His other hand grips the love handle above my hips in a way that makes me proud of the curves I've acquired since my army days. My heart has never hammered this hard in my chest from an invitation.

Mouth parted, he looks to be searching for words. "I really like my piano," he finally says.

My heart skips a beat, and I grip his arm. Unable to look him in the eye over the silly little trinket that kept me occupied the other night, while he was miserable. I avert my gaze, but can't fight the smile his praise brings me.

"I need to fuck you," he whispers.

I couldn't possibly have heard what I think I just heard. When my gaze snaps back to his, though, his hand moves lower, covering my ass. He gives it a squeeze that makes my cock flex behind the fabric of my underwear as he leans in.

"Need to be *here*," he murmurs and brushes his lips against mine. His index finger trails down between my ass cheeks, and he looks into my eyes. "Do *you* want me there, Lucas?"

I'm not a monk. I love sex, but I don't think I've ever wanted it so badly—even though I have no idea if it will feel as good as his fingers did. But I want Andrew. I want to be the first man he's ever been with. I want him to be mine.

Stepping back on wobbly knees, I hook my thumbs under the waistband of my underwear and drag them down. I hope the look I give him tells him my answer before I bend over. There's nothing worse than underwear lying around on the floor. Communal living in the military taught me that, so I slide them off at the ankle and toss them where they land on the top of my suitcase, hoping I still look sexy. He lets out a stifled groan that makes me shudder. Turning, I climb onto the bed and wait on my knees, unsure of what to do next.

I can hear his soft exhale from here. Watching his towel drop, my skin goes up in flames. All of *that* is for me. I'm sure he's bared himself a hundred times for others, but this time, right now, it's just for me.

He moves to his bag, rifling around in it until he produces his bottle of lube. Thank goodness one of us is thinking clearly enough to be prepared. When he slides a knee onto the bed, I'm determined not to be a statue and take the bottle from his hand. Lying back, I draw my feet up to the base of my ass so I can access what he asked for. Spreading my knees, I feel so exposed, but in a way that makes me feel desirable, as though I possess something valuable. Maybe it's the way his jaw drops as he stares at me when I dribble some lube into my hand and run it between my cheeks. I've never touched myself there intimately. Watching him watch me removes any thought of inhibitions.

Shannon asked me a few times if I wanted to watch her pleasure herself. I declined, thinking it felt like an invasion of privacy or would make her feel like our regular foreplay wasn't enough. Looking back, I realized maybe I'd disappointed her by turning her down.

As Andrew grips his cock and gives it a slow stroke, looking drugged, four years of feeling inadequate evaporate. She and I just weren't the right people for each other. Because right now, I know I could watch Andrew do that—and let him watch me—for hours.

Picking up the lube bottle, he murmurs, "Get your hole, handsome."

Handsome… I know he's never said the things he says to me to another man. It gives them importance, the way they slip effortlessly like that from his lips.

Circling my ring, I press inside. It's instantly apparent that it's easier and feels better when he does it, but I don't want to give up. Staring at the sheen on his cock from the lube he's applying, the sensation transforms into something more sensual, knowing that he'll soon be inside me. Except…the longer I stare at his slow strokes, taking him from root to tip, I grow wary of the geometry. He's not overly well-endowed. It's just an average-size cock. It's not even as thick as mine. Yet, a sliver of worry snakes its way through me. Will I be able to do this? Physically?

He distracts me by bending down. His face presses to my navel, against the side of my cock. He buries his face in the thatch of hair there, a feature I once thought he was mocking me for, and groans. My tense breathing turns into a gasp of pleasure. The next thing I feel is his slick fingertip circling the edge of my stretched ring. Planting his other hand on the bed, he works a path of kisses up my body until his breath mingles with mine.

His mouth melds to mine like melted butter, less commanding and greedy than usual. "Want some company?"

It turns out that wasn't flirty commentary for him joining me for a kiss. His fingertip presses against mine, where my body is hugging me. The idea of both of our fingers inside me at the same time has me swallowing against a glob of lust. I nod.

Expression attentive, he holds my gaze like he's intent on reading my every reaction to make sure I'm okay. It's a picture of the sweet Andrew, the one who's turned me into a heart-eyed fool. I feel the press of his fingertip and exhale. My ring stretches and burns, but then it gives way, and he joins me. The contrasting angles of our fingers have me expanded more than he ever has. It's all I can do just to breathe. Closing my eyes, I zone in on the moment. A mix of imagination and feeling the reality sheds the discomfort, and a groan peels out of my throat when his fingertip traces my gland.

Close suddenly doesn't seem like enough. Reaching up, I grip his hair and pull him to me. Tasting his tongue, hints of his beer and burger, I pour the anguish of my maddening need into his mouth. Pretty soon, my forearm is strained from trying to flex and add to the motion inside of me. Abruptly, he pulls out and stares down at me.

"That's enough," he pants. "I'm going to come just from listening to you if you keep that up."

I wanted more. I nearly forgot there's more to come. Withdrawing my finger, I watch him slide his knees underneath my thighs and shift my hips to help him. Everything is still so new—the heat from his cock so close to mine, the way I'm lying like this. I feel like I'm discovering sex for the first time, but at an age where I can truly appreciate it. It's like getting a do-over.

He dribbles more lube onto his cock and runs his hand over it. With what remains, he makes a languid pass over mine.

"You good?"

Good? I'm dying here, teetering on the edge of a cliff somewhere between want and anxiety.

"Fuck me," I urge, even as my face burns from the boldness of my demand.

You'd think I just made the air thicker the way his nostrils flare. Running his hand down my thigh, he uses his other to line himself up.

Hell, just the feel of his slippery cockhead against my hole has me sighing like it's a muscle relaxer. It's more than two fingers, though, so I lay my head back and close my eyes. There's pressure and then more. I fight not to hold my breath, but I can feel myself stretching to the point of concern. The sheets are balled in my fists to combat the slicing sensation that's threatening any bliss I'd previously found. Flaring my eyes open, I find his concerned gaze on me. I do not want to throw in the towel, but damn. I don't know whether I can do this. Averting my gaze to the ceiling, I focus on my breathing, gritting my teeth, but a pained groan escapes me.

I open my mouth involuntarily, trying to hold back the ceasefire I want to beg for, but feel a hand wrap around my waning cock. His thumb swirls over my tip.

"Lucas, look at me."

He sounds as strained as I feel. That touch, however, that request, and the look in his eyes as something gives way, has me exhaling as he passes through my ring. My muscles let up, and I find myself panting. I don't dare move. He's there. He's in.

Holding my gaze, he strokes my cock and slowly nudges his hips back and then forward a fraction. It's the most bizarre sensation. I can't even speak, only make peculiar noises—half cries of awe and wonder. It's not exactly physical pleasure, but rather an emotional one that has a message radiating through my body—*Andrew is mine.*

"Okay?" he whispers, face flushed.

I make an unintelligible reply and nod, my head rattling vigorously. I am so *not* okay. I'm completely consumed. When he nudges deeper, his warm hand still on my cock, the message amplifies—*and I'm his.*

Gripping his arm, I silently beg for his mouth. To my surprise, his eyes are closed. He looks like he's having an out-of-body experience. With a tight hold on my hip, he lets out a shuddered breath and looks at me. Pride swells in my chest. *I'm* doing that to him.

Releasing my cock, he bends down and sloppily carves out my mouth. His hips begin to move, compounding the sensation of fullness. It seeps through every inch of me. The friction passing over my gland sends a storm of pleasure through my entire body.

"Fucking hell, Lucas." His voice is choppy against my lips. "You should have stopped hating me sooner."

Typical Andrew—hiding sentiment behind the blame of others. He knows damn good and well that our hate was a two-way street, instigated by him. I try to laugh, but it's just another breathy noise. The past is distorted now. Four years of exchanging glares and avoiding each other feel like an alternate reality now. I couldn't hate him now if I tried. I'm so full. Full of Andrew. The cliff I was teetering on crumbles, and I freefall. I hope like hell he catches me because I'm lost forever.

Chapter 25

"You should have stopped hating me sooner," I tease, but it's not even a joke.

How did we get from there to here? From there to a place where he's trusting me with his body. A place where we're sharing something that feels like a lot more than just fucking.

He makes another breathy noise that sounds like it was meant to be a laugh, but he's just not capable of it right now. I want to hear him. If I don't, I'm afraid I'll start babbling all the nonsensical things running through my brain like *mine, mine, mine.*

"Say something," I beg against his neck, doing my best to control my slow thrusts. He doesn't. He just lets out a warbled moan, grips my biceps, and raises his feet off the bed. Hooking them over my hips, I gulp for air at the new angle, the new depth.

Shit. He shouldn't have done that. My balls are about ready to explode.

A person who feels this incredible should come with a warning label. The brush of his sac against my navel each time I bottom out, the feel of his soft tuft tickling me, the restriction of his channel from my base to my tip, and the way he looks so lost… My God, each time I look into his eyes, it's like seeing a silent request for me to both find him and never retrieve him from whatever plane we've discovered.

"What does it feel like?" I plead, trying again.

"Good," he pants, closing his eyes and digging his fingertips into the back of my shoulder blades. "Too good."

It is, and I'm happy with his report. While he's the kind of person who'd settle for mediocrity and give thanks for it, I'm still the opposite. What the hell am I going to do if nothing after this ever feels the way this does?

"There's no such thing," I inform him.

He chuffs like he thinks it's more of my greedy sarcasm. I'd frown if every cell in my body wasn't lit up with pleasure. He deserves *too good*, and the fact that he doesn't know it has me groaning in frustration. I bury the sound in his mouth, gripping the underside of his knee and letting my hips give in to the sweet torment that is everything Lucas. His noises erupt when I come up for air—maddening little half-moans that tell me he's enjoying the new pace. He stares between us at the slap of our bodies, his face painted with fascination and desire.

I can feel the tension coiling in my lower back. Can feel my toes starting to curl. I've gone so hard that it's to the point of pain.

"I'm going to come," I warn him, because that's all it is, a warning.

I don't know how this is all supposed to go down, but I don't want to pull out of the happy home he's made for my cock. When his gaze flicks to mine, I hold it. The urge for him to see me come undone is powerful. His eyes scan my face as if he's looking for any sign of change, anticipating my threat.

He wants to see it too. That's all it takes.

I come, looking into Lucas' bewildered eyes, watching surprise flash over his face. His mouth falls open, and he lets out a strange little cry. He was the storm that built this fevered pitch inside me. Now he's also the sanctuary from it as I release, shuddering violently. I want to hang onto the reins of the high, but have the wherewithal to scramble and get my hand between us, wrapping it around his cock. His fingers dig into my back. Eyes slamming shut, he arches his head back and pulses in my grip.

I didn't think I could be more awed by him, but he clenches around me over and over. It's a beautiful phenomenon, like his body is thanking mine. I ride as many waves as I can, blinking through our heady aftershocks until my arm gives way. Collapsing on top of him, I let my eyes slip closed and try to catch my breath.

Too good, just like he said. When his fingers finally go slack on my back and my cock has somehow slipped out of him like it's afraid more would kill it, I ease onto my side. I find those dark eyes of his sliding to mine, curious and half-lidded. His chest is still rising and falling along with his stomach, where the soft hair is slick, stuck to his skin. We're both a fine mess, and the air smells like I detonated a Lucas bomb in the room.

With great effort, I rise on one elbow and lean over him, still feeling sapped from that stupid thorn. "Be right back," I whisper, planting a quick kiss on his swollen lips.

There is no grace in how I gangle my way to the bathroom. Frankly, I don't know how it's possible that I can walk right now, but I imagine Lucas is in a similar state—and with a sore ass to boot. I fetch two cloths and dampen them.

He gives me a strange look when I return and hand one to him, but says, "Thanks."

"You good?" I inquire, flopping back on the bed and motioning to his lower half with my chin.

If I went too far, I want to know. I realize I have no idea what the aftereffects might feel like for him.

"Yeah," he's quick to answer. "Yeah, everything's…fine." Wiping ourselves off in silence, he adds offhandedly, "Kind of glad I didn't eat much."

It's a welcome bit of amusement and has me making a mental note for next time. "Well, don't forget. We have cake."

His eyes light up as they flick to the table. "That sounds really good, actually."

"Not complaining about my snacking anymore, huh?" I tease, bumping his shoulder with mine.

I remember another surprise I have and reach for my phone, pulling up the tickets from Mason. When I explain the reason for the gift, he pinches his eyes shut and lets out a puff of breath.

"So, make sure you put me on your calendar for Wednesday," I inform him casually.

"You…want to go with me?"

Why does he look surprised? Who in the heck else would he take to a monster truck rally?

"Are you planning on taking your other boyfriend?"

Smirking, he chuckles, but then his expression falls as he stares at the screen of my phone. "Ah, crap," he whispers under his breath. "That's the night of the bachelor party."

Is he serious?

"You're actually fucking going to that?"

Frowning, he looks away in thought. "Yeah. I want to be there for the guys."

I know he means his new brothers-in-law to be, but has he forgotten that bachelor parties are for men? I know what other man in his life is going to be there—the dreaded ex-best friend who stole his girl. Again, he's a better man than I if he wants to put up with that for a night.

Stowing my phone back on the nightstand, I console myself with the knowledge that I can easily find tickets to a different show to surprise him with some other time. I have to bite the inside of my cheek to keep from laughing. Look at me, wanting to book a night of monster trucks in my future.

Sighing, I relax and run my hand over a dry patch of soft hair on his stomach. "Well, if you come to your senses, you could take a wrong turn on your way there down Arlie Lane instead."

He shoots me a questioning look. Is it because my hand is venturing into post-coital cuddling territory, or does he not know where I live? I guess I never realized the latter. "House three-oh-two," I clarify, waggling my eyebrows. "I stay up late."

He stares at me for a moment. A strange, sickening sensation builds in my chest. I'm about to pull my hand away, wondering if I've just been shot down, but he glances at his stomach and gingerly covers my hand with his. It feels good and right, that simple touch, especially when his calloused thumb brushes over my knuckle.

"What are we doing?"

I barely hear the question because it's mumbled so softly. His gaze is still fixed on our hands, but his thumb has stopped its stroking. I nearly forgot about that nervous brain of his, how it mulls over details. Is it years of looking out for two baby sisters that have him primed to prepare for disaster around every turn, or was it the war? It's so foreign to me. I wait for disasters to happen and then roll with them. This…us, is not a disaster. It's…just good, and I want to keep it that way.

"Getting along?" I throw out cheekily with a grin.

He seems to process that for a moment, gaze shifting to the ceiling, and he bites his lower lip. "Um. I've got to pick up relatives from the airport the next day, but maybe we could get lunch or something on Friday before I have to go to the rehearsal dinner." Glancing at me, he elaborates, "Celebrate the closings?"

I kind of thought what we just did was our celebration, but I'll take whatever excuse Lucas needs for us to get together again. I suppose navigating our new normal back in North Carolina might seem a little uncertain. Hell, this is new for me, too. I never even saw Veronica this frequently, and she's the closest thing I came to having something like a relationship.

"The fifth?" I clarify, already excited about it.

"Yeah."

The fifth… Why does that date stick out? Fuck.

Sighing, I scrub at my eyes. "Ah, I can't. I've got a family luncheon thing. I've been threatened into not missing it. Plus," I add, shooting him a smile, "I should probably thank Shaw and Terry for the lifeline in person."

Okay, maybe it's a little embarrassing to admit that I'll be thinking about him when I'm not with him, but I'm trying to let him know I'm not blowing him off on purpose. He picks up on my insinuation, and his face goes an adorable shade of red.

Ha! Wait until he meets them in person. As I sit up and sling my legs over the side of the bed, I stare at my feet. Lucas meeting Shaw and Terry someday… I wait for the hypothetical to freak me out, but it doesn't. He'd probably get along great with my cousin, to be honest.

Look at me, already acing this not-being-so-fake thing. Maybe dating wouldn't be so difficult, after all.

"I can text you when I get home, though," I reassure him, grabbing some boxers on my way to the table. "Unless you're busy stuffing bags of rice or something."

There was a time I was sick of hearing about his wedding worries, but now I can't wait for the damn day to be over and done with. Maybe he'll be more relaxed when the babies get it done and are off to start their new lives with men of their own to take care of them instead of their big brother. It's infringing on my future Lucas time.

"Yeah." I hear the sheets rustle when he gets out of bed. "Yeah, sure."

I wonder what he looks like in a suit. Does one even wear a suit to a wedding that's being held in a barn? Wait a minute…

"So…it's a wedding," I preface as he joins me at the table and we uncover the cake servings. "Do you have a plus one?"

Scoffing, he picks up his fork. "No. I have too much shit to do to have a plus one," he grumps.

I try to ignore the sound he makes when he closes his mouth around a bite. As a shudder sweeps through me, so does a sense of relief. I shouldn't be jealous if he did, in fact, have a plus one. The event was planned back before our fake-boyfriend days. He should have one if his ex is going to be there with his ex-best friend. Dignity and all. Kudos to him for being a confident single-looking badass, though.

I mean, I'd go…if he asked. But he didn't, so…whatever. I get it.

Maybe that would be weird. Him having to explain it to the babies and all on their big day. Would they be cool with him being with a guy? I want to ask, but don't want to ruin the evening.

Holy shit, I think my brain is on a fast track to upgrading from the *'getting-along'* zone to the dating zone. Staring at my cake, I have the urge to laugh out loud. I think I'm all right with that. In fact, I think I'm eager to storm that track with a damn monster truck as I glance at the sated-looking man with sex-tousled hair across from me.

Chapter 26

Watching my brothers-in-law stumble into their house after Tyler finished puking next to his mailbox, I realize that going to the bachelor party probably wasn't the best idea. Their slurred apologies as I drove them home, about the evident tension in the air between Mark and me, were an unnecessary mark of humiliation that I was trying not to acknowledge even existed. I thought everything was fine, and that it was just me being paranoid, but apparently, even drunk, the future grooms picked up on the same avoidance from Mark that I did. The last thing I wanted to do was make Ty and Ricky uncomfortable at their own bachelor party.

If you'd asked me if I'd have ever thought in a million years that Mark's cousin, Paul, would be there, I'd have answered swiftly in the negative. All the years we were friends, he couldn't stand the guy and bitched about him whenever he had to see him. Watching them bust up like two peas in a pod all night was surreal, to say the least. I made an effort to say hello, but it was apparent I was like an awkward guest someone feels obliged to be cordial to. After a '*friendly*' nod, the pregnant pause made that clear. Neither made an effort to speak to me, or even glance my way, for the entire evening.

When the boys were in close proximity, they lit up with jokes and conversation, yet it was as if I were invisible. I was fine chalking it up to two people I don't care to associate with and leaving it be at that. Hearing that the boys picked up on it, however, was a thorn I didn't need twisted into my side. I don't want their pity. I'd have to care about the slight to need it. It just chaps my ass that if Mark is harboring some resentment toward me, he could have the decency to at least fake our truce for the boys' sake for one evening. Julia and Ty have known each other since they were kids. They should be allowed to be in love without drama between their brothers. Mark better not have set a precedent for the wedding. I'll never hear the end of it from the girls if they're watching me like a hawk to see if my feelings are hurt. Do they think I'm that fragile?

When I pull into my driveway, I breathe out a sigh of relief and grab my phone off the center console. The big wraparound porch with its swing looks serene under the bright moonlight. It's much too large a house for just me. I know that, but I take pride in knowing that it's mine, considering the meager beginnings I came from. Or at least it will be someday, whenever I get the loan paid off. I've sometimes wondered if Shannon's cold feet started when I bought it. It doesn't matter now, though. I'm stuck with it and decided that being proud is better than feeling stuck with something. Sometimes, pride isn't a bad thing.

Making my way inside, I head straight for the bedroom, my footsteps echoing across the hardwood floors down the hallway. Flipping on my bedroom light, I'm grateful for the sight of my mattress, eager to fall onto it after the night's events. If only… The temptation is just par for the course tonight.

I have damage control to do, thanks to a frantic call from Jolissa earlier, informing me that the band we hired for the wedding just canceled. I am going to be up, scouring the internet for last-minute replacements I can call when the sun comes up tomorrow.

The toe of my boot bumps into the box of rice baggies I made up for the girls, making me chuckle. Steel-toe is my first thought, seeing the dent I left in the cardboard box and remembering how Andrew looked that day in the Northern Territory.

It's strange how my time with him on that trip almost feels like a vivid dream rather than a reality I just lived. The last two days since we got home have been non-stop chaos with wedding prep, giving me very little time to process where I stand with him.

He gave me a hug at the airport when we were about to go our separate ways and murmured close to my ear, "Don't miss me too much."

I watched him grin and turn away, wondering what it meant, especially after his confusing post-sex behavior that night in Darwin. Why did he ask if I have a plus one for the wedding? Was that his way of telling me not to get attached?

Why did I ask him what we were doing?

I don't have time to dwell on his vague response of, '*Getting along.*'

Except I can't help it. Was that supposed to be a clear message? Is that all it is—getting along? Because…I kind of thought it felt like more. Or hoped so, anyway. By the time I made it home from the airport, I'd let reality sink in enough that I felt like I'd been kicked by a mule.

But then, he texted me yesterday. I half-expected him to go radio silent. The way my stomach leapt into my throat and my breath caught just from seeing his name is probably something I should work on controlling after the wedding is over until I know what in the hell we're doing.

Everything in my suitcase smells like you, he wrote. Maybe it was more than sex for him if he took the trouble to send that. Except, I started wondering if it was a complaint rather than his new playful teasing.

Then it's an improvement, I had written back, figuring that was a safe reply.

This morning I had another one from him. It was a picture of a granola bar. The sight of his fingers in the shot should not have had the effect on me that it did. I felt giddy at seeing any part of him. Giddy that he thought of me enough to text me, even if it was a stupid message.

Stole this. #sorry #hearthealthyhasnoaccountfortaste

Waking up my phone, I tell myself it's because I need to get a head start on looking up bands or DJs to right the epic fuck-up that is sure to ruin the reception. It's true. I do. Seeing several messages from Andrew, though, is an easy distraction. They have me hopeful that I was wrong. That I wasn't just a fling.

ANDREW: Are you done bachelor-ing yet?

ANDREW: Did you forget how good I look naked, or were you scarred for life by my toe injury? I'm telling you, it didn't fall off. Plus, I can still hit that spot you like without it.

ANDREW: What time are you coming over? Are you going to leave me hanging?

As I read the stream of messages, my facial muscles go slack. I think I just got a booty call. Three impatient booty calls, to be exact. Revisiting our hotel conversation, I suddenly feel like a damn fool.

I invited him to lunch to celebrate our closings. I know he said he had a family lunch thing to go to, but all I've ever heard him do is complain about most of his family. If he refuses to work for them, you'd think he'd have no qualms about missing a lunch he doesn't want to go to. I suggested lunch, and what did he do? He suggested I miss the bachelor party to apparently come over to his place and let him fuck me again. He was already planning it before we left.

Suddenly, everything I was confused about doesn't seem so confusing anymore. The way he joked about thanking his cousin for the prostate advice and made fun of me for stuffing rice bags. Yeah, I did stuff rice bags, but that's not the point.

Not in the mood. Wedding problems.

Rattling off the message, I hit send and toss my phone on the dresser to get out of my boots. I no sooner get only one set of laces undone before it buzzes to life again.

ANDREW: Dude, they didn't call it off, did they?

Dude? I went from sweetheart to dude. And why is his first assumption that the girls called off the wedding? Is that some kind of crack about me and Shannon? Does he think everyone in my family leaves or gets left at the altar?
Closing my eyes, I take a breath. I'm still spun up from the bachelor party and worrying about how I'm going to save the reception. Maybe I'm jumping to conclusions and am still programmed for pre-fake boyfriend Andrew.

No, the band canceled at the last minute.

I get my other boot off and just start on my pants when another message comes in. Is it too difficult for him to call me?

ANDREW: Have someone stream a playlist. Problem solved. What time will you be here? Or do I need to send an Uber?

I could be drunk for all he knows. I just came from a bachelor party. Typical old Andrew. Never thinking about anyone but himself and never taking anything seriously. He once spouted off to me that women want *Tiffany's* and shit like that, and yet, streaming a playlist is good enough for my sisters now because he's horny?
I'm sick of it. All of it. Is there a sign on my forehead that says I'm shit and people can walk all over me? Mark, his stupid cousin, Andrew, heck, maybe even Shannon, now that I'm on a roll. Silencing my notifications, I toss my phone on my nightstand and make my way down the hall to my home office. I have a laptop in there that will be free of communications from the aggravating, selfish man on the other end of my phone that I don't have time to deal with right now.
As I power it up, I try to push everything from my mind. The blissful thoughts, the sensual words, his moments of openness, all the things that made me lose my head and think our time together meant something. The big, fat red warning signs that told me this is what the outcome would be come flooding back to me. He's a womanizer. Throwing a man into the mix wasn't going to change anything. Andrew doesn't know how to do anything else. It was me and who I am that made me think differently. It was a great physical connection, but just physical.
"You idiot," I chide myself.

For a brief moment, I thought I saw another layer to him. There are more layers than I suspected, but still only two sides to him, apparently. One in bed and one out of bed.

Chapter 27

ANDREW BROADHOUSE

licensed agent

Sucking on the end of my fingertip, I pull it from my mouth and blow on the blister where a needle from my artificial Christmas tree poked it. Maybe I lit a few too many candles in anticipation of Lucas coming over last night. My bedroom looked like I was prepared for a seance. A seance that never happened and ended in physical misery.

Ouch! That hurts.

Sighing, I glance down at my phone. No new messages. Still. I'm starting to worry. Did he slip in the bathroom from the way he takes off his pants, fall, crack his head open, and is now lying there in need of medical attention? What other explanation can there be for ghosting me?

He stopped answering my text messages last night and didn't pick up when I called. Which is fine. Maybe he fell asleep. He went to a bachelor party, after all. But that's no explanation of why he hasn't answered yet. I've been waking up at the crack of dawn, feeling invigorated since I got home. Maybe my adjustment to different time zones is still in effect. Lucas was always early for work, though, so I assumed he'd be awake by now, especially since he's in wedding mode. I called him when I got up, and the call went to voicemail again. I left one, but he still hasn't called me back.

Admiring the way his little piano looks front and center on my tree, I smile to myself. I don't have any showings lined up, so I needed something to do to kill time. Christmas in July it is.

Padding my way to the kitchen, I pour myself a cup of coffee. I could probably get dressed, but I have nowhere to be, and these sweatpants are mighty comfy now that I've cranked my air conditioning to give my living room a winter effect.

I wonder if Lucas wears those cheesy Christmas sweaters with all the embroidery work on them. I can just picture it, and oddly enough, I think he could be the only person to actually pull off looking good in them.

Checking the time, I see it's eleven o'clock. There is no way he's not up and at 'em by now. Pulling out my phone, I try again.

It rings several times rather than going to voicemail, which gives me hope. Finally, he answers, causing a big, stupid grin on my face.

"Would you stop fucking texting and calling me? I don't have time for this today."

Damn. He sounds like he hasn't had his morning granola yet.

"Whoa! Someone's hungover," I tease, imagining his close-cropped hair a fine mess the way it was that night in Darwin.

"I'm not hungover. I barely drank," he grumbles. "I told you, I have to try to find another band for the reception at the last minute."

"You're serious?"

"*Yes*, I'm serious. The girls wanted a band, so I'm going to get them a band."

"How the fuck are you going to find a band in like forty-eight hours? Why would you do that to yourself?"

An exasperated sigh floods over the line. It's like a claw reaching across the miles, pulling at my guts, hearing how worked up he has himself. "Just forget it. It's not your problem."

"Yeah, but I'm trying to help."

I don't understand the sardonic laugh I hear next. "*Help*? Is that what you call leaving me a stream of texts and voicemails to come over and let you fuck me when I have shit to do?"

Whoa! Is that what he got from that?

I wouldn't have said no to sex, but I just wanted to see him. Tempting him with offers of sexy times was supposed to be the lure to get him in the same room as me, so I could see his grumpy, bearded face again. I'd have been fully satisfied with just a sniff and a snuggle. Someone has a case of the *Brother-zillas*. Geez.

"I was being flirtatious," I defend. "And I *did* try to help. I told you—just find a young person to stream some shit. There's technology at everyone's fingertips now, and you can pair a phone with speakers. It's not like you need to kill yourself to find a DJ at the last minute, and bands are *always* a bad idea. Name one wedding you've been to where people said, '*Oh, my God, that band was amazing!*'"

"Andrew! Just…stop."

Damn. I think he just used his army voice on me.

"Okay, stopping."

"No, I mean…just stop all of it. *This*." Another of those frustrated sighs comes over the phone. "You and me. What the fuck are we doing anyway?"

I thought we were on the road to monster truck season, but apparently, I was wrong. I don't get it.

"We're…"

Before I can come up with a guess that might appease him, he cuts me off.

"See? You can't even name it. We're… It's just… What's the point? We're too fucking old to…whatever this is. Or at least, I am. I can't be like you. I…I'm not…*you*."

Like *me?* What does that mean?

As I stare dumbly into my coffee cup, I have a feeling it means some of the less pleasant things he said in that sunroom in Harlow's Landing the night of the power outage, the things he said before the redeeming qualities—coward, cynical, dishonest. But that's what's so confusing. I thought he said I'm not really any of those things, even if I spent most of my life trying to convince my family that I was. Something twists in my chest contemplating that I've lost whatever appeal he found in me. How is that possible when I'm still riding the high from our time together?

"What are you saying?"

"I'll just…see you at work, and we'll go back to trying not to kill each other," he mumbles, sounding as defeated as I feel. "That's where it would have ended up anyway, right? I've got to go."

I don't know how long I stare at my silent phone, but at some point, I stagger my way out of my kitchen. It feels like my monster truck just crashed into a damn mountain.

Chapter 28

A knock at my door disrupts Elvis Presley as he croons out '*Blue Christmas*' through my stereo system. That I streamed…*easily*. I release the throw pillow that I've been clutching to my chest like I'd been electrocuted and scramble to the door. Lucas… Is it Lucas?

Please let it be Lucas.

Wrenching open the barrier, the fading afternoon light is still brighter than my darkened living room, causing me to shield my eyes. When I drop my hand, it's not the face I hoped to see.

"Surprise!" Veronica cheers, holding a gallon of Rocky Road in one hand and flashing open her jacket with the other, revealing a silky lavender chemise. "I got back early, and thought I'd surprise you," she adds, sauntering inside.

"Oh…it's you," I mumble, feeling like karma just played a terrible joke on me.

"Don't sound too excited," she laughs, shrugging off her jacket. "I'm surprised you're up, actually. I figured you were napping, and I'd have to call your phone until you came stomping to the door." Eyeing my miserable state up and down, she smirks. "Or am I not far off?"

Moving forward, I give her a peck on the cheek before rounding the couch again. "I'm kind of busy actually, but…thanks for stopping by. Welcome back."

Reclaiming my warm spot on the couch, I hug the throw pillow again and pull a blanket over me.

"Busy, huh?"

Peering up at her, she looks equal parts bemused and puzzled. Averting my gaze, I shrug and stare at the flickering flames of the fireplace scene broadcasting on my television.

"Jet-lagged," I offer, hoping she'll get the hint.

The couch cushion by my feet sinks down. Actually, she half-sits on them, forcing me to move them out of the way. I feel a hand on my hip, and fingertips playfully walking up it.

"Too jet-lagged for a quick reunion?"

"Not in the mood," I mumble, remembering the text Lucas sent to me last night. He was trying to brush me off even then.

Her hand freezes and then moves away. "Wow. That's a first."

It's quiet. Peering covertly from under my blanket, I hope she doesn't suddenly get all clingy on me. She's never asked for more, but she's also never shown up unannounced. Glancing around, she frowns at the array of storage boxes I dragged out that hold my ornaments. "What's with the Christmas tree?"

"I was feeling festive."

Rising, her heels clip against the hardwood floor as she walks over to it. "You must have run out of festivity if there's only one ornament on it," she says with a laugh.

My breath catches in my throat seeing her fingers clasp the little piano. It sways under her touch, and I can just picture the hook I placed on it sliding off the branch, sending it sailing to the floor. I whip the blanket off and pop up. "Don't touch that! You'll break it."

Flinching, she releases it. My heart is in my throat watching it sway momentarily, but then I realize it's safe. With open, raised palms presented in front of her, the universal sign for not posing a threat, she looks at me strangely.

"Are you sick?"

"No." I feel sick. Sick to my stomach. Sick over how something I thought was the beginning of the best semblance of a relationship I've ever had turning so quickly into a big fuck off. Why was he so angry?

A soft gasp has my gaze snapping back to Veronica. "You met someone…"

It's not a question. It's more of a discovery.

Fine. Ten points to her.

Whatever. It's better this way if she's shown up like this. It'll make things easier.

"Yeah." I shrug. "You're off the hook. Free to go find all your Mr. Wrongs and Mr. Rights."

"Wow!" I don't know why she's giggling. "Congratulations."

"Thanks." I don't know what I'm thanking her for. A few days ago, I was thankful. Today, I just feel like I got hit in the balls with a listing sign.

"So…why the long face then? You don't have to put on an act to get rid of me, you know. I get it."

"I'm not." I sigh, sitting up. Great. Now I have guilt to add to my kicked balls. "I know you're cool." Fingering the edge of my pillow, I try to find some vague explanation that won't invoke too many questions as I stare at the moisture forming on the outside of the ice cream container. "We had a disagreement, is all. Thanks…for the Rocky Road, by the way."

I realize it's gone quiet again and find her smiling thoughtfully at me. "She's good for you," she says like it's another discovery, but the words sting.

I watch her move to the back of the couch and don her jacket, a sign that she's leaving. Thank goodness for small mercies. I don't feel like wallowing with company around. I rise out of respect for our friendship and help her.

Turning, she gives me a pitying look, but with a hint of an amused smile, like my misery is somehow adorable. "Andrew, I don't know what happened, but if you want her badly enough, just do what you do best instead of burrowing into your couch."

If she has any kind of answer that will fix this, I'm all ears.

"And what's that?"

She lets out an amused puff of breath, like it should be obvious. "Be a complete pain in the ass until you get what you want. Move hell or high water."

I'm not even offended. Just more depressed. That was the old me. The me I was before I became Lucas' fake boyfriend for a few weeks. I used to get what I wanted, but now the one thing I really want doesn't want me back.

"What if…he doesn't like when I'm a pain in the ass."

She gapes at me, and I can't understand why, until I realize what I said. *He*…as in a *he*, not a *she*. Yeah, that probably caught her off guard, considering how much she knows I like women.

Her brows quirk, however, and her amused smile returns. "He must have liked something about you to get his hooks in you this deep." Her hand cups my cheek, and this time I do see genuine empathy in her face as she adds gently, "Figure out what that is and use it."

How does she know so much about relationships when she's spent the better part of a year just knocking boots with me in her free time? Tugging on the lapel of her jacket, I offer her a half-hearted smile.

"Did you find Mr. Right in Brussells?"

Shrugging, she chuckles. "No. A Mr. Maybe and one Mr. Not A Chance In Hell."

Ew. Ouch. I grimace on her behalf. "Well, happy hunting. And thanks again for the ice cream and…the advice."

Fat lot of good it will do me, but again, I'm not in the mood to be the old asshole me. Canting her head, she studies me again. What is up with that?

"You know…if it doesn't work out with *your* Mr. Right…you should give me a call about that offer you made me before I left."

Oh, God. Does she think she sees something in pitiful-depressed me that's a game changer?

"Um, why don't you leave before I have to block your number?" I joke.

Laughing, she moves to the door. "Relax. I'm pretty sure you're off the market, and I won't lose any sleep over it. I promise. Goodbye."

Strange woman. One of a kind for sure. I hope she finds her Mr. Right sooner rather than later.

Carting my melting ice cream to the kitchen, I mull over her advice. Lucas did like things about me. I know he did. He said so himself. Aside from my cock, kisses, and my looks, he also liked not having to be responsible all the time, the way he's having to be right now. Him and this freaking wedding. It's ruining him. Who in their right mind thinks they can find a decent band in forty-eight hours? The only band I know is…

The ice cream falls from my hands and splatters all over the floor. Leaping over it, I barrel into the living room to fetch my phone and shut Elvis up.

"Drew! How's it going?" Mason answers on the first ring, the way normal, not pissed-off-at-me people do.

"Mason! Good. Great." What the fuck am I saying? "Actually, no… No, it's not. I've got a problem. Are you back in the States yet?"

"Yeah. Why?"

I proceed to tell him about Lucas' band cancellation debacle and that the clock is ticking. I realize, as I ask him if there's any chance he could make an appearance, that it's a ballsy request. Platinum-record-selling bands don't exactly double as wedding singers. This very well might cost me a big chunk of my commission, but I don't care. It's worth the ask.

"Ah, that's awful. I really wish I could help, but I'm sorry. We've got a big network interview tomorrow. It's in our contract, so we can't miss it."

Fuck. What was I expecting? Freaking Veronica. Does anyone give good advice these days? Now, I'm embarrassed that I asked a former client, who just spent a giant chunk of change on three properties, for a favor of epic proportions. I lied to him and his husbands, and now I'm calling in a favor I don't deserve. Ugh. No wonder Lucas doesn't want me.

"No. I get it. I'm sorry to have even asked. I know when you said if we needed anything, you probably didn't mean something equivalent to donating a kidney, but it's just that Lucas is… He… Well, he's a fucking perfectionist who only thinks about everyone but himself. He promised his little sisters that he'd find them a band for their wedding, and he's the kind of guy who follows through when he makes a promise, even if it's an unattainable one. I know he's making himself sick over this, and it's driving me mental. He's just so…so…fucking frustrating, it…"

"Hey, Drew." He laughs. Why the heck is he laughing? "It's all right. I get it."

Sighing, I loosen my grip on the phone and stop pacing. I forgot. He spent three weeks with Lucas. He probably picked up on his quirks, too. "You do?" I chuckle, rubbing my eyes.

"Yeah. You love him. We'd do anything for the people we love," he says simply. "Look at me. You think I like wilderness explorations?" he cackles. "I got acute dehydration and ended up with an IV bag from going on an expedition just to impress Dario when we first got together. And Keenan? I took him horseback riding. I'm fuckin' allergic to horses. I was so doped up on Benadryl, I could barely stay in the saddle. Love makes us daft and mental. I'm sorry, Drew. I'd be there in a jiffy if I could."

"No. No, it's okay. Uh…again, sorry I asked."

"It's all right. I told you. I get it. Best of luck. Okay?"

"Y-yeah. Thanks."

Love?

The accusation tumbles around in my head as I stare at my phone after we hang up. I know it's the lie I wanted him and his husbands to believe, but I understand the reason he's so convinced now. Because it's true.

Oh, God. I got it all wrong.

'What are we doing?'

For some reason, the replay of Lucas asking me that question makes me realize it was vulnerability in his eyes when he asked. I was so worried about coming across as too sappy that I didn't see it.

'Getting along.'

Ugh. I cannot believe I said that. And then…

Fuck. I basically asked him for a booty call with my slew of messages and voicemails. I probably sounded like the incomparable slut he thinks I am.

I drop onto the couch, feeling heavy and weak. All that crap I said to him about how we just jerked off from playing boyfriends and that I'm not real boyfriend material.

Shit. I fucked up.

I never imagined I'd ever fall in love. Finding out that I did just makes this fuck-up hurt even more. It turns out ignorance really is bliss.

Chapter 29

Picking at a platter of appetizers on the island counter in my parents' kitchen, I contemplate what looks good, knowing I should eat something. *Nothing* is the consensus I come up with. Nothing looks good. Love has officially ruined food for me. Love sucks.

The urgent clip of heels comes from behind me. I can smell my mother's flowery perfume before I see her. Dressed in white slacks and a soft yellow blouse, she looks like a woman who is confident that nothing will spill on her at a luncheon. Even food, apparently, bends to my mother's whims.

She's frowning at me. I can see it in her eyes. Her face doesn't move much from all the Botox. Years of trying to look good for my father, although she'll never admit it.

"What's the matter with you?" she demands, picking up a spoon to stir a bowl of dip, her manicured nails are perfect as always, making the utensil look out of place in her hands.

"Are you going to come outside or stay in here and mope? It's not going to kill you to spend an afternoon with your family."

Family…

I can see from the window that Shaw and Terry are here, sitting at a table by themselves on the lawn. I'm sure Chad will make the rounds and chat with them, but he and I are usually the only ones in my immediate family who do.

Uncle Lou called me on my way over here to inform me that my commission will be deposited on Monday. "You did good, kid," he said in that gruff tone of his that felt more like a hug than any I've ever gotten from my parents in recent years.

At least Lucas will be happy when he checks his bank account next week. That much made me smile.

"Is that what this is?" I ask, stuffing a shrimp into my mouth without even tasting it.

"What's the matter with you?" Chad's voice calls from my side, where I see him walk in with my father. Smirking, he grabs a bottle of beer from the fridge. "Real estate falling through?"

Does everyone think I'm pouting like the prodigal son? Not everything is about the freaking Broadhouse family. For fuck's sake.

"I just made almost a million dollars this month. Real estate is fine," I inform him without any fanfare. It's just a fact, but because he started it and the surprised look on his face satisfies my miserable mood, I suggest, "Maybe you should try it sometime."

Snorting, he still looks bewildered, like he knows I'm not shitting him about the figure. Face pink, he tries to hide it by taking a swig of his beer as he leaves the room.

My father's expression looks contemplative, but one look at my mother beating the hell out of the dip, and he makes a casual beeline for his den. Her gaze follows him like a hawk, an angry Botoxed hawk with a Tammy Wynette updo. It's a rerun I haven't missed, and one I blame for not knowing that love smacked me right in the face without me even realizing it.

Sighing, she sets her spoon down and wipes a nonexistent mess from her hands. "Well, if you're not going to eat, at least get yourself a drink before you go out there, so you can try to be social. Come on."

She stalks into the den after my father, and I groan under my breath. I don't want to be her lackey for whatever row she's having with Dad today, but I follow anyway because I have no energy to argue.

Nodding at my father, I drop onto one of the leather couches and watch my mother pretend she didn't march up to the bar just to be in the same space as him. She scoops ice into two glasses with the command of a general and pours us both a drink. Turning, she smiles as much as she can, back to being hostess of the year, and walks over to hand me a glass.

"So, what's new with you?"

Taking a seat opposite me, I catch her gaze flicking to my father to see if he'll join her. He stops next to his bookshelves and leans an elbow on one of them, causing a tiny furrow between my mother's brows. No wonder I don't know what love looks like.

"I met someone," I mutter, staring into the amber liquid that reminds me of the color of Lucas' eyes.

"Oh? Where?"

"At work."

Mom makes a *tsk* sound and remarks dryly, "Well, I guess you've learned nothing."

I feel like I've been chopped up in a blender, and that's the starter conversation she leads with? And people meet people they work with all the time. For all they know, I could have wanted to marry that intern that I didn't even go out with. I'm so sick of feeding into it, though. I have no snappy retort today that will get under her skin.

'*At least I'm honest.*'

Lucas' words ring through me like a ghost melody.

"I really like him," I tell her, feeling bold.

"Who?"

"The guy I've been…" I'm not sure how to fill in that blank, and certainly don't want to say '*fucking*' because it was more than that, even if Lucas doesn't think so right now. "With," I finally settle on.

Maybe I shouldn't even be speaking to anyone at all today because it occurs to me I'm just staring at my drink with no concept of how much time has passed, too lost in my own thoughts. It's quiet when I look up. Dad looks a bit shocked, but also, strangely nervous. Mom lets out a fake-sounding laugh and then rolls her eyes.

"Is this your latest shenanigan?" She takes a sip of her drink and sits back, folding an arm over her stomach. "Well, try again. You won't be ruining our day. We're going to have a nice luncheon without any of your outlandish antics today."

Unbelievable. Even when I tell her the truth, she doesn't take me seriously.

Slumping back against the couch, I rub my thumb over the pattern cut into the crystal, imagining what it would be like to talk about a new partner with a normal family.

"He's a veteran," I murmur, deciding that pretending is as close as I'll ever get. "He flies for Uncle Lou. He's got two little sisters that he dotes on. And…he thinks the sun shines out of my ass." A sardonic laugh chuffs out of my lungs as I bring the glass to my lips. "God knows why," I mumble, taking a sip, but it's not funny anymore. It's just…sad. "And…I think I'm in love with him."

Scotch. Definitely scotch, I decide as the liquid burns its way down my throat. It's nice to feel something other than the ache in my chest for a moment. Glancing up, I realize I've done that thing again where I lose track of time.

Mom is staring at me, mouth parted like she just swallowed her tongue. Shit. I guess I pretended aloud. Dad tugs at the collar of his shirt, which isn't tight by any means, and turns to stare out the window.

"You have nothing to say? You always have something to say," comes Mom's anxious voice, but she's not looking at me. Huffing, she shakes her head and closes her eyes, muttering, "This is your fault."

Why do I feel like I missed something? Are they talking about something else, or did I only think I said all that stuff about Lucas aloud?

"*My* fault?" Dad exclaims, spinning around. "Oh my God, not this again."

"Excuse me?" I chime in, wondering what the hell I missed.

Mom rises from the couch and paces in the opposite direction of Dad, making a guttural noise and waving a dismissive hand. "You're just like your father. Nothing's ever good enough for you."

Just like Dad? I'm nothing like Dad. Everything is good enough for Dad. The man never complains about anything. "What are you talking about?"

"*One* time, Loretta," Dad interrupts, giving her a pointed look. "It was *one* time, *forty* years ago."

"I know how long ago it was! I was there!" Mom snaps, her hand balling into a fist at her side.

"Oh, for God's sake. *Now?* Do we have to do this right *here?* Right *now?*" Dad sighs, setting his drink on his desk and shoving a hand in his pocket.

"Apparently!" Mom squawks, extending her palm out toward me. "Our son has gone from a womanizer to…a…a *man-izer!*"

"What?" My confused retort is mirrored by my father. I glance between the two of them, feeling like I'm getting a case of whiplash. Rising, I hold up a hand, because clearly Mom is having a senior moment, or I fucking missed some huge connotation between how my being with a man has anything to do with my father. "Wait. What am I missing?"

"This has nothing to do with me," Dad says under his breath, eyes still locked on Mom. "And did you hear him? He said he loves the man. Maybe he's finally going to settle down. That's what you've always wanted,"—he gestures to her as my brain tries to process what I'm hearing—"but listen to you. You're still not happy. When will you ever let it go?"

Dad's…got no complaints about this? And he's standing up to Mom for once in his life. What is happening?

"Um…hello?" I pipe in, but they're like staring contest champions.

"With *my brother!* My brother, of *all* people!" Mom shrieks, stomping her foot like a debutante.

"Wait, what?" I am not fucking Uncle Lou. How in the hell did she get that from what I said?

"We were drunk!" Dad barks. "I *told* you that."

"You weren't drunk the *first* time!" Mom shoots back.

"That was before I even met you! I've told you this. It was just a fling."

Bringing her balled fist up to her temple, Mom's eyes pinch shut. "You kissed him at our wedding!"

Holy. Fuck.

"I was drunk!" Dad defends. "I didn't even think he was going to show up, and he came back from the service. None of us had seen him for a long time. I was happy. It was stupid. I know that. I was just saying goodbye. He pushed me away, and I was glad he did. How many times do I have to tell you I'm sorry? You're all I ever wanted. I've done everything I could to make it up to you for the last forty years."

It feels like I just walked onto the set of a soap opera that used to be my boring parents' life. "*You* and...*Uncle Lou*?" I babble, hoping like hell someone will finally make this all make sense.

Dad looks at me then. It's a look of guilt and shame. He groans and turns back to the window, swiping up his drink.

"Do you see?" Mom says, finally looking at me too as she gestures to Dad.

Dad lets out a snort and glances over his shoulder. "Yeah, do you see what I've been dealing with for forty years? Why I stressed to you to stop sowing so many wild oats because it might bite you in the ass someday?"

Mom growls, actually growls, and does that foot-stomping thing again. "Don't talk about me like I'm not here."

Turning around, Dad goes full Rhett Butler on her, commenting dryly, "Why? It would have the same effect."

I nearly gasp right along with Mom upon hearing that. Dad has never sassed her in his life. He just...takes it. Now at least I know why.

"How dare you!" Mom hisses all melodramatically, her face beet red.

Slamming his glass down, I watch Dad march over, closing the distance between them. I am completely slack-jawed, uncertain what to do as he cups her face in both his hands. They've never gotten physical before. What he does next is a new one, too. He kisses her long and hard until she comes up panting and gasping for air with a little whimper.

"I love you, Loretta Broadhouse. I've loved you since the day I met you. I've loved you for forty years, while you've beaten me over the head after finding out I had a one-night stand with your brother—a year before I met you—that *he* made me swear not to tell you about. I was so happy the day I married you, I wanted to kiss everyone in that damn reception hall. I love you even though you drive me crazy," he stresses, giving her a little shake. "I hope one of these years you'll figure that out before we die."

With that, he drops his hands and makes his way to the door. Turning at the last minute, he glances at me and clears his throat, looking a bit more composed. "Um...congratulations," he says, but then his gaze shifts to my mother and he adds, "Welcome to the club."

It feels like my brain was just chopped up in a food dicer. I turn to my mother. She looks ruffled in more ways than one, lips puffy from Dad's big-dick-energy moment. Her jaw is gaping, and I can see now that I was wrong about the Botox. She looks completely stunned as she stares at the place where he left. Should I fan her or something?

"Mom?"

Jumping, she looks at me and composes herself, tucking back a loose strand of hair. "Um…everything's fine." Walking over, she gives me a quick hug and a peck on the cheek. "Why…um, why don't you go say hi to Shaw and Terry? They were asking about you. You can tell them about your…work…man." She pats my hand and then hurries in the direction my father went.

I stand, stupefied, listening to the sound of her hurried steps down the hallway. "Jacob?" Her call echoes, sounding desperate, and dare I say, more loving than I've ever heard her utter it.

What the fuck just happened?

I lose more time staring at the empty doorway. It feels strange to be at the scene of the crime, so I wander dazed out into the backyard. I find Shaw and Terry sitting at a table, eating lunch, oblivious. How do I even recount what just happened?

"Well, well. Look who's back from the bush," Terry chirps.

Dropping into a chair next to them, I stare at the spread of plates on the red-and-blue checkered tablecloth. I can't do it. There's just no way to skirt around it.

"Your dad and my dad screwed," I blurt, looking at Shaw.

"I'm eating," he complains.

"I'm serious! Forty years ago, apparently."

Frowning around a bite, he spares me only a flicker of eye contact and continues eating. "Yeah. I know."

"You *knew?*"

Shrugging, he takes a sip of his beer like this isn't vital information. "I heard Mom and Dad talking about it once when I was a teenager, about why your parents never invite them to stuff." Frowning, he finally gives me his full attention. "You didn't know?"

How is this my life? I was always kind of jealous of Shaw's upbringing with his blunt and carefree parents, but now I'm sick from it. He knew the truth that kept my parents at each other's throats for years because his folks were honest, while mine chose to bury their secrets with fake smiles and table manners. If I'd known, I could have just slapped some sense into them. There's clearly no pining on Uncle Lou's end, the way he and Aunt Vera dote on each other. Shaking my head, I close my eyes, fighting a headache.

Did I know? No one tells me anything, apparently.

"No. I told them about me and Lucas, and Mom said it was Dad's fault," I explain.

"Oh my word, that woman can hold a grudge," Terry moans. Sighing, he adds, "Knowing that Lou and Vera are swingers probably doesn't help her paranoia, though, I guess."

Holy shit. What? But I don't get to ask because his eyes go wide.

"Wait! Did you just say you told them about Lucas, as in…you're officially a thing?"

Ugh. Shaw needs to consider his plus-one selection more thoroughly in the future. Talk about kicking a man while he's down and traumatized. "No. We're…nothing."

Terry winces. "Oh, no. You prodded, didn't you?" Gasping, he covers his mouth. "Did you not lube? I told you to use lube!"

"Again…I'm eating," Shaw whines.

The only thing official in my life is that I have no way to navigate it anymore. Dropping my head into my hands, I groan. "This is the worst day ever."

Terry's palm slaps the table in my line of view. The silverware clatters from the force. "Shut up! Stop it right now! *You're* in love!"

I don't remember telling him that. If I'm supposed to have some kind of reaction to his shocked expression, he's going to be disappointed.

"Again…worst day ever." Stealing his beer, I take a long drink. I set it down, fully expecting a typical Terry outburst, but instead, his pouty expression looks more like sympathy.

Reaching over, he lays a hand on my forearm.

"Oh, honey. What happened?"

Honey? Wh-what the hell is happening now? I can't take any more weird today.

Terry being nice to me is officially weirder than Dad having a one-night stand with Uncle Lou. Maybe even weirder than the thought of Aunt Vera lighting one of the candles I gave her for a threesome. The woman bakes me cookies and knits.

Except now Shaw is looking at me, too, like he's invested.

"I don't know." I throw my hands up and swipe Terry's beer back since apparently I'm off the hook for thievery right now. "He's freaking out over planning his sisters' double wedding and went off on me. Some bullshit about how this never would have worked, and he'll just see me at the office where we can go back to trying not to kill each other because *'that's what would have happened anyway, right?'*" I imitate his hurtful untruth. He once claimed that he was honest. Well, how does he know that's what would have happened? "He didn't even give me a chance," I grumble.

"Sweetheart, planning a wedding is like being in a cage match. Double wedding? Forget it. You cannot fault the man for being stressed out."

Hello, if anyone knows that Lucas can stress, it's me. I don't need Terry to tell me the obvious.

"I don't! I said I'd help, but he said my suggestions weren't helping."

"Okay, *talking* and *doing* are two very different things. Men, I swear." He sighs and rolls his eyes. "Take this one for example," he adds, gesturing to Shaw.

"What's that supposed to mean?" Shaw asks.

Terry folds his arms over his chest and bats a hand in the air, giving my cousin a knowing look. I don't believe this. Does everyone in my family stop to think about their own problems when I tell them I'm in the middle of a crisis?

"Hello!" I wave my hand. "Emergency here!"

Lolling his head back toward me, Terry takes a breath like I'm boring him. "Look, if you love your man, you gotta show him the love. I'm talking white-knight shit. Mani, pedi, massages." He rattles on, counting things off on his fingers.

We clearly have different opinions of the activities of white knights.

"If he's stressed," he continues, "destress that shit before something else does it for you, and you're just the guy who stood by and watched the dumpster burn. You ride up in there in your best shining armor and serenade that damsel in distress."

As I stare at the most obnoxious cousin-in-law on the planet, I have the urge to laugh. Maybe people are bound to give decent advice sooner or later.

"What are you doing?" Shaw asks as I pop up from my chair.

"I have to go. I know what to do."

"Oh, my God. Did I just save the day?" Terry claps excitedly.

He looks so hopeful. His eyes, so full of visions of happily-ever-afters for me. That's…really sweet. I never would've imagined him rooting for me.

"Fuck no. I'm the one who has to do the legwork."

Chapter 30

ANDREW BROADHOUSE
licensed agent

Walking out of Bob's Emporium, I now not only have a plan, but I have appropriate apparel for a barn wedding. Country gentleman apparel, to be exact, at least according to the logo on the receipt for my new duds. The reception should have kicked off right about an hour ago, per the invitation that I drove to the office yesterday afternoon to steal off Lucas' desk, since he still wouldn't answer his phone. Hopefully, he at least got my message that he could stand down on the hunt for a band and that I got it covered. There is no point in my running myself ragged if he gives himself an ulcer. Smoothing out the fringe on my khaki western shirt, I hope I look the part of a hired musician more than in the white dress shirt and black slacks I left the house in. The last thing I want to do is stick out like a sore thumb in Lucas' neck of the woods and embarrass him when I'm trying to win him over.

My keyboard is tucked safely in the trunk of my car, along with the amp and mic I had to go rent last night, since I have no idea what kind of setup I'm walking into at this hayloft extraordinaire. The things we do for love.

The peak of a giant barn, along with an array of cars in a parking lot, comes into view at the end of the lakeside road, letting me know my GPS was on track. I've found it.

No one starts dancing right away at these things. People always have to sit around and wait for the bridal party to arrive while they're starving, then they eat and suffer through speeches. I wasn't about to intrude in the middle of that and watch Lucas' head spin around. Timing is key in this thing.

Parking, I get out and hoist all my gear over my shoulder, grateful that I never pursued a musical career as I slog it across the parking lot. I'm freaking sweating under this cowboy hat already and haven't even reached the damn door. How sexy is that?

I have to say, though, that I look pretty fucking good in these boots. I swear they make my ass feel higher, perkier. That Bob knows what he's doing. Maybe his lot was empty because everyone in town was at the wedding.

Stepping inside, I get a whiff of Beef Wellington and fried chicken as soon as the air conditioning hits me. White-linen-covered tables litter the refurbished space that you wouldn't know was a barn unless you saw it from the outside or looked up at the rafters. Twinkle lights loop around them, casting an ethereal glow over the guests, who look to have just finished their meals, their attention now directed toward the bridal party table.

I don't see any sign of Lucas and wonder worriedly if I've just pulled a Mrs. Robinson. Except, there are clearly two brides at the head table. Two identical-looking brides, with the exception of their dress styles. One is giving a speech about a man who has played an important role in her and her sister's lives. I follow her gaze and find him seated at a large round table in the front next to an older woman who shares his dark hair. Damn, he looks good. His beige suit fits snugly on his thick biceps and thighs. His beard is freshly trimmed, along with his hair. The light blue tie around his neck lends a tone of innocence that fits his nature. And the humbled and heartfelt look in his eyes nearly brings a tear to my own.

Also, holy fuck, I'm going to kill Bob on my way out of town. I asked him to find me clothes to fit in with a country wedding in Bolton, not look like a fucking rodeo rider. Shit!

One of the baby sisters announces that they're going to cut and serve the cake now, so I make a break for it before I'm noticed. Slinking through the shadows, I head toward a small gaggle of people at the bar to hide. On my way there, I notice a setup in the far right corner. A band setup. What in the ever-loving hell? It's a full drum kit, a bass, a lead guitar, and a keyboard. Did he find a band after all? Only Lucas.

So much for saving the day. Fucking Terry.

Okay, fine. He's not to blame, but fuck! Can't a guy win at anything?

Now I look like a fringe-wearing ass, *and* I didn't do a damn thing to stop the dumpster fire. How in the hell am I supposed to explain what I'm doing here?

Taking a calming breath, I whisper my drink order to the bartender, hoping it will help calm my nerves. Think, Andrew. Think.

Maybe the band will suck, as most wedding bands do. I could be on standby and still save the day if necessary, and then Lucas will see that I not only have worth to bring to the table but that I'm not here for a piece of ass. Who in the hell subjects themselves to wedding reception song requests just to get laid? Again, though, I won't object to a good snuggle if he's up for it later on. Fingers crossed.

"Thanks, man," I tell the bartender, tipping him and trying to slip my wallet back into the tight-ass black cowboy jeans.

"Tell me that is *not* the entertainment," I hear a woman say conspiratorially off to my right.

A man snickers. "Just think. This could have been your wedding if you'd stuck it out with Lucas."

When their joint laughter follows, I slowly turn my head and locate them a few feet down the bar. A tall, slender man with dark hair, his arms around a curvy redhead, catches my eye in his mirth, but then looks away casually. I'd bet a granola bar that's ex and ex.

When I hear chatter behind me, I forget about the two douchesicles to my right momentarily to move over for more wedding guests. Except when I turn, I find a familiar face.

"Mason?"

"Hey! Drew!" He reaches for my hand, and it takes me a second to offer mine in return. Tugging me forward, he pulls me in for a hug and claps me on the back. "Hope I'm not too late."

"What...what are you doing here? I thought you couldn't make it."

"Didn't Lucas tell you? The network said they could send their reporter to do the interview on the road with us, so we did it on the drive down. We sent the crew ahead to set up," he says, gesturing over my shoulder to the meager setup. "Nothing fancy like our shows, but we didn't want to steal the wedding thunder, you know?"

Oh, my God. It worked? My lifeline worked? And Lucas knows about it?

Shit. I guess I never told Mason that it was a secret. He thinks we're a couple. Why would he think we keep secrets like that from each other?

"Shit, man. That's...that's great." I laugh. "That's fantastic. Thank you."

"No problem. We were able to work it out, so we did." Squinting at my gear, he nods. "What's with the keyboard? You going to join us?" he asks hopefully.

"Ah, no. No way. It was just a backup plan."

Grinning, he slaps me on the shoulder, and I realize that the rest of his band is standing behind him, peering out over the wedding guests. Jesus, I just met Renegade. "Lucas is a lucky man. If you change your mind, just come on up. We'll go get set up. I think they're about finished with the gestures now."

He nods toward the bridal table, where the babies and their husbands are wiping cake off their faces. When his bandmates file past me with hellos, I just stand there, stupefied.

"Nice look, by the way," he adds, flicking my cowboy hat before he joins them. "You'll have to tell me where to get one of those before I leave."

"Yeah, sure. Thanks."

I catch a hit of perfume and feel the back of a hand rap me on the arm. I find Shannon, I presume, at my side, Mark on her arm. "Was that Renegade? Like...*the* Renegade?" she whispers, eyes wide.

I can't believe this woman ever got to put her hands on my man. Glancing across the room, I see him about to take a seat with a plate of cake. His gaze catches mine, and he freezes. His brow furrows and his mouth parts, gracing me with a view of his sexy, confused face.

Unslinging my gear from my shoulder, I swallow against the dryness in my throat and thrust my shit at Mark. I'm fairly certain I bashed one of them in the shin with the amp, judging by the *'ouch'* sound I hear.

"Yeah," I concur. Glancing at him, I hang the strap on his shoulder. "Keep an eye on these for me, will you?" He accepts them dumbly, although both his and his girlfriend's faces say they don't understand why I'm asking. Straightening my hat, I tip the brim the way they do in the movies. "I need to go win over the guy you two jerks threw away."

Chapter 31

LUCAS EVERETTE

licensed agent

I swear that's Andrew. In a cowboy hat and boots. Is he…wearing fringe?

I set my cake down and start toward him. Everyone has risen from their places and started mingling around the cake line or the bar. It's like one of those movies where the crowd parts…until Julia slams into my side. The next thing I know, I've lost sight of Andrew.

"Is that Renegade?" she shrieks in my ear so loud my eardrum throbs.

Chuckling, I give her hand a squeeze on my arm. I hardly believed it myself when Mason called me before I was going into the church this morning. I was so blown away by his offer to come play at the reception that I didn't even think to ask how he knew we needed entertainment until the call was almost over.

Andrew. Of course, it was Andrew. How else would he have found out?

I've been waiting for this day for almost a year, but all I could think about during the ceremony was that Andrew gave a damn enough to call Mason for me. I wasn't about to tell the girls until I knew it was a sure thing. I'd only told them I *might have* acquired a band at the last minute and that their friends wouldn't have to wing it by streaming songs all night. Seeing the gear set up over at the side of the room when we walked in, though, had me laughing under my breath; I was so damn relieved.

I had a message from Andrew last night saying he had the problem solved, but I sure as shit didn't think this is what he meant. I mean…it's

Andrew. Then, when Mason called this morning, I had no clue what I'd even say to Andrew after the way I dressed him down the other day on the phone. I have a lot of crow to eat.

"Renegade is *really* playing at my wedding?" Julia asks again, bouncing up and down energetically.

"I heard your band canceled," comes a familiar voice, and there he is. His gaze shifts from Julia to me, and he continues somberly. "They were the only one I knew. I hope that's okay."

Is he…asking for my permission? God, he looks good. Stupid, but good.

"You look familiar," Julia pipes in, glancing between us strangely.

"Um…this is Andrew. We…work together."

And he touches me. And I like it, I don't add.

"And you just called up Renegade and made it happen?" she asks with a hint of her usual mirth.

"I know how this one worries," he teases, crooking his thumb at me. "Nothing but the best for his baby sisters."

I do *not* worry. I'm just…responsible.

Great. Why is Julia looking at us with that weird little grin?

"Well, you're not at all what I expected," she says, taking a gander at his get-up and giving me a look that says she bets twenty bucks it came from Bob's Emporium. I shake my head, asking her not to go there right now and get another of those peculiar looks.

"Thank you," she finally adds, remembering the manners I taught her.

"Congratulations." Andrew nods, tipping his hat like he's taken on some cowboy persona by wearing that outfit.

Flashing me a smile with a twinkle in her eye, she grabs the skirt of her dress and twirls off to no doubt freak out with her sister and the boys. That leaves me and Andrew. Alone. In public. In a room full of my family. Andrew…in my world. I still can't believe he's here.

"Hi," he says, sounding more vulnerable with one syllable than I've ever heard him.

"Hi," I parrot back, and then we stand in an awkward silence. I take him in slowly again, from the fringe across his chest to the pointed toes of his cowboy boots. "What are you wearing?"

"Distinguished country gentleman shining armor. I can explain later."

Am I supposed to know what that means?

Before I can find more small talk to get to the things I want to say, he lets out in a rush, "I'm here to help. What do you need?"

Is he kidding me? He already did me the biggest solid anyone's ever done in my life. I nod toward where Mason and his guys are tuning their instruments and then shake my head. "Nothing. Um…I'm sorry, I didn't get a chance to call and thank you."

Nodding, he just smiles at me, looking pacified. "You look good," his voice comes softly.

"Thanks. You look…ridiculous."

He also looks handsome, especially when he smirks. "No. That's impossible."

Oh, brother. And that's why I didn't need to compliment him. I roll my eyes and fight a smile. It doesn't seem right to laugh and joke after the way I went off on him, considering what he just did for my sisters.

He steps forward suddenly. "I can't look bad when I'm next to you, Lucas. The way I feel inside whenever you're around…it's so big it feels like it radiates and makes anything it touches look like gold."

The way he feels inside? A flutter sweeps through my stomach, which is very inopportune since today isn't about me, but what's a guy supposed to do when an idiot walks in wearing a cowboy hat and says something like that?

Clearing his throat, he takes a step back and tugs at his cuffs. "Look, I don't want to ruin their big day, so I'm going to get out of your way, but I'm here if you need me. I'll just lurk in a corner and make sure all the champagne glasses are filled or something. But, um, when this is over, I was wondering if it'd be all right if I asked you out on a date?"

"A date?"

"Yeah. The kind where I ask you to keep being my boyfriend." His tongue comes out to wet his lips. "Because…you were really good at it." His mouth quirks up at the corner, but it's not a mocking Andrew smirk. It's a smile from a man who I think is trying to pour his heart out. "You've got the job if you want it."

He…wants to be my boyfriend? For real?

He's already had my ass, so if he wants it again, he certainly doesn't need to take me on a date, which disintegrates my previous theory of him using me for sex. I'm not about to tell him how many times I had to watch '*Jerry Maguire*' with my mother over the years or that he had me at Renegade. Even after that phone call from Mason this morning, when my heart flipped, I assumed it might still be an uphill battle of him being insensitive. Except, I think he just informed me he's going to stick around like the pain in the ass he is and help at the reception whether I like it or not. Like a boyfriend would. A good one. If I wasn't gone for him before, there's no turning back now.

A microphone squeals, making me nearly jump out of my skin. Mason's voice booms over the speakers. He introduces himself and the band, as if it were even necessary. Andrew and I exchange amused looks as the three hundred and twelve guests lose their minds around us. I'm going to have to do the stand-in for Clark for the father-daughter dances soon, but it feels like so much more needs to be said before I lose sight of him.

He shifts in place, motioning over his shoulder, looking anxious. "I'll just, uh, go sort the coats, charm the old ladies, and, you know, other wedding stuff."

It's such a bizarre state to see him in. The thought of him walking away, even a foot, tugs at my heart. "Do you want a drink?" I ask over the noise.

Smiling, he steps closer and takes off that stupid hat, looking relieved. His gaze canvases my face. It has the same look it did the night we made love in Darwin as he shakes his head. "Just you," he whispers. I know damn well and good that I'm mouth-breathing right now. He must notice too because he inches closer so our chests are touching and murmurs, "Just *only* you…for as long as you'll put up with me, Tufty."

The backs of his fingers brush mine. For once, I don't feel like less or like I'm in this alone. I can't *not* touch him, so I weave my fingers through his. His breath hitches, and he squeezes his around mine, searching my eyes.

"I'll be better," he assures me in a rush. "You make me want to be better."

I'm shaking my head before he's even done speaking because he's already better, or maybe he already was and just needed to know this wasn't a game anymore for me, either. When did I start fingering the tassels on his shirt?

"Better is overrated."

"I don't know. It looks pretty good from where I'm standing."

We sort of gravitate toward each other then, unavoidably, until our lips are nearly touching. Two victims of a heady spell. He's the first to pull back, drawing me out of the fog.

"Sorry," he chuckles, his gaze darting around, "I want to kiss you so badly."

Shit. I would have let him, having completely forgotten where we were. I look over at the bridal table and find Jolissa, Julia, and the boys staring at us slack-jawed. Fuck. Fucking fuck.

"Shit," Andrew whispers, releasing my hand and stepping back. "Busted."

"Uh, yeah. There will be questions. Lots of questions," I mutter, already imagining the girls putting me in the hot seat for all the dirt. I will be buried with that dirt clenched in my fist, if I have anything to say about it. There are just some things little sisters don't need to know.

"I can help field them, if you want," he offers, which is as sweet as it is unexpected, even if his mischievous grin has returned.

I can only imagine what he means. I distinctly remember what he told Mason about how our fake relationship started, so I decide to turn the tables on him.

"How you followed me around with those big puppy-dog eyes for weeks before you finally got the nerve to ask me out?"

He laughs, and it's the most handsome sight I've ever seen. Nodding, the look in his eyes turns tender again, though. "Yeah, more or less. I didn't know what hit me."

Isn't that the truth? I'm about to become a puddle of emotions on the floor, but luckily, Mason announces that it's time for the special dances, so I'm forced to pull myself together.

"Um…I have to—"

"No, I understand. Go. Go ahead."

"You're staying, though?" I ask hopefully.

"You're not getting rid of me, sweetheart."

I wasn't about to try denying anything to my sisters, but it would have been pointless with the way I'm smiling like a loon after that parting. The thing about twins is that no matter how much they try to say they're different in so many ways, they're still siblings. So, I dance my way through two dances, fielding the same questions.

Why were you holding hands?

Are you dating? How long has this been going on?

I thought you hated the guy. What happened?

Is it serious?

Julia was the only one to veer off-course with, "Well, he's way better looking than Shannon."

It was surprisingly less uncomfortable than I imagined it would be. Much less so than the actual dancing. I gave each of them a final twirl, as previously instructed—like they think I have two left feet because, in all fairness, I do—and was left with whispered demands of, "You'd better introduce me."

I walked off the dance floor feeling dizzy only to run into my mother for the third round of interrogations. She looked confused about why she hadn't met him yet if I was '*sort of dating him.*'

"Well, does he want to come sit and eat cake with us?" was her final take on the entire conversation. That's it. Not even a question about why I was suddenly with a man. I will never understand the women in my family.

"Mom…I don't know. Can I just go find him? Why don't you talk to Aunt Charlotte? I think she was looking for you."

Making my way through the crowd, I shake hands and offer thanks for congratulations as I search for Andrew. It shouldn't be so difficult to find the only man wearing a Western cowboy-style shirt at a formal wedding reception.

I finally find him at a table with my great-aunt Katherine and great-uncle Louis. He has a chair pulled up between their two wheelchairs and is listening intently to whatever my aunt is saying. He glances up as though he senses my presence, which sends a rush of shivers over my skin, and smiles.

"Never go to bed angry," Aunt Katherine stresses to him with her bony hand.

Uncle Louis adds, "And always kiss her goodnight."

"That sounds like excellent advice," he agrees, patting them both gently on the shoulders as he gets up.

Quirking my brows at him, I don't get any sort of explanation other than a smile. Bending down, I place a kiss on my aunt's cheek and speak loud enough so she'll hear me. "You look very nice tonight, Aunt Katherine."

She eyes me up and down for a second. "Thank you."

I nod and then look at Andrew, hoping he's up for escaping with me momentarily. Something latches onto my wrist, however.

"Bobby," Aunt Katherine calls up to me. "Tell your mother that I want to be home by seven o'clock. I have to feed Biscuit."

Biscuit? What the hell is a Biscuit?

"Her cat," Andrew supplies.

I'm pretty sure Biscuit had a different name the last time I saw her. Also, I look nothing like my cousin Bobby. He's bald and has a mustache.

"Um, sure. Okay." I pat her hand and glance around for my cousin or his mother, except then I feel something tug my other wrist as soon as she lets go.

It's Andrew, angling his head toward the door. "Her daughter literally just told her she'd get her home in time like five minutes ago," he confides to me under his breath. "Come on, *Bobby*. Walk me to my car?"

He smirks at his own joke, but my heart sinks hearing that he's leaving. I nod, though, making my way toward the door with him. He stops and picks up what looks like a keyboard carrying case, slinging it over his shoulder. There's an amp too, which he grabs with his other hand and then checks to see if I'm following him as he heads outside.

"What's with the gear? Is it Renegade stuff?"

He chuckles and kicks a rock across the parking lot, his cheeks turning pink. "Well, to tell you the truth, I didn't think Mason was coming. He said he couldn't make it when I called him the other day." Glancing at me sheepishly, he continues and holds out an arm. "So, the best I could come up with was a one-man band. I just overestimated what one should wear to a barn."

My footsteps slow momentarily as I piece together what he's saying. The fringe makes sense now…sort of. I mean, this is Andrew, after all.

He would have played for my sisters? *For me*? I can't believe he would have done that. I'm kind of sorry everyone won't get to hear how talented he is.

We walk in silence until I realize we're at his car, a vehicle I used to despise seeing. I still despise it right now because it has the ability to take him away from me.

The humid air, along with my nerves, has me starting to sweat. I shrug out of my suit jacket and roll up my sleeves while he stows his gear. When he closes the trunk, he gives me a once-over and smiles that new sheepish-Andrew smile. I hope he hasn't lost all his spark from my tongue-lashing the other day, although it was really sweet seeing him socializing with my older relatives.

"What were you and my aunt and uncle talking about?"

"I asked them what the secret to being happily married for sixty-five years was."

I know they've been together since the beginning of time, but I hadn't realized it's been that long. Hearing that he chatted with them long enough to find out makes me want to hug him.

He inches closer. "I don't want you to go to bed angry with me to-night. Or any night. I'm sorry. I didn't..." He shakes his head, searching for words. "I didn't think you'd want more. Frankly, I didn't know how to give more, but I want to."

Damn. He's really breathtaking when he's not pretending to be an asshole.

Clearing my throat, I close the distance. "Then you'd better kiss me goodnight," I suggest, taking my Uncle Louis' advice.

I could melt just from the touch of his hands on my cheek. "I missed you, Tufty," he whispers at my lips before touching his to mine.

The kiss is soft and thoughtful. It's our first outside of work, with no doubt about its authenticity. It calms my soul like the piece I've been searching for all my life has finally been found. I grip his waist, not want-ing to let go. It's perfect.

"Luuucas!"

I'm thirty-seven years old and can still recognize my mother's voice from a mile away, even if it wasn't hollering across the parking lot at full volume. I jump, stumbling backward.

"Jesus," I pant, clutching my chest.

Locating her standing outside the reception hall's door, I watch her wave her hand, beckoning for us to return. Right.

"Sorry," Andrew laughs nervously. "Um, I should probably go, so I'm not distracting you. I can come back later and help clean up if you need it."

He shifts from one foot to the other. I watch in awe at how his nerves are making him just as clueless as I felt the last few weeks. Smiling, I hold out my hand for him to take. He looks at it, confused.

"My mom wants you to come sit and eat cake with us."

His jaw goes slack, and his brows rise, glancing toward the door. He lets out a disbelieving puff of air and smiles. "Seriously?"

"Yeah, and then later," I add, capturing his hand, "you can give me that goodnight kiss."

His smile grows as he realizes I duped him into more than one kiss. He glances at his feet, shaking his head, and I hear him exhale. Looking back up, he grins and chuckles.

"That sounds like a really good deal."

Smirking, I start us back toward the hall and nod. "It is. Fifty-fifty split."

"Guess I should see this thing through to the end. Think we can pull off looking like a couple of happily paired guys?"

The way his grip on my hand tightens belies his humor, telling me how much it means to him for this to happen, so I squeeze back. Except, I owe him a few zingers for the shit he used to say to me.

"Yeah, as long as we can be as disgusting as we can and you act like you give a damn about me."

"Tufty," he prefaces, "that won't be a problem."

Chapter 32

ANDREW BROADHOUSE
licensed agent

"Can't believe you're in my house," Lucas slurs as we bump into the wall on the way to his bedroom.

I can't believe what a happy drunk he is. And heavy. It's like he's lost all control of his muscles along with his anxiety. Panting, I clutch his wrist tighter where it's slung over my shoulder and steer us through the doorway he said leads to his bedroom. It smells like Lucas in here, and there are several little wood carvings on one of the dressers. At least the directions to his room were better than the ones to his house that he gave our taxi driver.

"Can't believe you're in my room," he murmurs against my neck, inhaling deeply. "Dreamt about you being in here."

Oh, really? We *will* be discussing that later.

My leg bashes into a chair, toppling a cardboard box onto the floor. I catch sight of an open sack of rice spilling out along with tiny organza baggies. My boot crunches some grains as Lucas' momentum takes us toward his bed.

"It's a nice room," I say, coddling him. "I love what you've done with the place."

His arm bashes me in the back of the head when he spots his mattress and dives toward it, landing with a belly flop. Crawling forward, he sticks the bubble butt in the air and then flips around so he's sitting on it. I nearly get dinged in the nuts when he kicks off his dress shoes. Leaning back, he rests his weight on his hands, but his torso still sways. He smiles, but it's clear he's still trying to focus on me. Such a mess—a big, sexy, adorable mess.

Now that he's stationary, it seems safe to move back in. I step forward and start working on the buttons of his dress shirt. We lost the tie earlier at the reception when the guy who claimed to have two left feet suddenly turned into a dancing machine.

"All right, party animal, jammie-time," I inform him.

Grinning up at me, he scoots forward. "You want to see me naked?"

"Maybe some other time… like when you're sober. Right now, I just want to get us tucked in."

"You're staying?"

God, he's killing me. I've never seen this man smile so much. He's a happy teddy bear tonight.

"Someone's got to make sure you don't end up on the floor with a face full of rice."

"*You* tried to make me sleep on the floor once," he grumps, giving me an accusatory look.

I did, didn't I?

"Which was wrong of me," I admit as though I'm speaking to a child. "But hey, you ended up in the bed anyway."

"So we'd look like we were having sex," he says, shifting back to his playful tone.

He flops back on the bed and thrusts his hips up in the air when I tug his pants down over them. The bulge of his half-hard cock nearly bashes me in the face, and I swear under my breath. I hear a moan and glance up to find him running his hand down his happy trail.

Fucking hell. Alcohol is definitely *not* heart-healthy. Mine is doing somersaults over the things coming out of his mouth right now.

I wrangle his socks off him and fling them over my shoulder. I may be in love, but I'm not a maid or an ex-soldier with laundry rituals. Also, I had a buzz of my own before wrestling this handsy grizzly bear out of the cab and up his front steps. I am one urban cowboy in dire need of sleep.

I start on my shirt and catch his hazy eyes watching me, his hand slowly massaging his junk. Lord, I'm almost afraid to get in there with him. I might not make it out unscathed, and then I'll have one more thing to feel bad about.

"Mm," he groans at the sight of my bare chest, sending a wash of pride through me, but then he busts up, laughing.

"Can't say I've ever gotten *that* reaction before from stripping."

"There's a cowboy in my room." He giggles. "Cowboy stripper."

"Wow. You are on a roll," I deadpan, trying not to laugh. "And only half a cowboy. I gave Mason my hat, remember?"

"Still mad about that," he mumbles, licking his lips when I undo my belt buckle.

Damn. I need to deflect.

"Go on. Get under the covers so I don't have to haul you up there." I gesture with my chin to the head of the bed.

He grunts a pouting noise, but then belly crawls his way to the pillows. "So tired," he murmurs. "I'm never getting married."

I know he means the planning part of it, but I feel a bit slighted. I wonder what it would be like to be married. Cuddling in the morning, driving to work together, and shopping for coffee tables. Chuckling, I shake my head at myself, realizing the image I see is with him, and kick my pants off. God, I have it so bad.

"I'll get you a wedding planner," I offer, sliding in under the covers.

"Like a wedding bitch?"

"Language, Lucas," I scold, sounding like my mother, but it's too funny to hear him be so unfiltered. "I don't think that's what they like to be called, but yeah. Someone to do all the planning so you don't have to stress about anything." I raise my arm to wrap it around him, but he burrows into my chest before I even lay it across his back.

"No way. I'd do it myself. They'd screw something up."

Snorting, I shake my head and rub his back. I guess his future dream wedding is back on. Rolling back, he glances up at me. The next thing I know, a hand is pressed against my face. His fingertips nearly poke me in the eye as he drags his sweaty digits down my face. When I open my eyes, he's grinning at me like a fool.

"What?" I laugh, my breath catching in my throat. Is he going to tell me I'm the one he pictures in that dream wedding he supposedly doesn't want?

"You're in my bed. Like seeing you in my bed."

It will be my mission in life, henceforward, to get him to loosen up this much without alcohol. Pressing a kiss to his forehead, I assure him, "I like being in it."

When I draw back, his mouth moves in. "Want you," he murmurs, kissing me. It's sloppy, and yet it's still as sweet as he is. His hand moves lower, though, trailing over my cock and giving it a squeeze. "Want you, Andrew."

Fuuuck. This is payback for every rotten thing I've ever done or said in my life.

Capturing his wrist, I bring it to my chest and kiss his knuckles. "Not tonight, sweetheart. I don't put out before the first date." Or when people are inebriated, but I'm not about to listen to an intoxicated man try to convince me he's not intoxicated.

"Since when?" He frowns.

Ouch. That was some drunken honesty.

"Since now."

He tries to be all coy, sliding his fingers from my grip and nudging his hips forward, but I catch his hand again before it passes my belly button, intertwining our fingers. Huffing, he rolls closer, burying his face in my chest.

"You're mean," he mumbles against my skin.

Kissing his temple, I agree sympathetically. "I know."

When he stays still and quiet, I feel my body relax. Maybe the beast has finally decided to hibernate. Gingerly, I slip my fingers from his and wrap my arm around his back to hold him close. Something creeps up on me that feels a lot like gratitude as I hold his warm body in my arms. I get to be here. Get to hold him. Like this.

Smiling, I place a soft kiss on the top of his head, recalling our evening. I still can't believe I got invited to sit with him and his mom.

I remember how my stomach was in knots as we approached the table, hand in hand. I've never met the parents of anyone I've been intimate with. I certainly wasn't expecting to be welcomed into the family tonight.

"Don't volunteer for anything," Lucas whispered as we approached her.

He should have elaborated more and sooner. I see now why he takes responsibility for his family so seriously. That woman roped me in without my even realizing it. I ended up with a date to help clean her gutters, paint her fence, and look at her faulty washing machine. I don't know shit about washing machines other than how to call for a repair. Still, it was nice to be relied upon and trusted. I'll have to try that out on Loretta sometime and see how it goes.

And the babies? Well, they're adorable little bundles of giddiness and mischief. Granted, I know it was their wedding day, but I can tell they're rays of sunshine year-round. I'm glad Lucas has had that in his life. They pretty much adopted me. I think it was mostly my dancing skills, but seeing the way their brother smiled at me with his puppy-dog eyes might have had something to do with it, too.

"Ask me now?" Lucas pleads, interrupting my thoughts. I thought maybe he'd fallen asleep, but I find him looking up at me with a seriousness in his eyes that belies his inebriated state.

"Ask you what?"

"To be your boyfriend."

He went from wanting to save a horse by riding a cowboy to wanting to watch '*The Notebook.*' What am I going to do with him? Also, I can't ask him right now. Not like this! I came up with the perfect date plan while we were at the reception.

I know the man pretends to love granola, but I also discovered he has an affinity for cake. The way he moaned over that slice in Darwin— he did the same thing tonight with the wedding cake. I was going to take him to this wood carving place I've seen and then out to my favorite restaurant in Wilmington, which has the best better-than-sex cake that lives up to its name.

"Why don't we wait until your head is clear?" I suggest tenderly.

"Don't need to. My heart is clear."

Jesus. Who can argue with that?

Swallowing, I brush my nose against his and close my eyes so I don't end up crying. "Yours always has been."

"Ask me," he whispers.

"I wanted to make it special and take you on a date."

His brow furrows, making him look equal parts confused and annoyed. "You're still going to take me on a date," he insists.

Oh my God. He's become a boyfriend monster already. I bark out a laugh, but he just stares at me as though he doesn't understand what's so amusing.

"*Ask me.*"

For Pete's sake. He's not even going to remember this tomorrow. I want fully alert Lucas to be the one to answer me, even though I like every side of him.

"Lucas..."

"Please?" he begs, sounding so sweet, I don't know how anyone could deny him anything. "I don't want to wait another minute."

I'm not laughing anymore, not even on the inside. Because I know exactly how he feels. And it's like Mason said the other day, we'll do anything for the people we love.

"Lucas...will you be mine?"

His brow furrows in confusion. "I already am."

I try not to laugh. I really do, but my head rocks back and my stomach shakes against his. I can barely catch my breath, but I have to reel it in when I see that crease in his brow and find him looking at me like he still doesn't understand the joke. Stroking his beard, I murmur, "That must be why I love you."

It's not until I've pressed a kiss to his lips that it occurs to me what I've said. Shit. I was also going to save that for a more coherent Lucas. When I pull back, he's smiling again.

"You're in love with me?"

I think I said '*love*,' which sounds like a level below *in* love. As I gaze at him, however, I know I'm absolutely at whatever the highest level is. I nod and give him another soft kiss.

"Yeah, Tufty. I'm in love with you."

His arm squeezes me tightly, and his head ducks underneath my chin. "Then ask me," he repeats.

Fucking Lucas and his boyfriend kick. I guess boyfriend status trumps love when you're three sheets to the wind.

"Lucas Everette...will you be my boyfriend?"

"For real?" comes his muffled, disbelieving voice against my sternum. I guess some people just need to hear the words.

"For real. I want you to be my real-life boyfriend."

He lets out a strange groan against my skin that sounds like it's the equivalent of '*aw shucks*' and then sighs a contented sound. I think I finally appeased him. Stroking his back, I smile into his soft hair and wait for his answer.

And I keep waiting.

His arm feels heavier on my ribcage than before, and I think his breathing has changed. Pulling my head back, I find his eyes closed.

He freaking fell asleep on me. Now I have to do this all over again tomorrow. I mean, I still plan to anyway. He's getting that date. It's just... he made all that fuss and then left *me* hanging. Drunken Tufty does not play fair. Judging by the little smile on his face, however, I'm pretty sure I know his answer. It's a really good answer that sends me to sleep with a smile of my own.

Epilogue

As Andrew turns onto the freeway, my eardrums are still vibrating from the monster truck rally. I didn't hate it. Would I go again? If he's with me, I suppose, but only if he admits that he's now a superfan. He bought more memorabilia than any parent there did for their children. Either he's hooked or he has a junk-buying problem. He said he bought them for me, but I wasn't the one screaming at the top of my lungs and waving Digger's flag in the air like a maniac. That sight alone was worth sitting on hard bleachers for two and a half hours.

So, yeah, I'd go anywhere with him. The big idiot. I'm so stupidly in love, it's comical.

As of tonight, I've officially had a boyfriend for two weeks. It's been full of date after date, followed by night after intimate night. Laughing, snuggling, loving, talking, and more loving. We've been big on the loving part, and not always physical. I'd feigned ignorance of our conversation the night prior, after the girls' wedding, but I remember what I heard. Granted, some of it came back to me slowly and in flashes, but I knew it wasn't a dream. Andrew is in love with me. It wouldn't have mattered if I hadn't heard it, though. I can see it in his eyes and in the way he treats me. Sometimes, when we're making love, he looks at me like he's holding his breath, and I imagine it's him hoping that I'll say it next. I've never been one to play games, but it's different this time around. Andrew's the last partner I'm ever going to say it to because he's the last partner I'm ever going to have. I know that to my bones. So, I've been waiting for the perfect moment.

Glancing over at him, his hair blowing in the breeze from his open car window, a big grin on his face, I think tonight's the night. I can't contain it any longer. He looks so damn happy, almost like a kid on Christmas, as though the night couldn't get any better. He loves to surprise me with things like taking me to that wood carving place on our first date and buying these monster truck show tickets for tonight. I want to surprise him too, even though I don't see how it's not obvious that I'm over the damn moon for him.

"Hey!" he yells, clearly temporarily deafened from the night's loud event. "Are you sure you're okay from earlier?"

If by earlier he means when I met his parents at lunch, I'm not sure why he's asking again. They were all right. It was a bit strange at first, like I was eating lunch with two people who were strangers to Andrew. His parents were very affectionate with each other, and his mom was super attentive and sweet to me. Andrew had just stared at them for the first five minutes, as though he was seeing them for the first time and was unable to speak. He loosened up eventually and started rambling on excitedly about some of our outings together and about my family, smiling proudly each time he looked at me. When we left, he seemed a bit dazed for a moment and then turned and gave me a long, silent hug outside on their doorstep.

"Thank you," was all he had murmured into my neck.

"Yeah. I told you. I enjoyed it," I assure him. "They seemed really nice." Something seems off, however, considering his previous description of them. "Do they still give you grief about working for your Uncle Lou?"

He lets out a breathless laugh as he reaches for my hand. "No, come to think of it. They haven't made a peep since the wedding. Some… *things* came to light. It looks like they're getting along better, too," he adds off-handedly. "A lot better. *Gross.*"

"What's gross about your parents kissing? Are they one of those couples who kiss all the time? Because, I mean, we're kind of one of those." I smirk, not even embarrassed about it.

I can't help it. I like kissing him.

"Fuck no. They were at war my entire life. They started getting along only recently."

I can't see that, but I don't think he's being dramatic. He's toned down the drama level when it comes to serious topics. Ask him to compare two television shows, however, and you get an hour-long diatribe.

"What happened?"

Turning onto the road toward his house, he shakes his head and makes a noncommittal noise. "I don't know. Something about a disagreement with Uncle Lou," he mutters. "I don't want to bore you."

"I'm not bored." I laugh. "You're never boring, that's for sure."

"Bore…traumatize, whatever." He waves a hand. "Trust me, you won't be able to look at your boss or my father the same way again if you know. Can we please talk about something else?"

Damn. Now, I really want to know, and I'm not even a nosy person.

Speaking of never being looked at the same way, and Lou, though, I still don't think he believes that we're dating. On our first day back in the office, we decided to do the professional thing and went in and told him. He just stared at us for a moment and then snorted.

"Yeah, sure," was his initial response, I think.

"No, we're serious, Uncle Lou. We're dating."

He stared at us, his gaze pinging back and forth for a moment, and then threw a hand up. "Get the fuck out. I don't know what you're trying to pull, but I don't have time for this shit."

We tried a few more times to assure him it wasn't a prank, but the door got slammed in our faces after we were swiftly told to get back to work. He's been eyeing me suspiciously each time I see him ever since, like he thinks I'm in cahoots with Andrew and something is going to pop out of the wall and grab him. I'm about to ask Andrew to start acting like an asshole at work again just so he'll stop. It's freaking me out.

"We could talk about how this is only the second time I'll have spent the night at your house," I suggest as we pull into his driveway. "Are you embarrassed about your Christmas tree?"

"No," he responds swiftly.

Liar. That was a happy surprise on the night of our first date. I about broke down and professed my love right then and there when I saw the little piano I carved hanging on it, but I bit my tongue when I considered how much thought he'd put into the evening. I wanted to spread out the happy memories.

"But I'm warning you," he adds as we get out. "I think the only food I have is some crackers and ice cream."

Smiling at him over the top of his car, I know his pantry is bare because he's been warming my bed in Bolton each night. I love that he's so comfortable there. He says it feels more like a home, and frankly, having him there makes it feel that way. He even says he doesn't mind when my mother stops by unannounced—which I really need to freaking talk to her about, by the way. Damn my luck that she likes Andrew so much.

"It's not my fault we've been stuck cleaning gutters and painting fences," I deadpan and make my way up his walk with him.

"Okay, fine. I know you warned me, but she never said her yard was that freaking big. I didn't know she had, like, five acres of fence. I'm going to be able to open a dojo in California soon with how many times I've painted the fence." Unlocking the door, he turns to me abruptly when we step inside. "Why? Are you sick of me using all your shampoo?"

I chuckle at the worry lines in his forehead. Insecure Andrew is a cute Andrew. Leaning in, I decide to let up on the teasing and give him a kiss. "No. Not at all."

Watching him unload all his monster truck crap onto his end table, I can't keep myself from smiling. That seems to happen all the time anymore. Some days, I go to sleep, and my face hurts because I'm just so damn happy. It's as difficult to believe it's because of Andrew as it is to believe it's possible to be this *stupidly giddy* as Julia once put it.

Glancing up at me, he freezes for a second and then laughs. "What? You don't like the hat? Come on. It's a cool hat!" he exclaims, picking up one of his treasures from the show.

I don't know why I've been waiting for the right moment. Every moment is the right moment to tell the person you love. Snickering, I shake my head and walk over to him.

"No, I was just thinking about the Hepperlys."

"If Dario has a cousin who wants to buy swampland in Arizona, he can fuck off right now. I've decided my wilderness expertise ends at fence painting."

Settling my hands on his waist, I shut him up with a soft kiss. "Actually, I was thinking about how grateful I am to them."

Setting down his ridiculous hat, he cups my cheek, all traces of humor gone. "Because you were able to pay off all your loans with your commission?" he asks gently.

There is that too, but God, I wouldn't even care if we hadn't sold anything together if it had all worked out with us ending up like we are. I'd have lived happily, with my credit stretched, knowing I got to come home to Andrew every night.

"Yeah, but they gave me something worth a lot more than that."

He gasps. "Did you get a fine parting gift that I didn't?"

"No," I laugh. "I got the same one as you."

His face scrunches up, so I squash down the butterflies in my stomach and clarify. "They gave me the chance to fall in love with you."

His lips part, and his eyes scan my face as though he's looking for a punch line. My stomach feels like it just flipped over, waiting for him to say something. He hasn't repeated the words he said the night of the wedding, but I just assumed he was playing it cool, as Andrew likes to do sometimes. Maybe I was wrong, and he thinks he spoke too soon. But then, a smile forms on his face.

"Love, huh?"

"Yeah."

He lets out a breathless laugh and squeezes my arm, glancing down. His grip fidgets on my biceps. I wait for more, but he just glances at me and then down again on a soft intake of breath. Is he…all right?

I'm yanked closer, and his mouth covers mine, hard. He cups my face in both hands, and the kiss softens, becoming deeper and more sensual.

When he comes up for air, he sucks in a breath and sniffles. My heart squeezes hearing that sound.

"You know, not to one-up you, but I told you two weeks ago. I was just waiting for the right moment to say it again."

"I know." I laugh, resting my forehead against his and closing my eyes to bask in the moment.

"You know? You said you didn't remember anything after we got back to your house."

"I was giving you an out."

"Who says I need an out? And wait a minute…why did it take you two weeks?" Pulling back, the worried mask covers his face again. "Were you…not sure? Because you don't have to say it just because I said it."

"I wanted to spread out our happy memories."

Groaning, he rests his forehead against mine. "You are so sentimental. You know that?"

"Says the man with his Christmas tree up in July."

Drawing back, his face lights up with defiance. "Hey! That's different. You held out on me. You're a tease."

"Patient," I correct.

Narrowing his eyes, he challenges with, "Cruel."

"Thoughtful."

"Mean."

Chuckling, I absorb the concealed joy rolling off him. I used to get so aggravated having verbal battles with him, but now they're one of the highlights of my day.

"Yours," I affirm softly.

Grinning, he squeezes my hip and tugs me closer, murmuring in front of my lips. "Damn right you are."

When his arms go around me, and his sweet taste touches my tongue, I melt into him. Now that I've shared my truth, it's like a dam has been broken. Maybe I am sentimental, because I swear I can feel the love flowing between us, wrapping around us.

He yanks my shirt out of my jeans and splays his palms across the bare skin of my lower back. His fingers knead my flesh the same way I'm practically clawing at his back to get him closer. Skirting my hand down between us, I rub the hardness behind his fly, still amazed that I'm no longer shy about being so bold with a man I never intended to even like.

He lets out a little growl and pulls back. "Go to my room. Now."

"You're so bossy," I laugh, still panting from our kisses even as his words send a punch of desire to my groin.

"Go to my room, Tufty, and I'll show you bossy."

I think that's a promise. I smile and start down his hallway. When I don't hear him following, I glance back. He peels his shirt over his head, and the look he gives me nearly scorches my underwear.

"You'd better be naked when I get in there."

Whipping my shirt over my head, I shuffle to his bedroom with hurried steps, unfastening my pants on the move. With my heart in my throat, I kick my shoes off, sending them flying. God, I'm trembling with eagerness so badly this almost feels like the first time. I shove my pants and underwear down in one swift movement, staring at the bed, searching for ways I can appear sexy. When I hear his footsteps tromping down the hall, my heart skips a beat. Time's up.

I panic, fling my jeans off my feet, and dive onto the mattress, landing on my stomach. Adjusting my dick underneath me, I get a tingle as it brushes against the comforter. We've never tried sex in this position. It's all I've got, so I fold my arms underneath my head and rest them on the pillow, eyes trained on the door.

Andrew appears in it a few seconds later, naked and hard. I know he said he's done with wilderness adventures, but he looks like a deranged Lucas hunter, and boy, am I *really* happy to be a Lucas right now. I lie still like good prey, trying to keep my expression innocent.

He reaches down and squeezes the head of his cock. "Fucking hell," he whispers under his breath.

I bury my smile in the crook of my arm. His heavy footsteps come closer, and the mattress dips. My legs are covered with his body heat. I feel the cut of his jaw on my ass. Something wet and slippery paints a stripe up my crease, and I gasp from the surprise.

My legs shift further apart instinctively. He did this a few days ago in the shower and left me a blubbering mess. I kind of wanted to ask where he's learning all his tricks, but they say not to look a gift horse in the mouth. If he had to text his cousin Shaw and his husband Terry, I don't want to know about it. We had dinner at their place the other night, and it was difficult enough to try to forget that they're the ones who told him how to find my prostate a few weeks ago. They seem like a really sweet couple, regardless of the way Terry seemed to get flustered when he couldn't push Andrew's buttons, but it's kind of difficult to forget that a person has given your boyfriend a lesson on your anatomy.

Groaning, I bury my face in the pillow, arching my hips up to Andrew's mouth. He grips my ass cheeks, spreading them apart, giving me the exposed sensation I got the other day. Except now, it's quickly replaced by the pleasure from his tongue as he swirls it around my ring and then makes little jabs at its center.

"Fuck, Andrew."

"Yes. Yes, we will," he teases. "But first…"

The tip of his tongue presses through my ring of muscles, slipping inside. It's not the heat I want to feel, but I am not about to complain. Especially when he reaches my gland. The strange sensation that I've grown accustomed to puts that terrifying pressure on my bladder but then mushrooms into bliss, bursting through my cock and balls. My hips buck back for more when his tongue retreats, my ass bumping him in the face. I don't care if I just ass-bulldozed him. He started it.

He pulls all the way out, though, leaving me feeling empty. I glance back, wondering what the problem is, just in time to see his hand come down on my ass cheek, giving me a little swat.

"Hold still. I'm not done yet."

Leaning toward his nightstand, his kneecap digs into the back of my thigh. I grunt at the discomfort, watching him scramble for a bottle of lube.

"Sorry," he whispers, moving his leg and settling back between mine.

His palm comes down again, but this time, it's softly rubbing the offended area. From here, I can see a condom in his grasp, and I'm grateful for it tonight. I have a feeling that afterward, I'm just going to want to curl up and fall asleep with him instead of showering. We've been learning a few things about the mess of anal sex and anal hygiene. For someone I could barely have a conversation with once, he's been incredibly thoughtful, always asking me how I feel afterward. I'm honestly too afraid to try it out of fear of hurting him, but I told him that if he walked me through it, I'd do it for him if he wanted.

Relaxing into the pillow, I hear the snap of the condom and then feel his lubricated fingers at my entrance. I melt further into the mattress when he dips them inside, coating me. He's careful as always, but I sense the urgency in him. I feel the same in myself.

"I'm good, Andrew," I whisper. "I'm ready."

"You're sure?"

"Yeah."

Exhaling, he lies down on top of me. The press of his weight alone supplies another aspect of arousal. I feel complete and safe, even though I wasn't afraid a moment ago. His arms drape over the back of mine, hugging me as he nuzzles the side of my face with his.

"Tell me again?" he whispers, a vulnerable contrast to his bossy display a few moments ago.

Letting my eyes slip closed, I smile, feeling the words before I even say them. "I love you."

Burying his face in my neck, he takes a deep inhale and squeezes me, just holding me like that for a moment. At this moment, I know nothing will ever come between us. The feeling is just too big, runs too deep, and is so mutually appreciated, it's the kind that lasts forever. When he angles his head to kiss me, I know I'll remember this day for the rest of my life.

Shifting his hips, his cock slips between my cheeks. He runs the tip through my seam several times until I start fidgeting, trying to nudge my hips back to capture him. He must finally get the hint, using his hand to line himself up. I'm so relaxed and open, I'm more than ready. Even the initial burn is a welcome sensation as he presses inside. I lie as still as possible with my eyes closed, feeling every inch as he nudges deeper, filling me. Panting, he settles his chest onto my back when his balls brush against the back of mine. His weight, the fullness, the emotions in my chest—they're almost a sensory overload.

I let out a little cry and clasp his fingers when he intertwines his with mine. It's not even the best part yet, but it's so good. I'm as close to the man I love, and as happy, as a person can be.

"Good?" he whispers in my ear, sounding strained.

"Too good."

When his hips retreat, I dig my toes into the mattress to arch my hips. His cockhead glides back and then forth over my gland, blossoming sheer ecstasy throughout my body. I feel his lips pressing kisses on the back of my shoulder.

"Love you too," he pants. "So stupidly in love with you."

The words somehow amplify the intensity of everything. I feel like his Christmas tree, lit up from head to toe.

"Andrew," I moan, sliding back to lift my hips higher.

He plants a hand on the mattress and slips his other around my waist, tugging my hips onto him with each plunge. I love how he can read me and know exactly what I want when I want it. I can feel how heavy my cock has gotten when it bobs from each of his thrusts. I have the urge to stroke myself; it'd be easy to get off if I did, but I don't want it to end. When my moans turn to breathless whimpers, I feel Andrew's palm wrap around me to put me out of this exquisite misery.

"No," I warn, tugging his wrist away with great mental effort. "Want to come without it."

He lets go and drops his other hand on the mattress, caging me in without letting up that perfect rhythm he's found. "You going to come just from my cock, sweetheart?" he rasps in my ear. "You love it so much, that's all you need now?"

I turn my head to say something, probably just his name again. That's all I can usually manage when he gets me like this, but I don't even get the chance. He takes one look at my parted, panting lips—my mouth-breathing, as he calls it—and seals his to mine. It's the final bit of connection I need. His tongue sweeping against mine. His taste.

I feel my sphincter clench around him, and I come with a groan. He presses his face against mine, giving a few more erratic thrusts before burying himself deep inside me. His cries mix with mine as I feel him pulse inside me. We shudder together, panting and rocking instinctively with the motions that brought us here until his cock slips free from me.

My arms give out. Andrew follows, lying on top of me, his chest heaving against my back. He's heavy, but I could fall asleep just like this without a bother. At one point, he rolls to his side. I hear the snap of the condom, but I don't even move. The covers shift a moment later, though, and I know I have to come back to life to a degree if I want to cuddle underneath them with him.

Rolling, I find a tender smile on his face as he waits for me to get settled and then tucks us in. Wrapping my arm around him, I nestle close, wondering how I got so damn lucky.

We share lazy kisses for a while until I feel my eyes starting to droop. I'm just about to close them when bright light illuminates Andrew's face. He squints along with me, and then his eyes go as wide as I imagine mine are. How in the hell did the light come on?

A noise by the doorway catches my attention. Andrew's body goes rigid next to me at the same time I flinch, spotting the figure of a man. "Terry?" Andrew screeches, scrambling back against the headboard.

"Jesus!" I yelp, sitting up with him and yanking the cover up higher.

Leaning against the doorframe, ankles crossed, his cousin's husband doesn't even seem to act like we're in the room. His attention is focused on the quart of ice cream in his hands that he's eating straight from the carton.

"So…I was thinking," he calls lazily. "Maybe we should try that place on Fifth Street for dinner next time. They do a great veal parm."

"Terry!" Andrew barks. "What the actual fuck? What are you doing in my house?"

Terry ambles forward and plops down at the end of the bed. I mentally cringe, wondering if he just stepped on my discarded clothing or if it's apparent that we just had sex. Carving out another spoonful of ice cream, he shoves it in his mouth and then looks up innocently, waving the spoon. "Oh…I was in the area and thought I'd drop by for a visit."

"At eleven o'clock at night? How the fuck did you even get in?"

Frowning as though Andrew just asked a foolish question, he bats his hand. "Please," he tsks. "For someone who works in real estate, you'd think you'd keep a closer eye on your keys. I do live only two blocks away from a hardware store, remember?"

Oh, wow. He *did* disappear for a while after our dinner at their house the other day. I just assumed he was tired of being social since Andrew seemed to have a stronger bond with his cousin Shaw.

Snagging a pillow out from behind us, Andrew gets up, holding it over his junk. I don't much like the idea of being abandoned naked in his bed alone with his cousin-in-law sitting at the end of it, but I hold on to my faith that he'll get me some privacy soon. What is the deal anyway?

"You freaking stole my keys?" he rages, snagging a pair of underwear out of his dresser.

"In case of an emergency." Terry smiles like an imp, telling me there must be something I don't know. This smells like revenge. Oh, great. What did Andrew do?

"Another dinner invite was an emergency?" Hopping into a pair of boxers with one hand, Andrew's eyes narrow. "Is that my fucking Rocky Road?"

"Mm," Terry grumbles, a dissatisfied sound. "All you had was this or crackers." Crossing his legs, he looks up brightly. "So, lovebirds. What are you two up to tonight?"

I'm pretty sure Andrew's head is about to spin around. "Get the fuck out!" He points to his doorway.

Terry gasps, but it sounds fake to me. "Rude! And here I thought you might be up for a game of cards or a movie marathon."

"You fucking knew we were going to the monster truck show tonight, and knew I'd be here, you ass. Hilarious. Joke's over now, though. Get the fuck out," Andrew continues, tossing the pillow at him.

"So inhospitable," he says, swinging his attention to me. "Lucas, you don't want me to leave, do you?"

"I..." Why am I being dragged into this? Of course, I want him to fucking leave. Naked here!

Andrew doesn't wait for a reply; he grabs a handful of Terry's shirt and hoists him up off the bed. Terry lets out a shrieking noise.

"Go! And give me back my fucking ice cream or I'll tell Shaw about the hair implants you got that time he had to go to London for work."

Terry sucks in a breath. "You wouldn't."

"The fuck I won't."

"Fine!" He pouts, shoving the ice cream carton at Andrew. "I'll just drop by another time."

"No! No, you won't!"

Stopping at the doorway, he glances back, giving us both a once-over, and shakes his head. "Baby gays, so sensitive." Flashing me a wiggling finger wave, he calls as he starts down the hallway, "This was fun, boys. Same time next week?"

Andrew stays frozen until I hear the sound of the door opening and closing. He drops his face into his hands and groans. "Oh, my God."

"Um, why do I get the feeling he was provoked?" I hedge, taking the cover with me to retrieve my underwear from the floor.

Andrew scoffs. "So, I may have walked in on them once. Maybe twice. Whatever. He's just being dramatic. You'll figure that out real quick."

He turns and opens his closet, pulling out his suitcase. After I get my underwear on, I notice he's stuffing clothing into it.

"What are you doing?"

"Packing!" he retorts like I should understand why. "We're not staying here."

"Andrew," I laugh. "I'm pretty sure he's gone. I can go check and make sure the door is locked if it makes you feel better."

"Did you hear him? He has a key now. There's no way I'm staying here with pain-in-the-ass Terry lurking around the city with a key to my house. The man is spiteful."

He's practically emptied his closet. I watch, baffled as he tries to smash the lid of his suitcase closed.

"You could just change the locks tomorrow," I suggest.

"Nope. It's ruined. I'm selling it. We'll stay at your place. We can put mine on the market tomorrow."

I don't mind him staying at my place at all, but as I watch him, I have to wonder. "For how long?"

Popping up, he frowns. "Why? Are you planning on breaking up with me?"

I have to hold back a snort. In Andrew-speak, this sounds like I may have just acquired a live-in boyfriend—indefinitely.

"No. It just seems a little extreme to sell your house when you don't have another one."

"Well, we spend most of our time at yours anyway," he rationalizes, tugging another suitcase out of his closet and moving to his dresser. "I think your mom likes having both of us close by, and I know you like commuting to the office with me. Don't worry," he finally looks up at me. "I'll buy my own shampoo tomorrow."

The idiot. If he wanted to move in, all he had to do was ask. I guess this saves us both a step, though, so I just smile. "You promise?"

"Yeah." He nods. "I'll pull my weight. Don't worry."

Tossing a stack of boxers into the last suitcase, he glances around in thought. His gaze moves to the hallway that leads to his living room, and he scratches the back of his head, mumbling, "We can come back for the Christmas tree tomorrow."

I walk over to the doorway and turn out the light. I ignore his questions as I head back to bed and get back under the covers.

"What are you doing?" he asks again.

"Andrew…"

"Yeah?"

"Get in bed. You can move in with me tomorrow."

The room is quiet. As my eyes readjust to the darkness again, I see him staring at me, perplexed. Maybe even looking caught.

Sighing, I pull the comforter back on his side. "If Terry comes back, I'll throw him out myself. Come on. I'm tired."

He moves after a moment and slides in next to me. I scoot closer and wrap my arm around him, grateful that the disruption and his subsequent relationship-protection measures are over. I feel his hand go to the back of my arm and rub it in soothing motions.

"You don't mind?" he asks softly.

"No."

"Don't you think it's a little too soon?"

I stifle a snort over how he's suddenly trying to make this decision sound like it was my idea. Because I'm certain that's how he'll tell it from now on.

"No," I reply simply. "I'm yours, remember? Aren't you mine?"

He chuffs and pulls me tighter against him. "Yeah. Sure am."

Shrugging, I close my eyes and tuck my head under his chin, just where I like it. "Then we might as well stick together."

I'm about to nod off when I hear him ask, "What if we have a fight?"

"Never go to bed angry—like Aunt Katherine said."

"Well, yeah, but it's bound to happen. Are you going to kick me out of your bed and make me sleep on the couch when it does?"

Yawning, I'd shake my head if I had the energy. "No. That's what pillows are for."

I drift off to the sound of his soft laughter. It's the sound of happy chaos that I'm looking forward to loving and living with for a long, long time.

Dear Reader

Thank you for reading *Contingently Yours*. I hope you enjoyed Lucas and Andrew's adventure. I wanted to write a double awakening story and can now check that off my writing bucket list. I hope it brought you some smiles.

If you'd like to connect with me or learn more about my works, you can visit me at www.diannaroman.com

Books by Dianna

The Shutout
The Fating
Silent Is The Heart
The Holidate Rescue

MEN OF OLYMPUS
You Again
Tough Love

BROKEN HEARTS
Until I Saw You
In The Eye Of The Beholder

CARVER BROTHERS
The Gentleman
The Idiot

BAD DECISIONS
Caged By The Stranger

GRAND VALLEY
A Fair Warning